IN THE
SHAPE
OF A MAN

PAUL CLAYTON

The author wishes to thank Stephen Gallup for help with this book.

CHAPTER 1

The San Francisco Bay Area of California, June, 1999

1015 Skyview Drive.

REYNALDO COLLINS' EYES OPENED WHEN he heard the radio alarm go off in his parents' bedroom. The music went away suddenly. A few moments later came the running of water in the sink. He knew the sounds by heart. Next would come the click of the medicine cabinet, the buzz of the shaver. As Reynaldo lay in bed he realized that the fog was outside. When the fog came and surrounded the house, little sounds seemed louder. He looked around. Gray light seeped into the room from around the edges of the shades on his window. He could see the rectangular shape of his Power Rangers poster on the wall, but could not see the Rangers' brightly colored outfits or read the words on the poster.

Reynaldo heard a door open. He slid out of bed and knelt, pressing his ear to his bedroom door as Daddy passed in the hall. He heard Daddy fill his water bottle at the kitchen sink. The refrigerator opened and shut. A few minutes elapsed and he heard the squeak of the handle on Daddy's briefcase, then the rattle of the chain lock coming off. The door closed and locked and Reynaldo slipped out of his room. He crept into the living room and parted the curtains slightly, his face curling into a smile. Daddy walked down the drive, fog swirling about him. Daddy opened the van door, then shut it with a hollow metallic clang. The engine started and the van slowly drove off, disappearing like magic into the cloud of fog. As the sound faded, so did the smile on Reynaldo's face. He heard a sound behind and turned. It was Mommy.

"What are you doing out of bed?"

"Sorry, Mommy."

"What are you doing out of bed?"

"I wanted to see Daddy go to work."

"What did I tell you about getting out of bed before I get up?"

"You said that you would put me down in the garage."

"Yes. Come on."

Reynaldo remained where he was. "Sorry Mommy. I won't do it again."

Mommy grabbed him by the arm and pulled him across the rug. "Sorry, Mommy," he said over and over as he held back.

Mommy's voice grew louder and her face turned bright red. "I told you, damn it!" She yanked the door to the garage open. It was dark. She pushed him down the three steps. "Now stay down there till I tell you to come up!"

He ran to the door as it closed, the darkness engulfing him. "Mommy! Mommy!" He pounded on the metal door with his fists, the sounds small and dull. "I won't do it again, Mommy. Please, Mommy, I promise!"

There was no response. There was nothing but his cries. In a few moments his eyes adjusted to the dark and his cries subsided. He went over and sat on the little throw rug in front of the bookcase, pulling his knees up to his chest. To his left, faint light lit up the frame around the door leading to the yard. He looked at the other end of the garage at the dark shabby door. There was a lock on it and every time Mommy put him down in the garage he wondered what was locked up in there. Monsters, maybe. His eyes focused on the padlock on the latch. He watched the door for a few minutes, afraid he would see it moving. It didn't and he calmed some. He wished Daddy didn't have to go away to work every day. He wondered for a while what Daddy did all day at work, and then he fell asleep.

A noise woke Reynaldo. The light was on and he rubbed his eyes. Mommy stood at the top of the steps. He could see his sister Christine sitting at the kitchen table eating something.

"Are you ready to be a good boy now?" Mommy said.

"Yes, Mommy."

"Come up and brush your teeth. Hurry up."

Reynaldo went up the stairs. His favorite show, Power Rangers, was on the TV. Christine watched without seeing him as she chewed her food. Reynaldo went into the bathroom and brushed his teeth. He returned to the table. His sister said nothing to him, nor did she look at him. He knew she was afraid to talk to him or acknowledge him when Mommy was mad at him. She would talk to him later.

Reynaldo turned around in his chair to see the TV. It was behind him. His sister could see it head-on, but he had to turn around in his seat.

Mommy poured milk into his glass and he turned around to her.

"I never wanted to adopt you, Reynaldo," she said. "Do you know that?"

"Yes, Mommy."

"Your Daddy did, but I didn't. I always thought there was something wrong with you and when your sister was born I knew it. She is a good girl. Not bad like you. Do you know that?"

"Yes, Mommy."

"You are always naughty, always making work for me."

"Sorry, Mommy."

"Now eat, and when you're finished, go do your work in your room."

Allen Collins drove the smooth expanse of Northbound 280 automatically. It was late Saturday afternoon. He hoped Reynaldo had not misbehaved today. Tina had seemed stressed lately, what with all the changes at her job and taking care of two kids. Allen noticed a red sports car racing up behind. He knew the driver intended to swing around him and then back into his lane to take the upcoming exit. As he watched the car draw closer, he did not turn his head to see it in the side mirror. When the car disappeared from his rear view mirror he jammed the gas pedal down hard, down-shifting the van into second gear. The van leapt forward, the car appearing beside him, racing to overtake him. The driver, a teen, stared intently at the rapidly approaching exit and then, realizing he'd never make it, turned his attention to Allen. Allen could tell from his peripheral vision that the driver was gesturing, probably flipping him the bird. At the last minute, the driver dropped back, beeped his horn, and took the exit, disappearing.

Allen smiled slightly, returning his gaze to the picture-postcard, tan colored summer hills of the San Andreas Wildlife Preserve on his left and the large expensive homes of Woodside on his right. Sometimes Allen entertained the fantasy that he had already died and that this life was a dream. I-280 became a viaduct over the abyss of Crystal Springs reservoir. To his left, Allen was aware of the blue of water. Just before the highway viaduct rejoined solid ground, Allen glanced to his right as he always did at the adobe monstrosity of a dwelling that someone had tagged as the 'Flintstone's House.' With its tan-colored mound shapes connected by tunnel-like corridors, it looked to Allen more like a futuristic lunar house than some sort of cartoon-themed attraction. The odd house marked the homeward stretch of his commute and he sighed inaudibly.

Allen had made this commute so many times over

the years that it seemed almost as if he went into a trace the moment he got on the freeway. He would notice one, maybe two landmarks like the adobe house, and then he would 'come to' in time to take his exit. More huge mansions passed in and out of view as Allen listened to the college jazz station. He had a sudden, bright thought about something important that he should do. He felt in his shirt pocket for his note pad while keeping his eyes on the road. By the time he got the pad out to write it down, the bright and shiny thing was gone, having sunk back down into the swamp of his mind. He attempted to pull it up, but it slipped below the surface and disappeared.

Allen was exhausted. He doubted it would kill him like it reputedly did the Japanese salarymen who suddenly and inexplicably collapsed, supposed victims of death from overwork. But his exhaustion wasn't trivial either, being somewhere in between, and severe enough that it was beginning to leach the color out of his life. He told himself that he really had a great life—if not for the long hours on the job. He'd been married ten years to an attractive, loyal wife, a competent mother to his kids. After a barren stretch of about eight years, they had decided to adopt a beautiful son, Reynaldo, now seven. And then, almost miraculously, a beautiful daughter, Christine, now five, had come along in the regular way. FMC Aerospace, where he worked, paid well and they lived in a nice, three-bedroom house in a decent neighborhood. They owned a van and a car. All he needed was a little rest. He would make time for that Sunday, he decided.

Allen half-listened to a discussion of the latest Clinton scandal and then found himself in the mob of cars exiting the 380 interchange. He merged to the right and onto Westborough Boulevard. Two blocks up he turned onto Hillside. The houses along Hillside were smaller and more modest than the mansions of the techno-riche along I-280, but it was a good community, Allen thought, crime free, with good access to the freeways.

Allen did not like working Saturdays, but if you worked in Silicon Valley, the much hyped *Center* of the technological universe, Saturdays were just another day. Allen sighed and turned his gaze to the iridescent red flags and fences of yellow netting that had recently been strung across the pristine canyons and tan grass-covered slopes of San Bruno Mountain. The little mountain range was the last stretch of open space between San Francisco and the peninsula bedroom communities, and Silicon Valley to the south. Now, after a very close vote in the South San Francisco City Council, they had allowed the sale of some of the mountain to developers. The plans were extensive—300 houses, 500 condos, a fire station and a small business park—enraging the open space advocates. A demonstration was planned; a lawsuit filed. Allen had mixed feelings about it. He would miss looking up at the hill and seeing nothing but tan or green grass, depending on the season, chaparral, jagged gray granite outcroppings, and red-tailed hawks hovering in the east-flowing air currents. But, he mused, like the crude bumper stickers proclaimed, shit happened, like old age and taxes. They had been lucky to have had the view for the last ten years. It had always only been just a matter of time. People were jamming into the San Francisco Peninsula like there was no tomorrow. And they needed houses to live in. And they had money, lots of it, to pay for them. Some of them even paid with suitcases full of cash. But for now, the mountain was quiet and untouched, with no bright yellow tractors and earthmovers in sight.

Allen turned down Skyview Drive. He tried not to stare as he passed the rental at 1030, but couldn't help it. The house hadn't seen a coat of paint in, probably, ten years, and the lawn had devolved into a square patch of smooth, hard earth, devoid of any living thing, even crab grass. Allen had written City Hall to find out who the owner was. Whoever they were, they had rented it out to a couple of twenty-somethings—punks, Allen guessed they'd prefer to be called—of the blue-haired, nipple-ring variety. Only, these two had red hair, or more accurately, hair that had been dyed the unnatural bright orange color of a Raggedy Ann doll's hair.

The girl—Allen had nicknamed her, Ann—sat on the steps of the house, filing her nails. They reminded Allen of the iridescent green Japanese beetles he would find clinging to his mother's roses when he was a boy. She appeared about twenty-five and filled out her jeans nicely. She would be quite pretty if she got rid of all the metal in her face and reclaimed her hair. Her skateboarding boyfriend, whom Allen had named Andy, wasn't in sight, but his pickup truck was. Painted battleship gray primer, it sat, hood up, without wheels, atop four cinder blocks, where it had been for the past two months. Allen tried not to stare as he coasted down the street to his driveway at 1015. Parking, he stared at the dashboard. Let it go, he told himself. At least his miserable excuse for a neighbor hadn't rented the house out to the local chapter of the Hells Angels. He turned the engine off and got out of the van.

CHAPTER 2

1030 Skyview Drive

TAWNY SAT ON THE FRONT step in the shade of the house, filing her nails. Tawny's real name was Judy Pulaski. Her dad had given her the nickname Tawny for her brown hair. She had dyed it red two years ago, the day after he died, and now she wore it cut close against her head, punk fashion. Her nose and lower lip were pierced and sported silver posts. Tawny pulled her pocket watch out and checked the time: 4:30. Her boyfriend, Rad Anderson, would be coming home in half an hour and she couldn't wait to run her hands up his muscled back, to kiss him.

Tawny looked up the street at the velvet-like tan flanks of San Bruno Mountain as a big 747 lumbered across the blue sky almost directly overhead, headed toward the Pacific and Asia beyond. Tawny felt contentment. This was the best part of her day. After finishing cutting hair at KoolKuts down at the Tanforan Mall, she arrived home around four every day, Tuesday to Sunday, to sit and watch the world go by.

Up the hill a gray minivan made the turn off of

Hillside Boulevard and slowly drove down Skyview. It was the yuppie guy that lived down the block at 1015. He came home the same time every day, sometimes even Saturdays, like clockwork. He glanced at Tawny and then checked out Rad's truck, which was up on blocks. Rad was going to fix the brakes and suspension, but they needed about two hundred dollars for parts. But the rent was due in a couple of days and there wouldn't be much left over for the truck. That was why Rad took the bus to work and back. Tawny wished they could put the truck in the garage where it wouldn't be such an eyesore. But that was where they kept Ketsel.

The van parked down the block. The yuppie got out carrying his briefcase and went in his yuppie house. Tawny continued to work on her nails. The Mexican woman came around the corner and started up the street. Tawny realized that, despite her thinking of this female as a 'woman,' she was probably the same age as herself. And yet Tawny didn't think of herself as 'a woman.' Not really. It was probably because she'd never had a kid, and here was this 'woman' with two of them and another one on the way. Tawny was pretty sure the woman worked at one of the houses around the corner as a domestic. She would be getting on the same bus that Rad would be getting off of, and Tawny felt a tingle deep down. The bus would be coming in exactly five minutes.

The Mexican woman and her two girls drew closer. Tawny noticed that the woman's belly seemed to bulge more than it had in the last month or so. She was about six or seven months along, Tawny guessed. The woman's two girls walked behind her. The older one, maybe seven, led her younger sister, three, maybe four years old, by the hand. It was cute to watch. Tawny wondered if she and Rad would ever get so far along with their lives that they would have a baby. She would have to get off the pill though. Then, every time they did it, it would be like a pull on the handle of a slot machine at Reno. She sighed. Didn't matter now. There was plenty of time. Tawny had never had a lover like Rad. He was so sensitive and warm. Her period still hadn't come, probably tomorrow, so they could make love. She smiled at the thought. They were young—she was twenty-seven, two years older than Rad—and they were having way too much fun to have babies. They didn't have a lot of money either. They rented, and they both had to work to pay the bills. But, she told herself brightly, they went where they wanted, when they wanted. They were enjoying their lives and in no hurry to acquire material things and deplete the planet's resources like the baby boomer yuppies.

A roar came from the top of the hill and she looked up. The big red, white and blue SamTrans bus pulled away from the corner. Then Rad came into view, crouching as he rode down the pavement on his skateboard like a surfer riding a wave to the shore. Spotting her watching him, he suddenly stood straight up and folded his arms campily. He leaned to the side and shot out into the street, turning in a wide arc. Brows furrowing in concentration, he crouched low and jumped, bringing the skateboard up with him as he cleared the sidewalk, then setting it back safely to earth. He jumped off and ran, kick-flipping the board and catching it with flair.

Tawny stood and Rad put his arm around her and deep kissed her. "Tawn!" he said upon pulling back, "how'd it go today?"

"Real good. Twenty in tips. How about you?"

Rad frowned. "The owner was in today and made us turn the sounds down. But other than that, it was gnarly." Rad worked at the custom skateboard shop inside Stokes Sporting World putting together and repairing skateboards. The job didn't pay much, but Tawny knew he loved it and so she never said anything about the money part of it. They got by.

"How's everything in the neighborhood?" Rad added.

"Oh, fine. You want to barbecue tonight? I picked up some chicken wings."

"Yeah. I'll fire it up." He pulled her closer. "But later, after I fire somethin' else up, you know what I mean?"

"Umm," she smiled, allowing herself to be led toward the door. "By the way, Mister Peepers drove by. You know, the yuppie in the van. It was like, what part of 'don't stare' don't you understand? His little beady eyes almost fell out from checking out the truck." Tawny laughed, but there was concern in her voice.

"Aw," said Rad disdainfully, "fuck him! He can't do nothin'. We ain't breaking any laws." As Rad steered Tawny toward the door, he looked at the Ford, making a mental note to check on the veracity of his comment later when he had the time. He believed he was in the right. After all, his dad had often worked on his trucks or boats or cars in their driveway, or in front of their house when he was growing up. South San Francisco, or South City, as the people who lived there called it, was all right with that. It had always been a blue-collar town, unlike "The City" of San Francisco with its many lawyers and business people. But in the last ten years a lot of yuppies who couldn't afford houses in "The City" and in Palo Alto and Menlo Park, were snapping up the South City bargains and putting their stamp on the place. Contractors like his dad were renovating and upgrading houses as fast as they could into big four- and five-bedroom jobs that would cost four hundred and fifty thou and up when sold. And, sadly, many of the orchards and plant nurseries that Rad had grown up around had been sold, knocked flat by dozers, and turned into developments for wealthy yuppies and immigrants, mostly Chinese. At worst, Rad theorized, Mr. Peepers might be able to make trouble for him with the landlord.

Rad slid his hand down Tawny's side, to where her hips flared out, and he dug his fingers in slightly, forgetting about trucks and boards of supervisors and skateboards and Mr. Peepers. All he could think about was sliding into Tawny. He'd loved her the moment he met her. So did his dick, becoming hard at first sight of her. And all he thought about was making love with her. Except for right after they'd made it. And then, after about ten minutes, he wanted to do it again. At the shop he thought about it a lot, whenever he wasn't working on a board. Skating and fucking. They were his life. Nothing else mattered and the world could go to hell.

As they went into the house the phone rang. Tawny picked it up.

"Hi, Terri. Yeah. No, not tonight. Maybe next week, okay? All right. Later."

Rad smiled at Tawny as she hung up the phone. "Let me guess... she invited you, a good Catholic girl, to a Buddhist meeting."

Tawny smiled. "Well, I'm not into the big organized religion thing anymore, but the Buddhism seems different. I'm gonna check it out sometime. But not tonight."

Rad nodded. Tawny's friend, Terri, had been trying to get Tawny and Rad to one of her Buddhist meetings for the last year. One of Rad's friends had been to a meeting and told him they chanted first, then gave testimonials, and then tried to sign everybody up for it. Rad had already told Tawny that if she wanted to go she'd have to go by herself. He too had been raised Catholic, but had let it lapse. And he wasn't interested in any kind of religion at this point in his life.

"Did the mail come?" he asked her.

"Yeah."

"Anything from Pygmy's?"

"No, Babe."

Two months earlier Rad had sent Pygmy's, a skateboard manufacturer, a tape of himself at a skate park, doing his stuff. It was some pretty gnarly footage. Tawny had shot and edited it and she was really good with a video camera. The tape had edge and a fluid beauty, with a nice soundtrack, a cut from the band, Garbage, that Tawny and he had picked out. He was hoping it would get him Pygmy's sponsorship for the X Games. All of the board companies sponsored skaters. If Pygmy's sponsored him, he had a shot. But if not, forget it. Without a corporate sponsor, you could literally be the best skater in the world but you'd never get into the X Games.

Tawny leaned close. "There you go again, fading on me. I'll make you forget about that shit." She grabbed his buttocks and deep kissed him. He picked her up and carried her into the darkened bedroom.

Much later Rad got out of bed and opened the curtains. The day's light had faded completely and harsh orangish, electric streetlamp light filtered in, illuminating Tawny's voluptuous body. He lay back down beside her and slowly rubbed his face against her breasts. The cool metal of her nipple ring tickled his skin.

Tawny ran her hands through his hair. "Your mom called earlier," she said.

"What did she say?" he said softly.

"She invited us to dinner Sunday... tomorrow."

"And?"

"I said we'd be there."

Rad sat up. "Shit, Tawny! I wish you hadn't." He got out of bed and started pacing.

Tawny shook her head slowly. "Babe, your mom is so nice to me... I couldn't say no to her again. I'm sorry."

Rad glared at her. "Well maybe you should go by yourself. I told you I didn't want to go over there."

"All right, Rad," said Tawny, a slight tinge of anger now evident in her voice. "Call her back and say you won't be there. But don't be a dick about this."

Rad said nothing for a while. Then, "Sorry. I shouldn't have jumped on you like that. Is my sister and her husband coming?"

"Yeah," said Tawny.

Rad thought about how when his sister Helen and her husband Roger and their son Jay were around, Rad's dad was a little more restrained. He wouldn't rag on Rad about Ridgeline College with them there. Rad had been enrolled at Ridgeline in their plumbing and pipefitting program. He had been preparing to go to work in his dad's contractor business. His dad had been paying his tuition and his grades had been good. He was just fifteen units from getting his certificate when he and his dad had had their big fight over skating, in particular, the X Games. Rad had talked about maybe taking a semester off to get in shape to compete. It was just an idea at that point, and he was just thinking out loud, but his dad had exploded and told him that if he took a semester off then he would have to go to work for somebody else and pay his own tuition. They hadn't talked since. Rad's mother called every week and he visited her sometimes when he knew his dad was working late. But he and the old man stayed out of each other's way these days.

Rad knelt to Tawny and kissed her. "C'mon. Let's get something to eat."

Tawny sat up.

"Shit!" said Rad guiltily, "I was gonna barbecue."

Tawny smiled. "This was more fun. I'll throw the leftover Chinese food in the microwave."

Later, after Rad had cleaned up in the kitchen, he came out into the living room. Tawny sat in the big red beanbag chair before the TV watching a music video. "I wonder if Gabriel came by to feed Ketsel?" he said to her.

Tawny frowned without taking her eyes off the TV screen. "Hmm, I don't know."

"You want to go see?" said Rad.

Tawny looked up at him. "Not really. But if you're going to, I'll watch you."

Gabriel had been Rad's roommate before Tawny had moved in. Tawny had never liked him, and neither had Rad, actually. But Gabriel had shared the rent, and so he and Rad had co-existed in the house, speaking only enough to make the arrangement work. They never hung out together, and when Gabriel's friends came over, Rad and Tawny usually went out or else just stayed in Rad's room.

Gabriel had a big snake for a pet—Quetzalcoatl, or Ketsel, for short—a Burmese python, which he kept in the basement behind a sort-of enclosure he'd built by sectioning off a ten-foot-wide portion of the garage behind a wall of 2x4s covered with chicken wire. He'd built a door into it so he could go in to feed the snake. Gabriel's cute little pet had not been the only thing to turn Tawny off to Gabriel. He was punk, with lots of piercings and tattoos, which didn't bother her; it was the really weird, black candle occult stuff he was into that left her cold.

Rad opened the door and went down the three steps

to the concrete floor of the garage. Tawny stayed just behind him. She was always nervous when she went in the garage, afraid Ketsel had maybe gotten out of his enclosure and hidden himself somewhere close to the door, ready to spring up at her, or drop down on her. She knew how they captured their prey, having seen it on the Nature channel, biting and quickly encircling it in their powerful coils, like a large, muscled man putting someone in a headlock.

They scanned the enclosure side of the garage. Ketsel usually camouflaged himself beside the old Persian rug they'd stripped off the corridor floor and put down there, or behind the wooden pallet on which Rad had piled their earthquake supplies, or around the water heater.

Ketsel had supposedly been twelve feet long when Gabriel left. They had no idea how long he was now. Gabriel had split when the rent was due, leaving Ketsel as his good faith deposit on his half of the rent. Although Gabriel came by and fed the snake occasionally, he had never paid Rad the back rent he owed, nor had he ever come by to collect his snake.

Rad spotted Ketsel back by the water heater, behind the tires, and went inside the enclosure.

On her side of the enclosure, Tawny looked at the growing mound of dirty laundry piled on the floor and up against the chicken wire separator next to the washing machine. She leaned down and start tossing some of the clothes into the washing machine. She noticed that a section of chicken wire bulged out near the floor where it had come loose from a nail, and she made a mental note to tell Rad about it.

"He has a little lump about midway," said Rad. "Gabriel must've fed him a nice fat rat last week."

"Uh huh," said Tawny. "When is he going to take him out of here?"

"I don't know. He hasn't answered any of my messages for the last month." Rad pulled the door of the enclosure closed.

Tawny threw a scoop of soap in the washing machine, dropped the lid, and twisted the knob. Water began running into the machine. "Let's go upstairs, Babe," she said.

CHAPTER 3

A<small>S</small> A<small>LLEN</small> <small>WALKED</small> <small>UP</small> <small>THE</small> driveway he wondered what was for dinner. Tina got home an hour earlier than him. That allowed her to pick up the kids at daycare and start dinner. As he opened the door he thought he smelled roast chicken. Allen had put on a few pounds in the years he'd been married to Tina, but he didn't care. Tina was a good cook and it was worth it.

He called into the kitchen, "Honey, I'm home."

"Hi, Honey," Tina smiled at him.

Allen put his briefcase by the door. Christine sat on the couch, watching TV. With her blond hair curled by Tina into little ringlets, Allen sometimes fancied she was every bit as pretty as the young Shirley Temple had been in her heyday. He called to Christine, but she was so engrossed in the cartoon she didn't hear him. Allen walked down the hallway and looked in Reynaldo's door. The little guy sat at his desk, pencil in hand, evidently working on some assignment that Tina had given him. Although Reynaldo was seven, he was still quite small for his age and people took him to be four or five. His hair was crew cut and accentuated with a little pompadour. His upper incisors were a little pronounced and he would need orthodontia in a year or two. But for now they only added to his boyish, Norman Rockwell painting-like good looks.

"How're you doing, Reynaldo?" Allen called in to him.

Reynaldo's handsome brown face curved into a smile. "Good, Daddy."

⌐◦◦◦⌐

After dinner Tina brought a tin box over to the table. She opened it and took out a chocolate cupcake, placing it before Christine. Allen was surprised when she covered the tin up and took it back to the counter. He frowned. "Uh oh," he said, "my little boy must be in trouble."

"Yes," said Tina, "he is. And he's not getting down from this table until he says sorry."

"Sorry, Mommy," said Reynaldo.

Tina ignored him.

"What did he do?" said Allen.

"Tell Daddy what you did," said Tina.

Reynaldo frowned and looked down at the table. "I made a mark on my desk, Daddy."

"No," said Tina angrily, "you put a hole in 'my' desk. It's 'my' desk, not yours!" She stared at him, then said in a mocking tone, "made a mark..."

"Sorry, Mommy," Reynaldo said, his handsome little brown face full of sorrow.

22

Tina turned to Allen. "He drilled a hole in the wood with his pencil!"

Allen tried to compose his face into an appropriately stern frown. "Oh, Reynaldo, what did you do that for?"

Reynaldo gave him a puzzled look. "I don't know, Daddy."

Tina glowered at Reynaldo. "Get down and go wash your hands. No desert for you."

"Yes, Mommy." Reynaldo slid from his chair and carried his plate to the countertop. He went out of the kitchen.

"Finish your work," Tina called after him. "I'll be in to look at it later."

"Yes, Mommy," Reynaldo said.

Allen spent about a half-hour on the dishes. As he finished up he heard Tina telling Reynaldo that he could now come out into the living room and watch TV. When Allen came out a few minutes later, the little guy was sitting alone on the couch watching TV. A golden retriever wearing a basketball uniform was sinking shots by leaping up and head butting the ball into the basket. "Reynaldo," Allen called, "what is that?"

"*Air Bud*, Dad. It's a movie."

Allen smiled as he watched for a few minutes. He recalled Belinda, one of the daycare teachers, being amazed at the fact that a little guy like Reynaldo had such an interest in basketball, and, despite his size, seemed to have some talent for it too.

Allen quietly backed out of the living room and went down to the garage to the little primitive study he'd built there. It was really just a reading space with an old La-Z-Boy recliner and a thick old-fashioned blue hook rug to keep his feet off the concrete floor. He'd set it off from the shabbier portions of the garage by a screen and a ceiling-high bookcase. Allen sat and read the newspaper.

A half-hour or so later a knock came at the door that led up to the kitchen. Reynaldo and Christine queued there to get their goodnight kisses. Allen got up and went and gave them both a hug and a kiss, then went back down to his newspaper. When he came up later, Tina was sitting alone watching a movie on the Lifetime channel. He sat beside her and half watched, half slept for the next hour, speaking with her during the commercial breaks. After they'd gone to bed, he was still awake when Tina finally emerged from the bathroom. As she slid into the bed beside him he felt a stirring. He ran his hand up her leg. "You tired tonight?" he said.

"Umm," she said, "not too…"

Afterward, Tina went into the bathroom. She always went into the bathroom afterward, Allen thought lethargically. He remembered the young women at college, how they would lie with him afterward, he in them, sometimes falling asleep in each other's arms. Not Tina. She was too obsessive about germs. She had to go wash everything off. He frowned as he listened to her libations. Theirs wasn't a perfect marriage, but whose was? He yawned. That's just the way it was with her; other than that, they were okay.

Tina came out and slipped into the bed.

"How's work, Honey?" he asked her in the dark.

"Oh," she said, "I don't know. I don't want to talk about it."

"You know," he said, "it's funny... When I came out of the kitchen, Reynaldo was watching a movie about basketball on TV."

"So?" said Tina.

"Oh, it's just that, for a tiny guy like him to have such a big interest in basketball, it's just funny, that's all. Did Belinda ever tell you how much he likes to play basketball?"

"Uh uh," said Tina as she pulled the covers up around her.

Allen laughed. "Belinda says he's quite good."

"Oh yeah?" said Tina disinterestedly.

"You know what, Honey?"

"What?" Tina yawned.

"We could put one of those portable basketball hoops in the back yard. That way he could get a little exercise and ..."

"No," said Tina. "He's not getting any hoop until he does better with his schoolwork."

"But Honey," said Allen patiently, "if he works out from time to time, he'll burn up some of that energy. Then he'll be able to concentrate better when he does his schoolwork."

Tina turned her back to him, shaking the bed. "No. He's not getting any hoops. Not until he does better with his schoolwork."

Allen said nothing further, instead turning on his side. When Tina made up her mind about something, it was almost impossible to budge her. They argued a lot about her treatment of Reynaldo and he had begun to worry about what kind of damage that might do to the kids. Parents were supposed to present a united front; he'd heard that on a family counselor's radio talk show. It made sense—a smart kid would look for an opening, a weakness to exploit and get what he wanted. And so Allen had decided to, as much as he could, leave Tina's arbitrary, and sometimes seemingly over-the-top calls, unchallenged, and then deal with her later when the kids were asleep. It had seemed to work in the beginning. But, he thought, maybe it hadn't. Maybe he had just been consoled by having a plan of action.

Allen sighed deeply. The hell with it. He'd have to work on her another time. He closed his eyes and slept.

CHAPTER 4

1030 Skyview Drive

RAD AND TAWNY WALKED UP Skyview to catch the bus to his dad's. A slight breeze washed over them, keeping the summer temperature to a tolerable level. Rad wished he was skating. That was his default go-to fantasy when he found himself in uncomfortable circumstances. Skating was his thing, the one thing he'd achieved a sort-of mastery over. So what the hell had come of the videotape he had sent to Pygmy's? God! If they would only sponsor him. Shit. He wasn't vain by thinking he was good. He was. Everyone knew it. When he went to the park all the kids moved off the course, too embarrassed to be skating at the same time as him cause they didn't want to look too bad. He'd work out while they all sat around on their boards, some, the young ones, watching him in open admiration, the other, older kids disdainfully looking elsewhere, as if they didn't care what he was doing, when he knew they did—a lot! Shit. You absolutely could not get into the X Games unless you had a sponsor. He sighed. Maybe Pygmy's would call tonight when he and Tawny returned home.

They reached Hillside Boulevard and stood waiting for the bus. Rad wished Tawny hadn't accepted the dinner invitation to his parents', but he'd long since forgiven her. She knew he hardly ever went over there these days. In fact, he only went when his dad's truck wasn't in the driveway. And then only to stay for ten, maybe fifteen minutes. His mom would always insist he have a glass of ice tea or something. Then he'd go. Rad thought that probably since Tawny's own dad had died and her mom lived so far away, she had transferred her affections for her own family to his. The thought that she had such respect and warmth for his own family moved him, despite his own troubles with his dad.

Rad stared across Hillside Boulevard at the little stand of ten or twelve eucalyptus trees and the tan velvety, gentle flanks of San Bruno mountain rising up behind them. The eucalyptus trees rose straight and tall, their mottled brown and tan trunks powerful and column-like. He thought the grove was like some kind of temple to nature, something like what you would see in Africa. He watched the long limbs of the trees bend slightly in the wind, shaking their leaves rhythmically like tribal dancers against the tan backdrop of the mountain. Nothing in the view had been changed by the hand of man as far as he knew. How many people had a view like that? Only a few. The rich. And him, when he stood up here waiting for the bus. And they wanted to tear it out and plant condominiums on it?

Rad looked left and right for signs of the coming development. There were no construction sheds yet, no little wooden engineer stakes driven into the earth, no fluorescent pink paint markings on the sidewalk. Nothing. Not yet. And Rad hoped it would stay that way for a long, long time. He had written letters to the editors of the two San Francisco newspapers, and so far neither had printed them. That had surprised him. The people in San Francisco were very progressive, and strong opponents of the deforestation in Indo-China and the rain forests of Brazil, and yet, here in their own backyard, the virgin slopes of San Bruno Mountain were about to be ravaged by developers and they didn't seem to be interested. He couldn't believe it. He decided to write another letter when he got back to the house later.

Rad watched two red-tailed hawks glide over the peak and follow the ridge down to his right. They hovered almost motionlessly over the plateau in the powerful current of air that passed overhead. Below them, some mouse or ground squirrel had no doubt frozen into motionlessness, calculating the distance to its hole. A couple hundred feet further up the hill, a shelf-like strata of black granite slabs jutted out from the tan, fur-like, grassy slope of the mountain. In winter, when the rains were particularly heavy, the tall grasses would turn emerald green and the run off from the canyon would spill out from over granite shelf, creating a micro version of the bridal veil falls at Yosemite Park for three or four days.

Tawny squeezed Rad's hand lovingly. "What's the matter, Babe? Miss your board?"

Rad looked at her and smiled sadly. "Nah. Not when I got my woman."

"Liar," Tawny said teasingly. She leaned up and kissed him.

The SamTrans bus appeared coming down the slope and they drew closer to the curb to board.

To Rad's surprise and relief, dinner was uneventful, almost pleasant, with only a slight edge to it due to his father's presence. His sister Helen and her husband Roger and their six-year-old son Jay provided the necessary insulation between Rad and his dad. Rad and Helen had fought like cats and dogs when they were kids. How he had hated her! But now they got along great. Helen was happy and she looked better than Rad ever remembered. It struck him that happiness can change a person's appearance. Although Rad admired Roger, he still felt a distance from him. Roger was about thirty-five, tall and slim. He'd had his thinning blond hair permed to make it look thicker in front. He was a nice guy, a successful accountant, and provided a nice life for Helen and little Jay, but he was a stranger to Rad. Helen had met and married Roger when she'd been going to school back East. Rad hadn't gone to the wedding; it had been just before finals and his grades had not been good. Then Roger and Helen settled down back in New Jersey. Jay was born. Then, six years later they moved to San Francisco when Roger's company transferred him. Rad knew his sister had made a good choice, or at the very least she had gotten lucky, and Rad loved his nephew Jay like the little brother he'd never had. But whenever Roger and Helen were over his mom and dad's place, Rad was always on his guard in case his dad took a shot at him in front of Roger. Dad had complained to Rad on several occasions about how skating was 'just for kids,' when in reality, the really good skateboarders were mostly all adults, if you considered early twenties to late thirties, adults. Kids could boogey in the parking lot, grinding and making noise with lots of attitude, but it took real talent and years of practice to get to the point where you could launch yourself from a half pipe and do a 360 air walk and land it without breaking your neck, arm, leg, ankle, wrists, or all of them.

Helen and Tawny got up from the table and started clearing the dishes. Rad was feeling good, like being in the home stretch of a PE run back in his high school days. His mom was a good cook with a repertoire greater than his and Tawny's combined, and there hadn't been much conversation around the table as everybody scarfed down her roast beef, twice-baked potatoes and gravy and asparagus spears topped with homemade Hollandaise sauce. He and his father had exchanged a few pleasantries and comments about the weather and the Forty-niners and that had been it.

Rad watched his dad pour himself a beer and sit back down at the table. Except for his beer gut, his dad was still in pretty good shape for a man his age. Rad figured it probably came from his long hours working on his feet and using his hands in his home remodeling business. He still had a head full of brown hair, although he was developing a bald spot at the top.

"Did you hear about all the houses they want to put

up on the mountain?" Helen called out as she rinsed off the plates and cutlery.

"They already have their financing," said Roger. He took a sip of his cabernet. "They have some Asian outfit backing them."

Dad nodded sagely, seeming to wait for Rad to weigh in before he said anything. Little Jay came over to Rad and tugged on his hand. "Let's play on the skateboard, okay?"

"Did you bring your board?" Rad asked.

"Uh huh," said Jay.

"Okay," said Rad. "I'll meet you out on the driveway in a minute." Rad looked over at Helen as little Jay walked off. "It's not a done deal," he said. "There's an outfit trying to stop it. They've got a protest march planned for later this month. I might join them."

His dad scoffed. "Hah! Protest march! That's not gonna change anything."

"Oh, Dad," said Helen. "You're just saying that because you're in the business yourself."

"No, no" said Dad slowly, taking no offense. "I only do remodeling, additions. Small potatoes stuff."

Roger sipped his wine, smiling at the exchange. "Is that right?" he asked. "You can't get any of the action?"

Dad shook his head. "Some big outfit like DeLoi or Rawlings will get most of it." Dad looked Rad in the eye. "There's too much money involved here, Rad. No bunch of flea-bitten wannabe hippies marching down Hillside Boulevard is going to stop it."

Roger laughed at the comment.

Rad smiled and took a sip of his Coke. There it

was. He knew he would not get through the evening without some kind of putdown from his dad. His dad could be outrageous at times, especially when he got excited. Still—flea-bitten hippies? Why did he always have to put things in such terms? Rad excused himself from the table and headed for the driveway to show little Jay some moves on the skateboard.

CHAPTER 5

1015 Skyview Drive

ALLEN LEFT THE HOUSE FOR his workout. As he fast walked up the street toward Hillside Boulevard, he looked nonchalantly at the other properties on the block. All were tidy and kept up, with, of course, the exception of the rental at 1030. Overhead, the boiling clouds of fog they got this time of year, rolled eastward, generating a steady wind and chilling everything beneath them. This was the first Saturday in a month Allen hadn't had to work. They had planned a family outing, but Reynaldo had gotten into some kind of trouble. Allen had awoken late and heard Tina questioning Reynaldo in his room:

"Why did you do it?"

"I don't know, Mommy."

"Yes you do know. Now why did you do it? Tell me!"

"I don't know, Mommy."

"Don't lie to me! You do know. Now, why did you do it?"

Allen had lain in bed for several minutes, listening. On and on it went, back and forth. Why the hell couldn't she just let it go? Kids do things sometimes and they don't know why. When he was a kid he had been throwing stones at cars driving by... until he hit one and the driver circled around, grabbed him, and took him to his parents. To this day he didn't know why he had done it.

Allen had been tempted to go out and ask Tina to lighten up. But that would have broken the so-called united front. He'd listened until he couldn't stand it anymore and then had taken his shower. By the time he came out, Tina and the kids had already had their breakfast and a pall hung in the house. Reynaldo was grounded for the weekend, confined to his room. And so they would all stay home.

Allen had his coffee alone in the kitchen as Tina went about her chores. She came through the kitchen carrying a hamper of clothes down to the garage to put in the washer. When she came back up he asked her if she needed any help. She ignored him. A moment later he heard her running the vacuum. After finishing his coffee he left the kitchen to use the bathroom before starting his walk. Christine was watching cartoons in the living room. Allen looked in Reynaldo's room as he passed in the hallway. The little guy's eyes were wet with tears as he sat at his desk working on his definitions. Tina had a regimen for Reynaldo that involved him writing down the dictionary definitions of about fifteen or twenty words in his best penmanship and memorizing their spelling and meaning. This sometimes went on for four or six hours. Then Tina would quiz him. If he could successfully spell the words and recite their meanings, he could go play or watch TV.

Reynaldo turned his head in Allen's direction, but Allen hurried past. He thought Tina's assignments were excessive, so how the hell could he look into those sad brown eyes when he was supposed to maintain the parental united front?

Allen decided to walk through the old downtown first before he power walked along Hillside. He turned onto Beech Street, then left onto Second Avenue, which ran through the oldest part of South San Francisco. The houses here were small and solid looking, like the houses in San Francisco, which were probably the same age. There were even several multi-story brick or stone apartment buildings of the type one might see in Philadelphia on the East Coast where he had grown up. But such solid edifices were rare in earthquake country.

Just past the Olympic gas station, Allen came to his favorite building—a brick three-story apartment house. He felt almost as if he had gone through some kind of dimensional warp and wound up back in Philly. One of the apartments on the second floor always drew his eye. Its sitting room picture window was framed by white brocaded curtains held open by pink velvet ties. Within this frame, two plush red upholstered chairs were turned slightly toward a table between them upon which sat a porcelain vase-style lamp with a lush fabric cover. It was, Allen imagined, exactly the kind of place that an old retired couple would live in. In their late seventies, having long contributed their time and energy to the community in the form of taxes paid, time volunteered socially, children properly raised and sent off to other parts of the country to establish beachheads of civility and citizenship, this serene couple now rested, occasionally looking out this window to ensure that the newcomers were now doing their part to bear up and carry forth the burden of good citizenship. Allen thought he had seen them once when he was walking by, but most of the time the almost-regal chairs were empty. Allen wished he knew the old couple. And he wanted what they had for himself someday, a quiet, bright, peaceful perch to look out in clean, respectful comfort onto the dingy chaos of the city's streets.

Allen walked up Acacia Street to Hillside Boulevard. He started fast walking against the traffic. After about five minutes he got his wind and settled into a good aerobic pace. As the road climbed higher, hugging the mountain's side, a BMW raced past—closer to the curb then necessary, Allen thought. He didn't look up, his brows furrowing unconsciously as he leaned into the cool winds buffeting him. Other cars raced past. He refused to look at the faces of the drivers, not giving them the satisfaction of a look. He had been in a hurry to get out of the house and he was wearing his dress-down working-around-the-house clothes, instead of his workout sweats. He thought that perhaps the drivers racing past him now assumed that he was of a low economic class walking hurriedly, not to burn off calories and reduce his cholesterol, but rather to get from point A to point B because he didn't own a car. Nothing could be further from the truth, he thought to himself. Another car raced by, the shock wave and the warm rotten-egg-smelling exhaust assaulting him. Fuck you, he thought.

Allen looked down the slope to his left and spotted the high redwood fence of the first house he and Tina had owned. On the other side of the fence a dog barked at him. He had had that fence put up himself. He had used some Chinese contractor Tina's friend had recommended. That was before the kids came along. Back then he and Tina had had their fights too. But usually they'd end up in the sack that night, making lustful kiss-and-make-up love to one another. Lately they'd slacked off a bit, he realized sadly.

Allen reached the summit of Hillside Boulevard. The road ahead sloped downward at a slight angle for about a hundred yards, and then began climbing again. On his right was the Mancini plant nursery with dozens of redwood tubs of potted trees lined up in orderly rows. Above the nursery, San Bruno Mountain rose gradually, the angle growing steeper at about fifteen hundred feet. There, granite outcroppings pushed through the soil. A dozen or so derrick-like microwave re-transmission towers capped the mountain.

Allen walked on for another quarter mile, coming to a small, round metal sign sprouting out of the ground next to the pavement—Colma City Limits. Bordering South San Francisco, the town of Colma had an interesting and unusual history. A tiny city, only eleven hundred people lived there, but over one and a half million reposed in its sixteen cemeteries. Known as the necropolis of San Francisco, Colma was home to the remains of Wyatt Earp, Governor Edmund Brown, A. P. Giannini, founder of the Bank of Italy, a Hells Angel buried astride his Harley Davidson motorcycle, Emperor Norton, Ishi, the last wild California Indian, and Tina Turner's dog, buried in the singer's mink coat, along with millions of lesser loved and/or forgotten souls.

Allen leaned slightly into the wind, enjoying its buffeting and the fact that by having to overcome its force, he was probably doubling his workout, his calorie expenditure. He came to the ornately-carved stone gates of Holy Cross Cemetery and paused. He breathing was labored and he wondered if part of that was due to some deeply-hidden feelings which the morning's disturbance back at the house had loosened in him. Or perhaps it was purely physical from the exertion, and his mind was mistakenly connecting it to the breathlessness of anxiety.

Why the hell did Tina have to be so hard on Reynaldo? And why did she let her anger get the better of her every time? He wondered what a therapist would have to say about that. He glanced at his watch. He'd been walking thirty minutes. The return would give him an hour total, his normal routine.

His eyes slowly panned the well maintained green expanse of Holy Cross Cemetery. If he cut through it, he could work his way back from there. It would be roughly the same distance, he calculated, and it would give him more to look at than just the road and the steady stream of Saturday people driving along Hillside Boulevard to their tennis lessons, or taking their kids to Great America, or Golden Gate Park or wherever. He started down the road into the cemetery.

Allen enjoyed the peaceful feeling of the cemetery. There were no cars racing by, no dogs barking at him, only the occasional distant prolonged whoosh of a jet high overhead. The blacktop road wound back and forth down the gentle slope of the hill. On either side, orderly rows of memorial stones marked the graves. Here and there a granite or marble mausoleum rose high up out of the earth to proclaim the wealth and prestige of its occupant.

Allen paused at a large, white marble vault topped with a statue of an angel. One of the wings had broken off long ago and the northernmost side of the sculpture was covered with a patina of green moss. An old, gnarled pine tree rose above it and the ground around the area was littered with a blanket of brown pine needles. It was an especially beautiful place and Allen was tempted to linger. But this was his workout and so he continued walking. Near where the road bottomed out, he saw a long, adobe-style cemetery maintenance building. On the other side of it, a red Honda drove down a road with a solid yellow line in the middle. Allen realized he was looking at Mission Road, which traversed most of the cemeteries. The car was headed in the direction of Daly City. On the other side of Mission Road, a high fence blocked off what Allen assumed to be train tracks. Back along Mission Road, in the direction of his own house, he spotted a ramshackle auto body shop with a corrugated tin roof and two dilapidated, rusting gas pumps out front. In the other direction he saw a large mustard-colored clapboard building with a sign out front that said McCoy's. What appeared to be a red and blue neon Budweiser sign glowed in the window, and Allen assumed it was a bar. He wondered how in Hades they got any business out here.

Allen looked at his watch. It was almost eleven. He could walk around the cemetery building and have a beer and sandwich at the bar. But he didn't want to be away too long, just in case Tina relented and released Reynaldo early from his detention. Then they could all go someplace and enjoy what was left of their Saturday. He walked on.

Allen came to a fork in the road and paused. The road was newly paved and the smell of asphalt filled his nostrils. The heat of the day was building and he turned in the direction of South San Francisco. At a point about a block away, the road appeared to angle up to join Hillside Boulevard.

The road climbed, then angled around, coming to an end after a quarter of a mile in a little cul de sac. It was evidently a new division of plots the cemetery had recently opened up.

Allen grew a little annoyed with himself. He wiped the sweat from his brow. Now he would have to retrace his footsteps. He scanned the fields stretching up and away in the direction of Hillside Boulevard. They came to an end at some kind of community garden. He could see orderly rows of poles set in the earth and what looked like a stable. He had heard that there was a 4H club up there somewhere. Maybe that was it. Allen was about to turn around when some movement caught his eye. A slick, fat earthworm writhed in the bright sunlight, then tumbled down a mound of freshly dug earth that was heaped up on the lawn. For some reason he walked up the new marble steps and onto the lawn.

Three graves had been dug in a row. Each of them was deep, Allen estimated, maybe six or seven feet. He thought of what his mother had told him when he was a kid about his Uncle John. As the story went, he had left the taproom in his cups, as they used to say, and taken a shortcut home through the cemetery. Falling into a deep grave, he had been unable to get out. After struggling for hours he had finally given up, laid down and fallen asleep. The sound of approaching footsteps woke him. Someone stood at the edge of the grave in the gray light of dawn. Their face was obscured, but Uncle John had sworn that they'd had a clubfoot—the mark of the devil. By the time the workers found Uncle John later that morning, his hair had turned snowy white.

Allen stared at the graves. The one on the far right was smaller, child size, he realized with sadness. Some family must have recently suffered an awful tragedy. Three graves—a father, a mother, and a small child would lie here. He and Tina had two children and were a family of four. This numerical difference comforted him and gave him enough distance to imagine this unfortunate family's end. He pictured them in a car on a highway at night. They were returning from a weekend trip. The father was at the wheel, his eyes almost closed from exhaustion, the bright pinpoints of headlights doubling, coming together, moving apart, fading. The mother and child slept in the back seat. The engine droned and the man's eyelids drooped. He opened them suddenly as blinding light flooded in. Cursing explosively, he jerked the wheel hard. The car swerved, then spun, disorienting the occupants as it hurtled through space. The woman screamed in horror, then the car landed on its roof, snapping their necks in an instant. Then silence. Allen felt a chill and turned away. He went back to the road and started walking.

CHAPTER 6

O N SUNDAY, RAD AWOKE TO the sound of Tawny showering as she got ready for work. He looked at the clock: 8:14. He swung his feet over the bed and went out to the kitchen, putting on a pot of coffee. It had been three months since he'd spoken to the guy at Pygmy's. They should have called him back by now as to whether or not they were going to sponsor him. He went into the living room and took the man's card from his wallet. He dialed the number. The phone rang once and a voice came on. "Raines here."

Rad stared at the card, momentarily tongue-tied.

"Who is this?" said Raines impatiently.

"Hello, Mr. Raines," said Rad. "Rad Anderson. I'm the guy from South San Francisco that sent you the tape. I was wondering if you guys had made any decisions yet on who you're going to sponsor."

"Huh? Those letters should have been mailed out three weeks ago."

"I never received anything," said Rad.

"Shit," Raines muttered at his end. "What did you say your name was again?"

"Rad Anderson."

"Hold on a minute."

Rad waited. He heard the squeak of the faucet as Tawny turned the water off.

Raines came back on the line. "Sorry, Anderson. They didn't pick you. You're probably the best skater of the bunch, but I don't think you have the image they're looking for. Who shot the video?"

Rad felt stunned. He had a lump in his throat the size of an egg. "Huh? Oh, my girl did."

"She's good, man."

"Yeah," said Rad.

"Well," said Raines. "Sorry."

"Yeah," said Rad, "thanks."

In what had become his knee-jerk reaction to bad news, Rad grabbed his board and went outside to work it out. Motion did it for him. It was his drug. Motion or Tawny. But he couldn't share this with Tawny yet. It hurt too much. He had to grind off some of the sharp edges. As soon as he got out the door the sun hit him full in the face and he sneezed. He sat down on the steps, his board on his lap, and stared up at San Bruno Mountain. 'Move!' his mind told him, 'Just move,' but he just sat there, staring at the soft tan velvety flanks of the mountain. Mr. Peepers drove by, glancing at him surreptitiously. Rad had a momentary out-of-body experience, seeing himself from Mr. Peeper's perspective as he sat on the steps like some little kid waiting for his friend to come over to play with him.

Rad tried to deny the truth of the image, but it was too strong. He got up, leaned the board against the door, and started walking up the street. He felt odd without his board clutched in his hand. As he walked his eyes were again drawn to the mountain.

Reaching the top of Skyview, Rad stood on Hillside Boulevard, watching the high tan grass on the mountain move in waves, like some otherworldly sea. About two hundred feet up the slope, a grove of tall, dark green eucalyptus trees drew his eye. He stared at them and then looked beyond, following the hill up to its peak. A jet circled high overhead, its engines inaudible.

No one climbed the sides of this beautiful mountain, Rad realized. He'd never seen anyone up there. Nobody cared about it. Not really, not enough to be on it. He had a sudden impulse to climb it. He frowned. Maybe he'd have a vision, like Moses or something.

Rad waited for a break in the traffic and ran across the boulevard. He started up, following a rocky rubble-filled, dried-up streambed up the hill. The morning's chill was almost gone and the sun was beginning to heat the air up.

The streambed meandered off to the left and a faintly discernible trail continued straight up the slope. Rad walked slowly through the cool, dark aromatic shade of the eucalyptus grove. The path was littered with long strips of eucalyptus bark, crunchy brown leaves and acorn-like seedpods. The darkness was comforting and he was tempted to linger. But that was not what he needed now. On the boulevard below, the noise of the traffic had softened and was like the gentle sighing of a river or the surf. His anger and disappointment flared anew and he felt like hitting something. "Fuck it," he said softly. "Just fuck it all!"

He walked out of the grove into bright sunlight. The air was warm and dry. He had an easy go of it for the first third of the way up. The path was dry and rocky and he trod slightly hunched forward, short steady steps like a mule. The thick, still slightly-damp knee-high grass was sprinkled with golden California poppies and some purple wildflowers Rad didn't know the name of. Below and behind him, South San Francisco was a flat gray grid of streets and buildings. Above, a jet plane banked in a tight turn after having taken off from SFO, the sound of its engines muffled by its altitude.

He reached the first peak and paused to catch his breath. A broad grassy valley dotted with deep green chaparral stretched below about two thousand yards to the north. From it the fingers of the mountain rose up to the top. To his left, the tan squiggle of the trail ran out onto the nearest finger of the mountain, running level for about five hundred yards, then rising and disappearing behind a large rocky outcrop. Overhead, another jet, its twin engines mounted on its vertical stabilizer, banked into a tight turn, its long, skinny aluminum fuselage gleaming brightly in the sun.

Rad resumed climbing. The wind came up and began whipping about his ears. To his left and right, deep valleys yawned full of grass, rocks and chaparral. Ahead, the mountain rose slowly, the trail etched into its center. Along the way, great shattered gray rocks rose here and there out of the tan hill like the battlements of a demolished castle. Anise and sage crowded the trail, giving off an aromatic air.

It was very quiet. Rad realized that he had achieved an increasingly unique modern experience—that of being truly alone—unless, of course, there were people on the other side of the rocks ahead, which he doubted. He was like a solo sailor out of the shipping lanes; if something were to happen to him there was no one close enough to help him. His fists clenched reflexively, the idea thrilling him. He stared at the rocks, looking for any sign of movement.

He began walking again. The trail ran parallel with another dried-up streambed and angled up. The footing was bad and Rad slipped several times. The grade was steep now and his breathing was coming hard, his heart pounding. He thought about turning around and going back. This was stupid. Did he expect to find a gray-headed old wise man sitting cross legged at the top of the mountain, waiting to ease his mind and help him unpuzzle his life? Of course not! So what the hell was he doing? It didn't matter now. Only getting to the top did.

He paused, breathing heavily. Two or three hundred feet below, a red Coast Guard helicopter was passing through the canyon. Rad thrilled at the sight. He saw the red choppers almost every day as they headed out toward the coast to patrol the beaches. Now he was higher than they were.

He continued climbing. After another ten minutes he crested a steep rise in the trail and saw a pile of rocks crowning the peak. He pushed on toward it.

Rad's breath was wheezing out of him when he reached the peak and he was amazed at how difficult the climb had been. He sat on a flat rock in the sunlight, his chest rising and falling. He was thirsty, wanting only clear, cold water, and lots of it. To his left lay the gray concrete bowl of Candlestick Park and a marina with 40 or 50 sailboats, their masts like a forest of white trees and the deep blue of the bay beyond. On his right, the sun reflected blindingly off the Pacific Ocean. Almost directly below, the gray grid of South San Francisco came up against the soft green of the cemeteries of Colma—the orderly lines of polished tombstones glinting in the sun like parallel pools of water. He was reminded of the pictures he'd seen of rice paddies in Vietnam, his father's pictures.

Rad studied it all as the wind mussed his hair and the sun beat down on him. Slowly his breathing returned to normal and his strength returned. His head seemed to have emptied out. He had no profound answers, no insight. Nothing. But, strangely, he didn't care. His disappointment had left him and been replaced by a kind of physical joy, a delight in his life and the young, strong body which had brought him up all the way up this high. He tried to pick out the house he and Tawny lived in, but couldn't. When she left for work, she must have wondered where the hell he had gone, puzzling over the fact that he'd left his board behind. How many times had he done that? Never. He decided to call her at the shop when he got back to the place.

He started down. Later, as he neared the roadway

of Hillside Boulevard, he wondered where his answer was. He felt silly. There was no answer. Just like there was no sponsor. And he would not participate in the X Games and that was that.

He ran across the boulevard and walked down the street to the house. On an impulse, he stopped and turned around to look back at the mountain. It was beautiful and voluptuous; but it was also helpless. Suddenly he knew what he would do.

The article on the housing development was in Sunday's paper. The paper was still in the garage somewhere. He would find it and get the number for that outfit, Mountain Saviors, or whatever they called themselves. He would help them oppose the goddamn greedy developers and save the mountain.

CHAPTER 7

ALLEN SAT ON ONE OF the two tiny yellow plastic chairs, his knees almost as high as his shoulders; Christine sat in the other. On the floor around them were the Barbie and Ken dolls, assorted doll clothes, a Ken and Barbie toy convertible car and, of course, Barbie's house. Allen couldn't recall which one of them had come up with the idea, but their play always consisted of him and Christine, each holding a doll up like a marionette and having a dialogue—simple things like:

Christine as Barbie, "How was your day, Daddy?"

Allen as Ken, "Fine, Honey. How were things at the house?"

Allen was always charmed by these play sessions. Christine liked them and wanted the interaction and he always consented, although he had fallen asleep during them once or twice, only to be brought back by a petulant, 'Daddy!'

This time Allen fell silent for longer periods as he wondered and worried about the fate of his family. On a few rare occasions Tina had yelled at Christine and she had cried fearfully. But there had been nothing like the anger and seemingly-hateful behaviors that Tina exhibited toward Reynaldo. And this fact nailed down one truth for him—if he did break the family apart and file for divorce he would never get custody of his daughter. He knew it deep in his bones, because the bulk of Tina's abuse had not been directed at her. But—there existed the very real possibility that he could lose Reynaldo as well. After all, if he divorced Tina he would be a single man, and he couldn't imagine a judge giving custody of a child that had been treated as badly as Reynaldo had by Tina, to a single man. Allen had tried to temper Tina's behavior, of course, but would that be enough to dissuade some judge from taking Reynaldo away from them both and giving him to an intact, loving couple, or putting him back into the system? Allen didn't think so.

"Tell me a story, Daddy," Christine said, breaking into his thoughts.

She had gotten out of her chair and pushed close to him. "Pick me up."

He picked her up and hugged her and his eyes teared up. He loved her deeply, but he didn't know how much longer he would have her.

Allen took the little note book and pen he always carried in his shirt pocket. He wasn't much of an artist, but he illustrated the stories he told to Christine with crudely drawn stick figures and she liked it.

"There was a little pig named Petey," he began, wondering where he could take it.

"Draw him," she said, snuggling close into him.

He sketched Petey on the lined paper, walking past some trees. "And when Petey was out walking, Sammy the snake saw him."

"Draw it," she said.

He sketched a long Adam and Eve in the Garden-type serpent hanging down from a tree, tongue flicking out. "And then Sammy captured him." Allen hurriedly scribbled ropes being wound around Petey the pig.

"And then what happened, Daddy?"

"Well, Sammy decided to cook him for dinner."

"Draw it."

Allen was sketching Petey the pig bound and sitting in a cauldron of boiling water when Tina entered the room.

"Time for bed," Tina announced.

Christine fairly leaped out of his arms.

In the dark of early evening, the police cruiser slowly drove down Grand Avenue as Allen sat in the parked van. The patrolman either didn't see him or didn't see him as any potential threat to the law-abiding citizenry, but Allen felt odd sitting in the dark and so he started the van up. He and Tina had had another fight and he had decided it was better to get out of the house and let things cool off. But where the hell could he go and who the hell could he talk to? He remembered the bar he'd seen from his walks in the cemetery—McCoy's, or whatever it was called. It was on Mission Street in an old, mustard-colored wooden Victorian building.

Allen put the van in drive and turned onto Mission. He drove past some long low buildings and realized they were part of El Camino High School. He drove further, figuring that the bar had to be just up ahead. He saw a driveway on his right with a sign—All Saints Mausoleum. As Allen continued to drive slowly, he looked at the sharply defined squares and rectangles of the granite mausoleums off in the dark on both sides of the road. Joe DiMaggio and William Randolph Hearst were buried out there somewhere. He had always meant to go see their graves. Ahead on his right, he saw what he assumed to be Holy Cross Cemetery. A dim light appeared just past that on the left, below it a sign—McCoy's. He pulled into the parking lot.

The building was as wide as two houses, two stories with a peaked roof. As Allen walked up to the door he thought wryly that only the Irish would put a bar and social club smack dab in the middle of over twenty cemeteries. He went inside.

There were no customers at the bar. On the other side, an ancient-looking bartender sat on a stool before the tall pull handles of the beer taps. He nodded noncommittally at Allen. Gruff male voices came from the back room, then the crack of a pool break and the dull thud of a ball falling into a pocket. Allen slid onto a stool near the bartender and ordered a pint of lager. The bartender wordlessly leaned in to a shelf below the bar and took out a pint glass. He slowly filled it. Something about the man's face intrigued Allen and he looked away, not wanting to stare. The man appeared to be about seventy, but he looked strong for his age.

Allen recalled his mother's term, an 'old bird,' then decided that that other term, 'old goat,' would better describe this man.

The bartender put the foam-dripping glass before Allen and he put a five-dollar bill down. The bartender's full head of gray hair was as curly and thick as a Brillo Pad. Deep crags had etched into his face, reminding Allen of those Hummel figurines carved from pieces of driftwood in Cape Cod. The man's wide nose appeared to have been broken once. High cheekbones, a jutting jaw, and innumerable wrinkles all testified to a hard life, perhaps as a stevedore or some kind of construction worker, or a sailor, some endeavor that had put him out to weather in the elements for long hours. Allen thought it was the kind of face a painter would like. Drama and struggle disfigured it, unlike Allen's own smooth, slightly baby-faced face. Allen remembered an illustrator friend who used to work at Lockheed who used to carve busts of famous people out of apples. He would then leave them sitting on his desk where they'd dry up, taking on a grisly look, like shrunken heads. The bartender's face had a similar look.

Allen felt like talking. He nodded at the ancient bartender. "Why in hell did they build this place here?"

For a moment the old guy appeared as if he wasn't going to respond. Then his bushy brows moved as he blinked. "When Colma was nothing but potato fields and pig farms, people used to stay here when they passed through on the old El Camino. It was what they used to call a road house."

Allen nodded. "When did they put in all the

cemeteries?"

The old guy frowned. "Oh, maybe a couple or so years after the big quake. They said it was for health reasons."

Allen looked at him quizzically.

"Up in Frisco, some of the bodies got thrown up from the earth during the quake, some really ripe ones."

Allen frowned with concern. "It must've freaked a lot of people out."

"No," said the old man, "not really. Anyway, it was really greed."

"What do you mean?" said Allen.

The old man glanced up at the college basketball game on the TV and then back at Allen. "Real estate rates were rising in San Francisco then, just like they are now. So they moved all the dead out of there, down to here."

"Really?" said Allen.

The old man nodded and went on. "Yeah, it was a good thing for South City, because most of the potato and pig farms had already gone south and we needed a new cash crop."

Allen laughed. The old man gave him a curious look, then went back to watching the game on the TV.

Allen sipped his beer slowly and wondered why he always seemed to be alone. He had no close friends anymore. Over the years, Tina had turned down so many invitations from couples he knew that they had stopped coming. Of the few friends he had brought home, she had always, inevitably, found some flaw or trait in them she didn't like, and would not have them over again. And Allen had no family on the West Coast. His only brother lived in Maine.

Allen couldn't remember ever feeling so troubled and isolated. When his mom and dad had died, the loss had seemed natural, in the normal scheme of things. They had both been elderly when they passed. But now he was trying to deal with a different kind of loss—the potential loss of his young family and all the comfort and security it provided—because if they couldn't work things out, divorce was the probable outcome. What the hell else could he do?

Allen ordered another pint of beer from the goat-like bartender. After he had drank down half of it, the bartender looked over. Cheering erupted from the TV and the bartender said what sounded like, "That's almost as good as doing something about it, isn't it?"

Allen frowned in puzzlement. "Huh?" he said. But the old goat didn't say anything further and turned away.

An hour later Allen drove back to the house. It was as quiet as a grave. He undressed in the dark and slipped into bed, falling asleep within minutes.

CHAPTER 8

1030 Skyview Drive

R AD WOULD NOT BE BACK for an hour and Tawny wanted to get caught up on her laundry. She decided to enter the garage through the back door. It was easier to spot Ketsel this way. She went out into the brightly-lit day and walked back along the side of the house. She put the key in the lock, turned it, and opened the door. Daylight flooded the back end of the garage. She didn't see Ketsel. She turned the light on and scanned the enclosure side of the garage, spotting him curled up in Rad's stack of tires. He was a good distance from the washing machine and she relaxed a little. Leaving the door open, she walked briskly over to the washing machine. Glancing back at Ketsel, she knelt to scoop up some clothes. She looked closely at the bulge in the chicken wire. It looked like it bulged out more now, but it was impossible to tell for sure in the dim light. As she scooped up some of the whites and dumped them in the machine, she thought she could sense the snake's awareness of her. She took another look. Even though it did not lift its head or move or make a sound, she knew it was contemplating her, and this unnerved her. It seemed to be bigger too. Rad said it was only ten or twelve feet. She thought it was a lot bigger than that.

Tawny threw a measuring cup of Tide in the machine, dropped the lid with a clang, and spun the dial to HEAVY DUTY. She looked over at the snake—still no movement. She wondered what would happen if the thing died. It would probably be weeks before they knew. She pushed the washer button in and water ran into the machine.

She retraced her footsteps to the back door, all the while keeping her eye on Ketsel. She knew all this caution was probably ridiculous, that it would not, could not, suddenly leap up and pour across the garage floor, burst through the chicken wire and wrap its coils around her before she got to the door. But the snake gave her the creeps now more than it ever did. She wondered if maybe the zoo would take it if Gabriel didn't return for it. Maybe they could even get some money for it. She turned out the lights and pulled the door closed, locking it.

Coming around to the front of the house, Tawny saw the Mexican woman and her two girls almost to the top of the hill. Even from the distance Tawny could see that the woman had gotten bigger. It would be no more than a month or so before she gave birth.

Tawny sat on the steps and wondered what a baby she and Rad had would look like. She looked up at the sky.

It would have eyes as blue as the sky and it would be chubby. She imagined it smiling. It would be beautiful; of that she was sure. The roar of the big SamTrans bus interrupted her reverie as it drove away. A moment later Rad walked slowly down the street without his formerly ever-present board tucked under his arm. She thought sadly how 'not him' this was. Ever since Pygmy's had turned him down he'd been depressed.

Rad smiled when he saw her. He pulled her close and deep-kissed her, temporarily dissipating her wondering and worrying. They went into the house.

All during their meal Rad seemed distracted and distant. Tawny had made one of his and her favorites, stuffed Cornish game hens, and Rad's quiet pensiveness had distracted from her enjoyment of the meal. Afterwards he offered to do the dishes.

"No, that's okay," she said. "Why don't you get the clothes out of the washer and put them in the dryer. And look at the chicken wire fence at the bottom of the washing machine. It looks like it's a little bulged out there."

"Okay," he said.

"I'll get the dishes," she said as he disappeared downstairs. She again thought about giving the snake to the zoo people, or maybe some kind of wild animal park. Surely they could get some money for it. She wanted to discuss it with Rad, but with him so depressed about Pygmy's decision, maybe this wasn't the right time.

Tawny wiped the drain board and went out into the living room. She parted the curtains and looked out on the dying light of day. Mr. Peepers drove by in his van with his wife and two kids. The boy was dark and looked like a Filipino, probably adopted. His handsome brown face got her thinking again about the Mexican cleaning woman and her two beautiful kids, and the one that she would soon give birth to. Tawny imagined having the woman and her children visiting in the living room with her right now. She imagined playing on the rug with them—and her own child! That would be wonderful. But, she reminded herself, it was totally impractical. How could she contribute to the rent and stuff if she had kids to take care of too? It wasn't do-able in today's economy. She let the curtains close and sat down on the couch. Rad came up from the garage. He gave her a little friendly squeeze on the thigh as he sat down and picked up the TV remote.

"Is that all I get?" Tawny said with a laugh, "a squeeze?"

Rad smiled without taking his eyes off the set, "for now." He clicked through several shows, settling on a sort of he-man fighting competition.

Tawny curled up beside him, browsing through a magazine as he watched. Several times she tried to engage him in conversation to no avail. It was like working in the shop and running her comb through an old man's thinning head of hair—there was no tactile feedback, nothing to build on. And she wanted so much to talk tonight. Maybe it was the snake. No. It was the children, she realized, and especially the Mexican woman's pregnancy. It had brought to the surface all her longings and fears, and dreams—and she wanted to talk them out. When her frustration with Rad's silence got the better of her she got off the couch without a word and went into the bathroom to get ready for bed.

Tawny was almost asleep when Rad pulled her close. She put her arms around him, luxuriating in his warmth. They made love and her concerns burnt up in their passion. Then, later, as their ardor cooled and dissipated, a vague worry slowly returned to fill the void inside of her. Rad reached for her later in the night but she turned away from him.

CHAPTER 9

O N SATURDAY MORNING, ALLEN SAT on the couch reading the newspaper as Tina rushed about fussing over the kids to make sure they were ready. They were going to the home of Tina's manager David Wu for a barbecue and lawn party. Allen felt good for a change. He and Tina did not socialize often and then usually only with Tina's family or close friends. Allen lamented that he didn't seem to have friends anymore, at least none that he could contact easily. He had a few back East, but he had long ago lost touch with them. But he did enjoy some of Tina's co-worker friends and looked forward to their two or three get-togethers each year. At these events Tina usually let down her guard a little and he could relax. The kids had figured it out too—with all the other adults around, they had a bit more freedom to play and have fun without upsetting Mommy and getting consequences.

Allen had met David Wu the year before at a company party. Unlike most of the Chinese in the

Bay Area, David Wu hailed from Shanghai and spoke Mandarin instead of Cantonese. His wife was Caucasian. David had received his MBA from one of the Ivy League colleges back East; Allen had forgotten which one.

Allen looked up briefly from the paper as Tina rushed back toward the rear of the house for something. They were only driving five-miles down the Peninsula to the next little town, but Tina prepared as if they were going on a day's journey. Finally Allen heard the porch door open, his cue that she was ready. He grabbed the sodas and two bags of chips Tina had volunteered to bring, and carried them out to the van.

After the kids had been strapped into their child safety seats, Allen drove up the hill. He eyeballed the house at 1030, as was his habit now, but Raggedy Anne and Andy were nowhere to be seen. Probably inside banging each other's brains out, he thought, or maybe they were hung over from dancing all night at some ecstasy-fueled rave party. Allen knew that his fantasies about them were partly caused by some generational jealousy. After all, his generation had been into some pretty self-destructive things too, and their long hippie hair and beards and bell-bottoms were just as childish and silly as nose rings and fire engine-red hair. He glanced briefly at the truck up on cinder blocks and the barren lawn, determined not to let it spoil his good mood.

The ride down 101 was uneventful. Most of the traffic was heading north for a Giants game at Candlestick. Allen took the Burlingame exit and soon they parked next to a nicely refurbished house on a quiet tree-lined street. Allen had looked at houses in this neighborhood after Tina and he had first gotten married. They were small, built pre-WWII, with out-of-code wiring. But even back then they were priced way beyond his and Tina's reach. Halfway between the cosmopolitan city cool of San Francisco, and the manic moneyed Silicon Valley, Burlingame was a much sought-after zip code for wealthy boomers with young families.

Allen grabbed the bags and took Reynaldo's hand. They followed Tina and Christine as they entered the back yard through the driveway. The lawn was lush and green. Allen noticed that David Wu had had a basketball hoop and backboard built against his detached garage. David Wu and a brown-skinned younger man stood next to a picnic table underneath a latticework arbor that broke the harsh sunlight into an easy-on-the-eyes checkerboard pattern. An old fashioned zinc washtub full of ice and beer and wine sat on the picnic table next to them.

Allen liked David Wu. He was personable, intelligent, well educated, without any trace of an accent. He had evidently come to the states at an early age and seemed more Americanized than any other foreign-born Chinese Allen knew. Tina had told him that David was some kind of big shot in the Democrat party and had a picture in his office of him and President Clinton standing together.

Allen nodded a greeting to the two men as he led Reynaldo over to the table and set the two bags down. "Reynaldo," said Allen, "do you remember Uncle David?"

Reynaldo shook his head shyly.

David Wu laughed and squatted down beside Reynaldo. "He was too young," David said. "A year is a long time to someone his age. Right Reynaldo?"

"I don't know," said Reynaldo.

Allen and David laughed. David stood and pulled one of the dripping bottles of beer from the tub and handed it to Allen. David indicated the man next to him. "Allen, this is Fidel Flores. He's part of the finance department gang."

"How're you doing?" said Allen, extending his hand. One night, a year or so earlier, as Allen washed the dishes, Tina had told him all about Fidel. Fidel was Filipino, in his early thirties, and unmarried, although he had a steady, live-in girlfriend.

Fidel shook Allen's hand stiffly, giving him an odd look. The look confused Allen at first, and then he recognized it to be disapproval. Fidel tried his best to hide it, but it was unmistakable. Allen had gotten that look a few times before, usually from strangers at the supermarket or the mall, usually Mexican-Americans or Filipino-Americans, all of whom assumed, wrongly, that Reynaldo was of their race. But he was not. He was Mixtec Indian, from the land of the Incas, a tiny, beautiful brown boy who had somehow managed to end up with Tina, Mexican-American, and Allen, Irish-American. Fidel's look seemed to say, 'What the hell is a kid that looks like that doing with somebody that looks like you?'

Allen smiled. This sort of thing no longer bothered him. As long as he wasn't being turned down for a job because of it, or denied a house in a neighborhood he wanted. And it lessened his guilt about his own prejudices. Everybody had them. Just the week before he had been walking through the parking lot of the mall when he saw two huge black teenagers, hulking in their baggy pants and their Raiders jackets, gangbangers, or wannabes—who could tell—following some frail, teen Chinese couple, all the while muttering, "chinka, chinka, chinka." The teens ignored them, chatting amiably as if they weren't there. What else could they do if they didn't want to get their asses kicked, or worse. And the Chinese had their prejudices and their own epithets for other races; Bokwei, or 'white devil' came to mind. Allen had had some elderly Chinese lady loudly and angrily call him by that slur once in a Chinese grocery store for some perceived slight. The only people who didn't have prejudices were saints and liars. Allen didn't know any saints, but there were plenty of liars strutting about these days, most of them in politics or heading up ethnic-rights organizations.

Allen thought wryly how Tina, by virtue of her Hispanic heritage and her surname—not her light skin, which would identify her as perhaps Castilian Spanish, but not Mexican—had gotten a pass from Fidel for having adopted little brown Reynaldo. But Allen, because of his Celtic name, light skin and blue-eyes, had not.

"Fidel," said Allen pleasantly, "we finally meet. Tina's told me a lot about you."

Fidel gave Allen a pained smile. "Oh? Not all bad, I hope."

"Nah," said Allen. Both men's' eyes disengaged to watch Reynaldo wonder across the lawn toward a solitary, gnarled tree. Allen thought it was an apple tree.

Allen took a sip of the beer and looked around. The houses across the way were small, maybe eleven hundred square feet at best, but in good shape. He'd heard they now went for over half a million. David Wu and his wife Colleen had no children, but had probably bought here because they planned on having a family. Tina had told Allen that the rumor was they were going to a fertility clinic.

Tina and Dolores Castillo came over. Dolores, Mexican-American, was the head secretary for the office. Dolores and her husband had raised six children and Allen wished he knew her and her husband better. But Tina had never invited them over and they had never been invited to the Castillo's.

After Tina and Dolores poured sodas for themselves, more office employees arrived bearing baskets and bags and they went over to greet them. Allen did not know any of them and stayed under the shade of the arbor, eating salsa and chips and drinking beer. He looked around. Tina was now helping another woman from the office at the barbecue grill. Christine was sitting on a little chair with another little girl who'd just arrived, talking quietly, and Reynaldo was still hanging about the apple tree, trying to figure out how to climb it. Allen put down his beer and walked over to the driveway and grabbed the basketball. He tossed it in Reynaldo's direction. "Let's go for the goal," he said to Reynaldo, inviting him to a little practice soccer session. Reynaldo kicked the ball towards the basketball court as Allen ran up and feigned a fierce defense. He let the little guy get past him and the ball rolled out onto the asphalt of the drive.

Reynaldo caught up with the ball, picked it up and shot for the hoop. Allen remembered that Belinda had said little Reynaldo had become their resident basketball jock. But the daycare basket was three or four feet lower than an official hoop.

The ball rebounded off the backboard below the hoop and bounced back toward the arbor. Fidel Flores left the couple he'd been talking to and picked the ball up as Reynaldo came running after it. The two of them walked back out onto the court. "Like this," Fidel said, showing Reynaldo how to line up the shot. He handed the ball to Reynaldo. Reynaldo leapt and launched the ball. It came close to the basket, but was still well below. Allen could see that there was nothing wrong with Reynaldo's aim; the little guy just wasn't tall enough. Allen hated to see him fail repeatedly and felt like going over to him. He wanted to involve him in another mock game of soccer, but not now with Fidel there.

Fidel dribbled the ball forward. He knelt and conferred with Reynaldo again, showing him how to line up a shot. Reynaldo's little body constricted then sprang. The ball shot up into a seemingly perfect arc, headed for the hoop, and then banged off the rim. Allen sighed. Reynaldo was too little. Give him a few years. What was the point?

Fidel again took the ball and ran at the hoop. His face focused on victory, he dribbled expertly, evading an imaginary opponent, and shot. The ball sailed up and dropped neatly through the hoop. Fidel passed the ball to Reynaldo, who again began dribbling it forward. As Allen watched them, he thought sadly how Fidel and Reynaldo looked more like father and son than he and Reynaldo did. The realization was so stark and undeniable that he had to look away. He was forty-six. Reynaldo was eight. Fidel was probably thirty-one, maybe thirty-two, a more fitting age match. And their skin tones were the same attractive nut-brown shade. Allen went back under the shade of the arbor and helped himself to another beer. Tina came over and stood with him for a moment. The slap and squeak of Nike shoes echoed off the court. "Do you want anything, Hon?" Tina said.

Allen no longer had an appetite. But before he could answer he heard David Wu shout loudly and excitedly, "All Right!"

"Yeah!" Fidel shouted.

Allen turned. Reynaldo was sitting on Fidel's shoulders, Fidel holding Reynaldo's ankles tightly. The little guy had evidently just sunk a shot from his new vantage. Fidel turned their way and waved. Reynaldo smiled, beaming with pride and excitement. Allen nodded encouragingly and took a pull at his beer to hide his pain at the sight. He thought if he had ever put Reynaldo on his own shoulders at home, Tina would freak out, complaining that it was too dangerous. As David Wu tossed the ball up to Reynaldo, Allen thought sadly how he never had the chance to play with Reynaldo like that. It seemed as if every time he wrestled with him on the rug or chased him playfully around the house, Tina immediately complained that Reynaldo might fall or that he was becoming too sweaty and might catch cold or that he was getting too excited and would have a hard time sleeping or that they might hurt Christine. Whatever. Tina would always find a reason to put a stop to it. Sometimes it seemed like she just didn't want him and Reynaldo to have any fun together. He had thought at first that maybe Tina felt he didn't play enough with Christine. But he did, sitting down with her and her dolls, reading to her on occasion. He loved Christine as much as any father loved his daughter. But no, there was something else going on with Tina about Reynaldo. Allen had always put it down to another of her idiosyncrasies. But now—watching Fidel running about with a squealing Reynaldo perched on his shoulders six feet above the concrete of the driveway—and hearing nothing out of Tina about it, he felt very bad.

"Allen," Dolores called over to him. "What do you want on your burger?" Allen suspected that Dolores had somehow picked up on his discomfort and pain while his own wife could not. He felt he had to get as far away from the basketball players as possible and so he went over to her. "Ketchup and onions."

Dolores handed him a burger on a bun on a paper plate. Allen thanked her and got himself some potato salad. He plodded over to the picnic table. Tina had wandered off again to talk to one of her other office friends. A few minutes later Fidel and David came over. Both men were sweating. Fidel lowered Reynaldo carefully to the ground. They exchanged high fives and Reynaldo ran out onto the lawn again. He and Christine and the other girl began kicking the basketball about, soccer fashion.

Fidel looked at Allen. "He can sink them, man!" he said, wiping the sweat from his brow with a napkin. "With a little help in the height department, he can sink them."

Allen nodded. "Yeah. I saw that. Thanks a lot. He got a big kick out of it."

David pulled three bottles of beer from the tub, twisted the tops and handed one to Fidel and one to Allen. David took a long pull of his, then looked at it appreciatively. "Man, that's good! I don't usually drink. I hardly ever go to bars. But this stuff really hits the spot now."

"Yeah," said Allen. "I've never been much on the bar scene either. But you know, I found this old fashioned Irish bar in an old hotel near the cemeteries. It's called McCoy's."

"I thought that place was torn down years ago," David said.

"No," said Fidel, "the lumber and feed store next door got torn down. They were both part of the same complex, the oldest buildings in San Mateo County."

David Wu shook his head. "No. I'm pretty sure it was the bar."

Allen laughed. "I think Fidel's right, David," he said. "I mean, I don't think I had that beer in the lumber and feed store..."

David turned to Allen, his face serious.

"David!" someone called, before he could respond.

Dolores Castillo approached. "David, sorry to interrupt. But can you come over and talk about the reorganization? Tina says we're going to start reporting to Cabral now. Is that right?"

"Excuse me a minute," David said to Allen and Fidel as he walked off with Dolores.

On the ride home, Allen turned philosophical. Yes, he told himself, Fidel had bonded more with Reynaldo today than he had. But he would have lots more opportunities than Fidel. And at least now he had some ammunition for trying to convince Tina to give Reynaldo more leash. Allen had long felt that the notes Reynaldo brought home from school for not staying in his seat, for talking out loud and all his other little misbehaviors at home, like drilling holes in the wood of his desk, or taking candy—all of it stemmed from his not having an outlet for his energy. Sometimes it seemed as if Tina expected Reynaldo to behave like Christine. Christine was perfectly okay with staying indoors all day and playing quietly with her dolls or watching TV. But Reynaldo needed to get out and run around, to burn up his boyish energy. Then he would be able to focus better on his schoolwork. Allen decided he would work on Tina in another few days.

Allen turned down Skyview. He looked over at 1030 as they rolled past. Raggedy Anne and Andy sat on their front steps. Allen had just received a letter back from the city with the address of the house's owners. He made a mental note to write them tonight. They had to get their tenants to fix the place up and get the truck off the front yard. As Allen was about to turn away, he noticed that for the first time that he could recall, Andy did not have a skateboard under his arm as if he were fourteen years old, instead of twenty-six or twenty-eight or whatever the hell he was. Allen pulled the van over in front of his own house.

CHAPTER 10

THE OFFICE OF JOEL BECKETT, psychologist, was on Lombard Street, one of the trendiest neighborhoods in San Francisco. After Allen parked the car he walked down the block, reading the addresses. The office was next to a hairdressing salon and Allen got a nose full of the pungent nostrums women used to take the spine out of their hair and bend it to their will. The house was one of those fine old wooden Victorians that San Francisco was famous for. But instead of housing only one wealthy family as in the old days, it had been subdivided into about a half dozen offices, indicated by the number of names on the brass plates mounted on the exterior. Allen punched the number Joel had given him into the keypad. A buzzer sounded and he pushed the door open. He slowly climbed up a steep flight of stairs. Joel had told him to be here at ten. It was twenty till.

The waiting room was as somber and serious as one in a Catholic rectory, with stucco walls painted ivory white and lots of dark genuine mahogany woodwork, probably logged out of central Asia a hundred years earlier and brought over on clipper ships. There were six offices, all of their doors framed with thick mahogany timbers, as was the lone window, which was set with stained glass and opened onto a light shaft. Allen sat on one of the four chairs and thumbed through an old copy of Architectural Digest. He noted the painted-over, capped iron pipe coming out of the wall about head high, no doubt an old gaslight had been mounted there a hundred years earlier. A few feet from where Allen sat, a small electrical device that looked like a space heater, hissed steadily. One of the office doors opened suddenly and a man Allen's age exited quickly, nervously avoiding eye contact. A moment later a woman who Allen assumed to be one of the therapists emerged and rummaged through some mail and magazines in the drawer of a small table. She smiled primly as she took her mail back into her office. As Allen settled back again, he looked over at the little heater on the floor, wondering why they would have a heater turned on today. He placed his hand next to it and felt no rush of warm air as it hissed steadily. He realized it was a noise generator, white noise, to mask the exchanges going on in the offices.

The door to another office opened and a woman exited hurriedly, leaving the door open. Dressed in running sweats, with unkempt hair and sallow skin, she appeared troubled and angry as she rushed toward the stairs, looking as if she'd knock over anyone who got in her way. After she'd gone, a handsome, elderly man appeared in the doorway and smiled. "Allen?" he said.

Allen nodded and got to his feet.

"I'm Joel Beckett. Come in."

Allen sat in a plush armchair across a glass-topped desk from Joel. The office was, for the most part, simple and business-like, with a polished wooden floor, framed degrees and licenses, and what looked like eighteenth century panoramas on two walls. Behind Joel, an array of African totem masks crowded the wall. Allen suspected that they had more to do with Joel's field than with any interest he may have had in art.

Joel interlaced his fingers and put his arms behind his head. "Well, I don't have to ask you what brought you here. You've already told me about your depression."

Allen nodded, not knowing how to begin. Joel seemed to be waiting for him. "Did you have children?" Allen asked him.

Joel nodded. "A son and daughter."

"If you don't mind my asking," Allen said, "how old are you?"

Joel smiled. "Seventy one. And you?"

"Forty-six."

Joel nodded, waiting again. Allen noticed a picture on the desk of an attractive woman who appeared to be about thirty-five or forty. "Is that your daughter?"

Joel shook his head. "Sheila. My girlfriend. We live together." He smiled. "We really should have another word for such relationships. My wife died twenty years ago."

"I'm sorry," said Allen.

Joel smiled. He swiveled his chair to the side, pulling open a drawer. He took out a small photo album and leaned across the desk to show Allen a picture of himself dressed in a suit, flanked by a young man and woman at some sort of function. "My son's graduation. He's a doctor now."

Allen nodded. He felt a little awkward at having asked, but he also felt a certain relief. He wanted to talk to someone who had raised children successfully, someone that knew what the hell they were talking about, not just on an intellectual level, but from their own experience. "I have a son and a daughter too," Allen said.

Joel nodded. "You told me."

"Yeah. My son is adopted."

Joel nodded, waiting for him to go on.

"One of the things that's been bothering me is the way my wife obsesses over my kids, especially my son."

Joel knitted his brows.

"I've tried to get her to lighten up, to give him more leash, but you know how women are."

Joel raised his eyebrows. "What do you mean? How are they?"

"You know how it goes, when it comes to the house, you know, where to hang the pictures, where to put the couch, women call the shots."

Joel said nothing.

"She's kind of, you know, the chief disciplinarian too, when it comes to the kids."

"What do you mean?" said Joel. "There's no abuse, is there?"

Allen shook his head and frowned at the word. He'd heard horror stories about parents who'd had their kids taken away from them by Child Protective Services just for spanking them. Tina was strict, but she wasn't abusive, at least he didn't think so. But some of these extreme CPS types might disagree. And if they did, would they try to take Reynaldo from them? Maybe even Christine? The thought was chilling. "No," he said, he hoped not too quickly, "it's not that. She's just, sort-of controlling. You know, she insists on what to dress them in, what to feed them. When it comes to stuff like that, women rule the roost."

"Not in all cases."

"I know, I know," said Allen nervously, "but isn't that the rule, in most cases, so to speak?"

"In most cases, there is a division of responsibilities, that's true. But in functional marriages there is agreement about these things. Have you discussed your concerns with your wife?"

"A little, but... she doesn't seem to want to discuss it. Sometimes I think it might be cultural. I told you she wasn't born here. She's from Mexico."

Joel frowned. "Go on."

"Well," said Allen, "maybe down there the men don't get involved in the child rearing as much. I don't know. But anyway, why won't she let him do anything? You know, soccer, basketball?"

Joel's voice was calm and reassuring. "I know a few people from that part of the world and I don't think this has anything to do with her culture. She's obviously worried about him."

Allen sighed in seeming exasperation, but he was actually reassured by Joel's statement that Tina was worried about Reynaldo. "Yeah, more like obsessed."

Joel didn't seem to be concerned. "Well, Allen,

you'll just have to work on her a little more. Until you can get her to come in with you, we'll have to come up with some strategies to help allay her fears."

Allen nodded. He found Joel's 'take charge' words flattering and he felt encouraged. He went on, "in every other respect, though, I think we've got a pretty good marriage, better than most, I suspect. Tina's a good homemaker. We have a very tidy house and she's very loyal. And we have a decent sex life."

Joel nodded and smiled. "That's always good."

"Anyway," said Allen, "that's not the only thing that's been getting to me lately."

Joel waited patiently for him to go on.

"The neighborhood I live in is going downhill a little I think."

"In what way?"

"Well, one of the homeowners moved out and rented their house to a couple of lowlifes. Now the place looks like God's Little Acre, only instead of bib overalls and corncob pipes, we got purple hair and nose rings."

Joel laughed and Allen felt better.

"And my job is starting to get to me. My boss is an ass."

"What do you mean?"

"He's a screamer, you know, dressing down his people in front of everybody, that sort of thing."

"How long have you been there?"

"Ten years."

"Any chance of changing companies?"

Allen frowned. "No. Our industry is in a down period now."

"Umm," said Joel. "Well, Allen, you've got a lot of issues we can work on. Let's try and prioritize them and work from there."

Forty five minutes later, when Allen got up from the chair, he felt rested and reassured. After they'd talked, Joel had had him count backwards, putting him in some kind of relaxed state.

Joel showed him to the door.

CHAPTER 11

RAD SAT IN THE BOWELS of the big, reticulated number 292 SamTrans bus as it roared and rumbled along Bayshore Boulevard. It was Saturday morning and Tawny was working at the mall. She never missed Saturdays because that was when she made almost fifty percent of her money. Thoughts of Tawny took Rad back to the house and that phone call. He could still hear Raines' voice as he blithely informed him that he hadn't made the cut. All the work he'd done on the board over the years, all his hopes and dreams, meant nothing. Neither did the fact that he was probably, according to Raines, who should know, the best skater who had submitted a tape. Despite that, it was no dice. No sale. Nada. At the time Rad had felt like telling Raines to go fuck himself, or putting his fist through the wall. Then later, he lamely thought of re-registering for classes at Ridgeline and getting his construction certificate. Then at least he would have some kind of goal. And when he graduated and went to work he could make some decent money. Working for whom, though? Not his dad. So whom? He frowned. But it didn't matter in the end because he'd been so pissed and depressed he'd never even put his application in at school. And then he'd started putting all his spare time into this new thing—helping to save San Bruno Mountain.

Bayshore Boulevard had been carved into the side of San Bruno Mountain. As the bus climbed the mountain, Rad looked down on Highway 101. 101 had been built in the fifties and used to be the major north/south artery in California. Now the newer I-5, about 50 miles east, claimed that title, but 101 still carried a lot of traffic, especially commuter traffic between Silicon Valley and San Francisco. Rad watched the cars and trucks flowing along the freeway below like logs in a log flume. He used to use these Saturdays to practice his stuff on the skateboard. Most times he'd take it into San Francisco to the Embarcadero. It was gnarly and usually the cops didn't bother you. And he drew a small crowd of regular watchers and wannabes. Tawny would meet him there about six and then they'd take a bus out to the Mission District to eat a Mexican dinner.

Rad looked at his watch. He figured he'd finish up with his Friends of San Bruno Mountain business and be back home by one or two. He wondered what he'd do till Tawny got home. He yawned. Maybe he'd take a nap. He'd gotten up way early to make this meeting and now he was growing sleepy. He looked out the window again at the San Francisco Bay stretching blue and bright in the morning sunlight all the way out to the east bay communities of Alameda and San Lorenzo. Rad took the Friends of San Bruno Mountain brochure from his pocket and read it again. The presentation and tour started at 10:00. According to the bus schedule, the 292 would drop him off at Guadalupe Parkway at 9:38. Then he would have to walk a little over a mile uphill to get there. He didn't think he'd have any problem making it on time.

The road began inclining upward more sharply and the bus's automatic transmission downshifted with a bang. The diesel engine roared as it pushed the massive bus higher and higher, 101 disappearing from view as the road turned westward. As the bus bounced and rattled over pot-holed asphalt, Rad stared out the window at junkyards, auto body shops, a trailer park and the occasional luxury condo, walled off from the other properties like medieval castles, their inscrutable black glass windows reflecting the distant blue of the bay. The road leveled and the bus shifted gears again, picking up speed. As they raced down an incline to a traffic light, Rad looked at his watch: 9:37. Right on time. He got up and pulled the cord.

The bus pulled over to the side of the road and Rad stepped off. He crossed the street and began walking up Guadalupe Parkway. There was no pavement, only a bike path. A minute or so into the walk his breathing began to labor; it was a pretty steep incline. Soon the bay again came into view behind him and he marveled at its beauty. He was struck by how much it reminded him of Southern Italy. Not that he'd ever been there, but he'd seen a movie filmed there and the San Francisco Bay Area had the same type of weather and views. Five minutes later he left Guadalupe and began walking down Decker Road, a wheel-rutted dirt road left over from the area's logging days. A hundred feet or so later and he came to a Forest Service building with a shingle roof and siding. About a half dozen people stood around on the little front porch. The door to the building was open and someone stood just inside, obscure in the dimness. A man in the doorway, a ranger in a uniform, was talking to whoever was inside.

Rad Joined the others on the porch—two middle aged couples about his dad's age and two girls of eighteen or nineteen from, Rad assumed, one of the local colleges, probably USF or UC Berkeley. One was taller than Rad, with wide hips, big breasts and short hair. She looked to him like the outdoorsy Greenpeace type. Her friend was Asian—petite, pretty and nicely shaped, with her hair in a black pageboy. Rad nodded a greeting at everyone. The ranger concluded his conversation and turned to acknowledge them all with a friendly nod.

"Well, it looks like you're it," the ranger said. "We usually get a few more." He walked to the edge of the porch and looked up toward Guadalupe. "David is usually here early," he said to them. "Oh, here he comes now."

A twenty or so year old Volvo turned off Guadalupe Parkway and came bouncing down the logging road, throwing up a cloud of dust. The car pulled up to the ranger station, stopped, and the dust cloud momentarily engulfed them. The driver pulled the hand brake and got out. Middle aged, with a receding hairline, blue eyes, a full gray beard and what remained of his hair pulled into a long ponytail, he nodded to the ranger and made a half-hearted effort to tuck his shirt in under his rather large belly. He reached back into the car and took out a clipboard and a pile of forms from the passenger seat. He turned to Rad and the others, "Follow me."

They walked down the road and the man stopped before a glassed-in posting board full of information on the history of the mountain reserve and its native flora and fauna. He put his papers and clipboard down and addressed them. "I'm David Hunsicker and I'm president of the Friends of San Bruno Mountain. You are all friends of San Bruno Mountain, I hope."

Rad smiled and nodded along with the others.

"Good," said David, "the mountain needs all the friends she can get right now with the damn lawyers and developers after her."

"You all want to introduce yourselves? Then we can get going on the little tour I give."

Rad gave his name after the two couples smilingly introduced themselves. The two girls were from UCSF. The taller of the two gave her name as, 'Cait,' short for Caitlin, and the shorter, pretty one introduced herself as Jenny Chin.

David led everyone off onto a trail that followed the gentle rise of a grassy meadow. After a slow meandering walk of about ten minutes they came to a thick, darkened grove of eucalyptus trees. Halfway through the grove, off the trail about twenty feet, a little shack squatted. Rad smiled at the sight of it, thinking how charmed Tawny would be by it. It had evidently been built by hand out of salvaged deadwood laid stick over stick without benefit of hammer, nail or plumb.

Jenny Chin turned to Rad and smiled. "It looks like something out of the Hobbit, doesn't it?"

He smiled, marveling at how pretty she was in the dappled light of the trees. "Yeah," he said. Then he thought guiltily of Tawny and looked back at the Hobbit house.

David nodded toward the dwelling. "That's where Lucinda and Larry live. They're squatters but they don't hurt anything so the rangers let them stay." David's brow furrowed. "They're undocumented. They don't seem to be home today. Maybe next time you come I'll have them give you a tour of their place."

Cait turned to Rad. "Undocumented? What's that?"

"It means they're illegal," said Rad softly.

David heard him and said matter-of-factly. "There is no such thing as an illegal human."

Rad tried to smile, feeling his face redden a little.

The male complement of one of the two older couples turned to him. "David is really passionate about the rights of the undocumented."

David looked up and swept his hand to indicate all the trees. "These eucalyptus are, of course, not native to the mountain. This entire copse is scheduled to be logged out in three or four months."

Rad was fascinated. He'd had no idea the eucalyptus trees were not native to the Bay Area. And he'd grown up here.

"So, what will happen to Lucinda and Larry?" Jenny asked.

"We're gonna have to relocate their house," said David. "I've been discussing with the rangers about where to put it."

David continued walking, pointing here and there as he discussed the various native flora and fauna as he led them up toward the top of the ridge. He pointed to a beautiful carpet of gold-colored plants covering the next ridge over.

"That's gorse, the worst of the invasive plants. It's been like a never-ending battle to get rid of it, but one of these days we will."

"How do you do that?" asked one of the older men, "Herbicides?"

David seemed to cringe at the word. "No!" he said emphatically. "It has to be removed by hand. We meet every Saturday morning at ten to work on it."

Jenny pointed back toward the eucalyptus forest. "The eucalyptus trees were so charming," she said sweetly. "I mean, that place was almost magical, with the light and the clean scent, and the little elves' house... Can't they just let the invasive plants mix with the native? Maybe they'll form new strains."

David smiled patiently and shook his head.

"You can't have a balance?" asked one of the older men.

"No," said David. "You might have what you think is a balance. But the hardier species will always crowd out the weaker and eventually dominate the environment."

"That's kind of sad," said Jen.

"Not really," said David, "that's nature. Plant and animal." He began walking again and they followed him, each quiet with their own thoughts.

As Rad walked along with the others, he was amazed by everything that David had told them. All his life he had looked at San Bruno Mountain and seen only tall grass, the occasional oak tree and the ubiquitous generic green bushes, which he hadn't learned were sagebrush until this day. Now he looked at the mountain with wonder and a kind of reverence

They reached the pinnacle of the ridge and David pointed to the distant housing developments surrounding the base of the mountain like a sea around an island. "South San Francisco and this whole area became San Francisco's dump," said David. "Whatever they didn't want... smoke-belching factories, stinking slaughterhouses, mines, a railroad switching yard, grave yards, garbage dumps, whatever, they relocated to South City and the neighboring communities. You know, Colma, with more than a dozen cemeteries, is a city of the dead, a necropolis. And so for that reason you have a lot of poor people living in the communities around this mountain, people that could never afford a place in San Francisco or Millbrae or Hillsborough. And that's why the developers have gotten away with all the pieces they've taken from the mountain. And that's why they think they'll get away with it this time. Because the people aren't organized." David looked a little saddened by his own words. Then he brightened. "But, we're not going to let them do that this time, are we?"

"No," everyone said softly. Rad said nothing. He was in a state of mild shock by what David had said about the surrounding communities being for 'poor people.' Rad rarely thought of class, his own or other people's. And this idea that he was poor or low-class, someone to be pitied or protected, shocked and bothered him.

Finally the tour was over and they headed back down the trail. At the ranger station, David told everyone the South San Francisco City Council was scheduled to vote on the fate of the mountain in three months time. "If we collect enough signatures of registered voters perhaps we can sway them in our favor," David said hopefully. "The damn developers are throwing money around like there's no tomorrow. But we'll beat them, right?"

Rad and the others nodded their assent. "So when do we begin?" asked one of the other men.

"Today," said David. He picked up a stack of petition forms and passed them around.

"There'll be a City Council meeting in the fall," said David. "That's when we'll deliver the signatures we collect. At that time there'll be an opportunity for anyone who wants, to speak to the Council on why they shouldn't allow the developers to destroy this mountain. I hope you'll all speak up for her. Will you?"

The older couples and Cait and Jenny all nodded assent. Then Jenny was smiling and looking over at Rad.

"Sure," he said.

David began writing down everyone's phone numbers. After Rad had given David his number, he started walking up the logging road to Guadalupe Parkway. A few moments later Jenny Chin and Cait drove up behind him in a little Toyota Corolla. "Would you like a ride?" Jenny called out the window.

"It's probably out of your way," he said.

"Where are you going," said Jenny.

"South San Francisco. Three, maybe four miles from here."

"Hop in," said Jenny

"Cool," said Rad, getting in the back.

They turned onto Guadalupe and started down the hill. Soon a powerful current of warm air scented with sage and wild flowers was pouring through the back window, buffeting Rad's head. Jenny said something to him he couldn't hear over the rushing air. He sat forward and she turned slightly to speak to him. He couldn't help but marvel at how pretty she was up close.

"Where to?" she said.

"Just follow Bayshore. I'll tell you where to turn."

"Where do you hang out?" she said.

"The Kat's Dawg. Ever hear of it?"

Jenny shook her head and glanced over at Cait who shook her head.

"It's in the SOMA," said Rad, using the hip acronym for the gentrified neighborhood of warehouses and defunct factories in San Francisco located South-of-Market Street.

Jenny nodded. "Where do you go to school?"

"I don't," he said. "I work."

Jenny nodded slowly, her face taking on a sage look, as if this was some new and lofty life-choice that she had only just now heard about. "Cool. What kind of work?"

"I build custom boards."

"Boards?" Jenny said loudly over the wind, "surfboards?"

Rad shook his head. "Skateboards."

"Oh. Sounds interesting."

Cait smiled, her parted lips showing big perfect teeth. She added nothing as she stared out the window at the blue bay stretching out before them.

Ten minutes later they pulled up in front of Rad's house. As the car slowed to a stop, Rad said, "Thanks for the ride."

He was walking toward the curb when Jenny called out something he didn't quite hear. He went back to the car and leaned into the window.

"Will you be at the next Friends of the Mountain meeting?" she said.

"Yeah," he said, again marveling at how pretty she was. "I'll be there." He smiled and turned and walked back toward the house. As he started up the steps he became guiltily aware of the boner glowing warmly in his pants.

CHAPTER 12

ALLEN WENT IN FOR HIS second appointment with his therapist on Saturday morning. He was surprised at how quickly he was warming up to Joel. Allen's father had been quiet, almost aloof, and he had never had an intelligent and attentive male confidant like Joel. Joel spent most of the session trying to have Allen see things from Tina's point of view and he encouraged Allen to help her more around the house. Then Joel put Allen in a relaxed state, as he called it. Allen had never been hypnotized before and when it was over he couldn't recall being unconscious or anything strange, although he did feel more relaxed and positive. When the session ended, Joel told Allen he wouldn't be able to see him next week because he had to have some tests done at the hospital.

When Allen returned home Tina was down in the garage doing the laundry. He wanted to speak to her about Reynaldo joining the soccer team. He had contacted the coach earlier in the week and he and Reynaldo were supposed to go to their first practice today. But if Tina wouldn't let Reynaldo participate, it was better that the little guy not even know about it in the first place.

Allen made sure that Reynaldo and Christine were engrossed in the cartoon show before he stepped down into the garage. He pulled the door closed so the kids wouldn't overhear. Tina was separating the whites from the coloreds and putting them in the machine's basket as Allen approached. She looked at him suspiciously, then continued with her sorting.

"Tina, remember I told you about that Tiny Tot soccer league in Daly City?"

Tina didn't say anything and continued to sort the clothes.

"Well, I got all the info from the coach," Allen said matter-of-factly, "and he said that Reynaldo would fit right in."

"Yeah? When is this supposed to start?"

"Today. The first practice is today."

"Today?" Tina frowned as she measured blue liquid laundry detergent into a cup. "He's too young."

"No he's not," said Allen, trying to keep the warmth in his voice; it wouldn't do to get her upset and have her dig in her heels. "He's seven and a half. They start kids when they're three or four. You should've seen them, Tina." Allen's eyes grew big as he warmed to the memory. "These little guys are hardly as big as the ball, but they can play! Reynaldo will be fine."

Tina dropped the washing machine lid with a clang. "Fine, huh? What if he gets hurt or sick? Are you going to take time off from work to stay home with him?"

"Sure," said Allen, wondering what kind of injury Reynaldo could possibly get from Tiny Tot Soccer. He looked quickly at his watch. "They start in about a half hour. You mind if I get him ready now?"

Tina picked up the clothesbasket and started past him. "Make sure you have him back in a couple of hours. He has his work to do."

Allen and Reynaldo drove down Skyline Boulevard toward Daly City. Allen saw the white blur of fog in the distance. The Bay Area had many unique micro-climates. Further east, the Central Valley baked under the sun, sending up columns of heated air. This updraft drew air horizontally across the surface of the Alaskan current-cooled ocean, condensing it into cold, clammy fog banks, which then rolled eastward, channeled by the different canyons of the Bay Area, forming vaporous rivers of fog. Along the way they chilled some neighborhoods down to the low 60s in the summertime, while other neighborhoods only two or three blocks away baked in LA-like temperatures in the mid 80s to high 90s.

A mile before Allen and Reynaldo reached the soccer field they entered the fog and the temperature dropped a good ten degrees or more. Allen recalled what Mark Twain had supposedly said about the fog, "the coldest winter I ever spent was a summer in San Francisco," or something like that. As the chill entered the car, Allen rolled up the window. A few minutes later he parked.

A dozen or so boys of various sizes congregated on the field. Two men kept an eye on them from the sidelines. The larger of the two wore a cap and had a whistle around his neck and a clipboard, all of which identified him as Chip Mikulsky, the coach that Allen had talked to on the phone.

Allen had Reynaldo put on his coat, which, he realized, would make it difficult for him to run and play. They walked over to Chip.

"I'm Allen Collins," said Allen, extending his hand.

Chip nodded toward Reynaldo and winked as he shook Allen's hand. "He doesn't look anything like you."

Allen was used to such statements. "He's adopted. His mother is Indian."

Chip glanced over at Reynaldo. "Ruby or feather?"

Allen smiled, but his face reddened at Chip's rude probing. "His mother is from Central America."

Chip nodded, again glancing at Reynaldo. "How old did you say he was?"

"Seven and a half."

Chip raised his eyebrows. "Kind of small for seven and a half, but I may have a jersey that will fit him." Chip walked off to the sidelines to a cardboard box sitting on the grass. He pulled out a red jersey with BULLDOGS proudly emblazoned on the front in gold lettering. He brought it over and handed it to Allen.

Allen wished the jersey's material was thicker. He looked at the boiling white mass of cold fog rolling by overhead. Shrugging, he helped Reynaldo out of his coat and into the jersey. He noticed Reynaldo's nose was already running. "Are you okay?" he asked him. "Are you warm enough?"

Reynaldo nodded, his eyes on the other boys. Allen

rolled up Reynaldo's sleeves, which were about six inches too long. Chip blew the whistle and the boys and fathers gathered around him. Chip looked at Allen and the other fathers. "We're just gonna let the boys run the ball today, drive for the goal. That's all."

Allen knelt down and conferred quietly with Reynaldo. "Just try and kick the ball. That's all you have to do. Can you do it?"

Reynaldo smiled as he looked at the other boys. "Yes, Daddy."

Allen held Reynaldo's coat as he watched from the sidelines. The boys ran after the ball, occasionally zooming in to kick at it. Most of them had full uniforms with shorts and white knee socks. Overhead the fog filtered the light to a pale grey, setting off the bright green of the grass. Allen drew himself into the folds of his jacket. He smiled as Reynaldo rushed in and gave the ball a good kick. His aim was off, sending the ball back toward the other goal. Regardless, the boys pursued it, driving it further away from its intended destination until Chip blew the whistle and set them off again in the proper direction. The practice lasted forty-five minutes and then Allen and Reynaldo got in the car and began the drive home. Allen wiped Reynaldo's runny nose before they went in the house.

Inside, Tina led Reynaldo off to his room and put him to work on his definitions. Allen got the newspaper and went down to the garage to read in his study. He was reading an editorial lamenting the lack of outrage over the Clinton scandals when the door opened and Tina glared angrily down at him. "He has a temperature!"

Allen put down his paper. "You're kidding!"

"No I'm not kidding. It's one hundred and two." She closed the door hard.

Allen sighed, knowing that this was one of Tina's big issues. Whenever the kids became sick she got manic. And all his efforts to calm her only seemed to make her more worried and excited.

He went up into the house. In Reynaldo's room, Tina was roughly yanking his red Bulldog jersey over his head. She tossed it to the floor and began tugging his undershirt up.

"Did you take your coat off?" she demanded of Reynaldo.

Reynaldo looked at Allen for direction as tears rolled down his face. Allen kept his face expressionless, knowing they'd have to tough this one out. "Yes, Mommy," said Reynaldo.

"Damn it," Tina muttered angrily.

"Tina," said Allen, trying to calm her, "I told him to take it off. You can't play soccer running around in a coat like that."

"Don't tell me what you can and can't do," she shouted. "He's sick! You know how much work he is for me when he gets sick!"

"He'll be all right," said Allen soothingly, "it's just a cold or something."

"Yeah! That's what you say." Tina turned back to Reynaldo. "No more soccer for you, do you hear me?"

"Sorry, Mommy," Reynaldo burst out, trying to dissuade her from her obvious, and, once she'd embarked on it, unalterable course.

"How many times have I told you not to take off your coat?" she yelled at him.

"Sorry, Mommy, I didn't mean it."

Tina pulled his undershirt off and pointed to the bathroom. "Get in there, damn it!"

Allen felt terrible. Partly it was guilt. Maybe he shouldn't have let Reynaldo play when it was foggy like that. But all the other little kids were playing! And if they got sick, would it be a big deal like this? No. It was an overreaction. Sometimes her responses to mildly stressful situations seemed way over the top. He resolved to again try and talk her into going to see Joel with him. He suspected that all this had something to do with menopause, or 'the change,' as it was called. But he could never tell her that. It was something she would have to hear from a professional, or maybe a relative or girlfriend. Maybe then she would seek help.

Allen recalled the last time he had been to his own doctor. He'd been waiting in the examining room and he could hear Dr. Waltz speaking with an older man in the next room. "It's driving me crazy," the man was saying with real concern in his voice, "she can't sit still. She's always fussing over things."

"How is she sleeping?" asked Dr. Waltz patiently.

"Sleeping?" said the man. "You've got to be kidding! She doesn't sleep and then neither do I."

"What's her doctor's name?" said Dr. Waltz, "I'll give him a call."

"It's a her, a Dr. Panang, over at..."

Tina took Reynaldo into the bathroom and slammed the door. Allen went out into the living room. The faucet squeaked rustily and water splashed noisily into the tub. Tina's angry words were dulled by the running water and the door as she continued to harangue Reynaldo. God, thought Allen, nothing like this had ever happened to him when he was a kid. When he or his brother or sister got sick, they got chicken soup, Vicks in the vaporizer, bed rest. They never got yelled out. Why the hell did Tina have to do this?

Allen listened to Tina's yelling, still audible over the rush of the water into the bath, and felt terrible for Reynaldo. He sat down on the couch and turned on the news. He watched but he really didn't hear what the anchor was saying.

Tina was struck by the brownness of Reynaldo's little body against the whiteness of the porcelain as he climbed from the heap of clothing into the tub. Snot glistened under his nose and his hands and feet were dirty. He always got so dirty. She picked up the washcloth and started scrubbing his face and ears, ignoring his cries.

If only she hadn't gone along with Allen on the adoption. If only she would have waited—what, another nine or ten months—she would have gotten pregnant anyway. And then she would have had more time and energy to devote to Christine instead of raising up somebody else's kid.

As she scrubbed him, she listened to his incessant crying and noted the dirt in the tub. And what an armful he was! Always lying, stealing. His room was always messy. Getting out of his desk at school. Coming home with notes. Trouble, trouble, trouble!

Tina twisted the faucet shut with a rusty squeak, grabbed a towel, threw it around him and lifted him out of the tub. She rubbed him down roughly, ignoring his cries.

"Go to your room and get dressed," she said. "And then finish your definitions."

Reynaldo's fever had broken by Sunday afternoon, but Tina had insisted that he was too sick to go to daycare the next day. So Allen took Monday off to take Reynaldo to the doctor. At six he heard Tina get out of bed and bustle about as she got Christine ready to go to daycare. He turned over under the warm covers. He couldn't call Doctor Goldman's office till nine. He half listened to Tina's libations, her preparations out in the kitchen, and then he fell back to sleep. He opened his eyes again a little after eight and got out of bed. Careful not to wake Reynaldo, he went out to the kitchen and closed the door. Savoring the morning quiet of the house, he put on a pot of coffee and called work to say that he was sick and would not be in. He went out through the garage to get the paper. When he returned, Reynaldo was standing at the kitchen door in his pajamas.

"Good morning, Daddy."

"Reynaldo, you're up already. How do you feel?"

"Good, Daddy."

"Good. Now go make your bed and get dressed. Then I'll make you something to eat."

"Okay, Daddy."

When Reynaldo returned, Allen took his temperature. It was now normal and Allen hadn't given him any Tylenol for the past six hours. As far as Allen was concerned, the cold or bug had passed and Reynaldo could have gone to daycare with his sister. Then he thought that maybe this could be productive. Maybe he could get some answers about his situation, like what was normal behavior for a kid Reynaldo's age. And maybe, what was normal behavior for a woman entering menopause. Allen made Reynaldo some toast and called the doctor's office, getting a ten-thirty appointment.

Doctor Goldman was a member of *Peninsular Pediatric*s, a bright, modern clinic with four full-time pediatricians. *Peninsular Pediatri*cs was usually busy and this was no exception. About eight mothers filled the chairs in the waiting room, half of them with babies in their arms or in little baby carriers at their feet. A half dozen children, most with runny noses, played in a toy-filled anteroom equipped with a bright red and yellow plastic brick play house. After Allen finished checking in, he turned to see Reynaldo happily playing with the other children. He cringed inwardly, hoping that Reynaldo wouldn't pick up a new bug, but he left him alone to socialize with the others. Allen tried to read a magazine for parents and quickly grew bored with it. He stared at the lone, fist-sized angelfish in the large aquarium built into the wall under the reception desk. Finally the nurse called Reynaldo's name and they went into the examination room. The nurse took Reynaldo's temperature and told them it was ninety-eight point four. She took his history and left them alone to wait for the doctor. As Allen waited, Reynaldo began pushing the doctor's little chrome wheeled stool around the room.

Doctor Goldman entered. A diminutive man, ten years younger than Allen, he smiled at Reynaldo and nodded a greeting to Allen.

"Well, how's my little friend doing today?"

Reynaldo looked at Allen questioningly.

"Tell the doctor how you feel, Reynaldo."

"I feel good."

Allen laughed and turned to the doctor. "Yeah, I think he's over it, whatever it was. But his mother insisted I bring him in."

Doctor Goldman nodded. "Okay, Reynaldo. Let's listen to your lungs."

Allen hoisted Reynaldo up onto the examining table and Doctor Goldman pulled up his shirt and placed his stethoscope on his bony ribcage. Reynaldo immediately began giggling.

"Tickles, eh?" said Goldman.

Reynaldo nodded.

"Okay, Reynaldo. Sit up and let's look at your tonsils."

After Goldman completed his examination, Reynaldo slid off the couch and went back over to the chrome, wheeled stool. He began pushing it about the room as Goldman wrote in his chart. Reynaldo climbed up onto the stool and moved himself along the floor by pulling on the table.

Allen thought how Reynaldo's inability to just sit still was a big part of the problem. Reynaldo's teacher would not tolerate it. Then she would send him home with notes which got Tina all ratcheted up. Allen nodded over at Reynaldo when Doctor Goldman looked his way. "Do you think he's a little too bouncy?"

Doctor Goldman turned to look at Reynaldo. "No more than half the kids that come through here. He'll grow out of it."

Allen nodded, feeling a little bit frustrated. It was not a problem for Goldman, but Reynaldo's teacher and Tina were a different story.

"Is there a problem at school or something," asked Doctor Goldman.

"We've been getting notes about his getting out of his seat."

Doctor Goldman frowned. "Has he hit or hurt any of the other children?"

"No."

Doctor Goldman shook his head. "Then I don't think it's a problem. As long as he's not violent or destructive. Sometimes the expectations on the part of the teachers are unrealistic. You can't expect all of these kids to sit still for hours on end."

Allen nodded. "I think he gets on the wife's nerves a little too."

"Why? How does she react?"

Allen felt the warning flags go up. Some would consider Tina's treatment over the top. Some not. "Ah, she just gives him time outs... stuff like that."

Doctor Goldman seemed to study Allen closely. "Well, we'll keep an eye on him. If this develops into a bigger problem we can try some therapy."

"You mean Ritalin?"

"That's an option too. And there are other medications. But we don't want to go there too quickly." Doctor Goldman started moving toward the door, signaling that the visit was over. He patted Reynaldo on the head. "Okay, Reynaldo. You're fine now. No medicine, no shots. Just a lollipop if you want one."

For lunch, Allen bought Reynaldo a McDonald's Happy Meal and they left for the beach in San Francisco. As Allen drove along Skyline Boulevard, he marveled at the cloudless pastel blue sky, the monsoon-soaked jade-green cliffs, and the deep indigo blue of the sea. In the seat next to him, Reynaldo stuck a French fry in his mouth as he looked out at the colors wide-eyed. A few miles ahead in the distance, Allen spotted a bunch of hang gliders circling the cliffs of Fort Funston like flies over a garbage pail.

Allen exited onto the Great Highway; the four lane road ran parallel with the beach. He looked at his watch: 2:00 PM. The day had warmed considerably. The weatherman had said that the temperature would reach the upper seventies. It felt like it had already.

"Look Daddy." Reynaldo pointed at the dunes on their right. A file of joggers wound around a path, up a dune and then down out of sight.

Allen nodded and smiled. The upset and craziness of the weekend was quickly fading. Both he and Reynaldo were feeling better. Maybe they would get through this. He scanned the beach on his left. In the summertime it would be crowded with sunbathers, all greased and tanned, very few of them venturing into the icy Pacific waters of Northern California. But now it was deserted, with only a few tracks in the wet sand. A half-mile out past the breakers, a dozen wet-suited surfers, dark dots in the water, rose and sank slowly as a large swell rolled beneath them. Further out, a lone container ship slowly turned in toward the Golden Gate. Allen made out part of the ship's name, Wang something-or-other, painted in white on the rusting bow. A dirty plume of diesel smoke issued from the ship's stack and moved sluggishly eastward.

Allen turned into the parking lot. Most of the cars were new except for an older, beat-up van near the entrance. He figured it belonged to surfers or the many homeless that hung around the beach. The homeless were a rough-looking feral bunch, hardened by their lifestyle. Once, while strolling the beach, Allen had come upon the evidence of one of their late night bacchanals—fast food wrappers, screw-top wine bottles, and used rubbers. He decided to park closer to the Cliff House. There would be foreign tourists there, walking down from their buses and the restaurants and souvenir shops.

Allen passed a newer van, its interior invisible behind black-tinted windows. He had a paranoid vision of several men crowded inside, videotaping his day at the beach with his son when he should have been at the office. He glanced over at Reynaldo. He still looked fine, showing no evidence of the bug he'd had.

Allen parked and took Reynaldo's bicycle from the trunk and set it on the pavement. Then Allen sat on the bench and opened the *San Francisco Chronicle*. He read a news story about a man who had been found dead inside the trunk of his own car.

"Daddy?"

Reynaldo sat motionless on his bike, propped up by his training wheels.

Allen put the newspaper down. "Yes, Reynaldo?"

"Can I play in the sand?"

Allen said nothing for a moment. Tina would freak if he got wet and he didn't want to have to deal with another of her over-reactions. "You're just getting over a cold, Reynaldo. You better stay up here." Maybe part of it was cultural, he thought. Tina evidently believed that kids got colds from not wearing enough clothing. Because of that, Reynaldo often went to school dressed in so many layers of shirts and sweaters that he looked like a tiny weight lifter on steroids. Allen had tried to explain to Tina that these childhood colds and flus were inevitable and that the germs got passed around at school from one snot-nosed kid to another. But she didn't believe him. Once, when Reynaldo had come home with the sniffles, Tina had gotten so angry she'd yanked all his clothes off and locked him down in the garage, naked. Allen had brought him back up and Tina became enraged at his interference. She didn't talk to him or Reynaldo for a week.

"Daddy," said Reynaldo. He sat stiffly on his bike. A warm breeze mussed his silken black hair. "I want to play in the sand. Please?"

As long as he played in the sand, Allen reasoned, it should be okay. The temperature felt like it was about seventy. "Okay, but don't get wet."

"Okay, Daddy." Reynaldo happily climbed off his bike.

Allen put the bike in the trunk and they walked down the steps onto the beach. The sand was warm; Allen could feel it through the soles of his shoes. He took Reynaldo's hand and they walked down to the water's edge. Allen looked out at the sea. It was flat and empty. He imagined himself alone out there in the water and felt a twinge of self-pity. He and Tina fought an awful lot now. He thought of perhaps calling his brother in Maine and talking things over with him.

"Daddy, can I take my shoes off?"

Allen tried to look stern. "No. And you have to stay on the dry sand. Mommy doesn't want you getting wet."

"Okay, Daddy," said Reynaldo sadly. They walked back from the water's edge a couple hundred feet. Reynaldo knelt and began scooping trenches in the dry sand with his hands. Allen spread the business section of the *Chronicle* out on the sand and sat on it. He opened the news to the story about the man found dead in the trunk, and tried to read. But instead he found himself thinking of his situation with Tina. If Joel could not help him come up with strategies to use with Tina, they would have to 'have it out,' as the saying went. This would lead to divorce. It was the last thing he wanted. Not because he didn't believe in the rightness of his cause, but because of what he could potentially lose. Allen imagined a stern judge looking down from the bench at Reynaldo. Would he order that Reynaldo be sent back to the county foster care system? After all, Allen and Tina had adopted Reynaldo as a couple, and the judge might not think a single father capable of providing a stable, proper household. And there was another danger. This was California—and if they ended up in divorce court he could very well lose custody of his daughter.

Allen glanced over at Reynaldo playing in the sand and then looked back at his paper. Unable to get back into his reading, he had a vision of Reynaldo being hustled into a car to be taken away into the cold vastness of the foster care system while he, Allen, ending up living in some dumpy little apartment, picking up his daughter at what had once been his home, every other weekend, like half the dads in California. Allen's eyes misted up. Jesus Christ! They'd only had Reynaldo four years; he was still a little kid, for crying out loud! Allen shook the thought off. It was overwhelming. Maybe he should look into retaining a lawyer. The more he thought about it, the more it appealed to him. He started writing notes about his situation in the margins of the newspaper. Finishing, he decided to finalize it at work and mail it from there so Tina could not intercept the reply when it came in.

Allen realized there were no longer any sounds of Reynaldo digging nearby. He looked up. Reynaldo was gone! Allen's heart started pounding as he scanned the beach. He spotted Reynaldo about a hundred feet away in the surf up to his knees.

Allen got quickly to his feet. "Reynaldo!"

Reynaldo waved, then turned away and waded further into the sea.

"Reynaldo!" Allen raced after him. "God damn it!" he said under his breath. Stories of bathers being swept out to sea by rogue waves filled his head. There were warning signs about such occurrences at all the entrances to the beach.

As Allen drew near, Reynaldo squealed happily and ran back out of the surf. Wet up to his chest, his pants drooped with the weight of the water.

"Reynaldo!" said Allen. "I told you not to get wet!" Allen shook his head in incredulity. Relief rolled over him, but how was he going to hide this from Tina?

Reynaldo's smile disappeared as he studied Allen's face cautiously. "I'm sorry, Daddy. The wave was big."

Allen looked at his watch. It was almost four. They would be getting home around the same time as Tina. Shit! He could hear her screaming already, "God damn it! You make so much work for me!"

Allen wondered if the episode could bring Reynaldo's cold back. "C'mon, Reynaldo," he said. "We have to get ready to go home."

"Aw, Daddy. Can't I play in the water some more?"

"Damn it, Reynaldo," said Allen, angry exasperation flashing through him.

Reynaldo's eyes grew large and frightened and Allen immediately tamped down his anger. It was Tina who deserved his anger, he thought, not Reynaldo.

Why the hell couldn't she just let Reynaldo be a boy? Let him play and get dirty like Allen and his brother had when they were growing up. It was what all boys did. Why the hell couldn't she see that?

Allen softened his tone. "It's okay Reynaldo. Just come with Daddy."

They walked back to their spot. Allen knelt to fold his paper. "Reynaldo," he said without looking at the boy, "we have to get you dry before we go home."

"Okay, Daddy."

Allen stood and turned. Reynaldo was sitting in the dry sand, digging. The white sand coated his body and clothing.

"Jesus, Reynaldo! Stand up."

Allen dusted him off as best he could. As they walked toward the parking lot he doubted that Reynaldo's clothes would dry in time. They wouldn't be able to run the clothes dryer without Tina becoming suspicious. "Jesus Christ," he said under his breath. There'd be hysterics tonight. Then Allen had a thought. Perhaps if he put the heater in the car on high for the ride home Reynaldo's clothes would dry out.

Before they got in the car, Allen had Reynaldo take off his shoes and socks. He wrung them out as best he could and laid them on the back seat. Later, after he exited the freeway, Allen pulled the car over to the curb and checked the shoes and socks. They were still cold and wet. He placed them on the dash of the car over the defroster vents and turned the blower and temperature up to the maximum. He got back on the freeway. Maybe if he drove around for another twenty minutes or so they would dry. Then he could tell Tina they had gotten caught in a traffic jam.

Luckily Allen managed to get home before Tina. He had Reynaldo quickly strip off his clothes. He shoved them in the washing machine, threw in a cup of soap and cranked the knob to Normal. Later that night Tina called to him from the garage. "Why is there sand in the drier?"

"Oh," he lied, "I took a quick jog on the beach. I washed and dried my running shoes in there."

He waited expectantly, wondering if she'd buy it. Then the drier lid clanged shut. He relaxed. It would be okay this time.

CHAPTER 13

T AWNY SMILED A GREETING TO Vince Rinaldi, the salesman from Circuit City, as he walked into KoolKuts. Vince's parents had left him a big house in San Bruno and he lived rent free. He often complained to Tawny about the taxes he had to pay on his house. It was a struggle for Tawny not to roll her eyes at his stealthy bragging. What Vince paid in taxes was nowhere near what she and Rad paid in rent, and Vince was renting out one of his rooms, providing him further income. The last time he was in he'd bragged to Tawny about his plan to convert his house into two apartments.

Vince was about ten years older than Tawny and one of her regular customers. He was always hitting on her, despite her having told him several times that she had a boyfriend. Cocksure that his good looks, charm, and financial prowess would win her over eventually, he never gave up. Actually, Tawny didn't mind. Vince held no great attraction for her and she enjoyed the attention and he tipped well.

Vince smiled and sat down to wait. The other stylist, Flo, was outside in the mall on her break and

Tawny had Grace, an older lady, leaned way back in the chair for her monthly dye job. Grace was one of Tawny's neediest customers. Sometimes she wore Tawny out with her depressing talk of her dead husband or the son that never came to visit her, or her dreams of death and dying. But she was well off and tipped well, always ten dollars exactly, no matter how much or how little Tawny worked on her. But she took a toll, leaving Tawny drained of spirit. Tawny shrugged. A cup of coffee would help bring her back to life. And besides, it was all in a day's work.

Tawny watched the pedestrian traffic in the mall as she washed Grace's hair and prepared her tint. Putting on her gloves, she worked quickly and soon she was nodding over at Vince to take a seat in her chair. He got to his feet and walked over gracefully. Sitting down, he carefully checked himself out in the mirror and then looked at Tawny.

"How's it goin', Babe?" he said.

"Goin' good," she said. "How's it goin' for you?"

He nodded and smiled aggressively. "Good, real good. You still hooked up with the skater boy?"

Tawny nodded. She didn't like the name that Vince had tagged Rad with, but that was partly her fault. One day she had been in an overly chatty mood and had told Vince that her boyfriend was a skateboarder who might be in the upcoming X Games in San Francisco. Forever after Vince disparagingly referred to Rad as 'the skater boy.' Tawny put up with it because he was a good customer.

"I just bought a place up at Clear Lake," Vince said.

"Real nice, with a deck in the back that looks down on the water. Maybe you and the skater boy could drop by some time."

Tawny smiled as she went to work on Vince's locks. "Maybe," she said as she pulled the comb through his hair. The comb moved easily through his crown, too easily. She frowned. That was too bad. He'd probably have a bald spot there before he was forty. But he didn't know that yet. As Tawny moved about the chair, several times she had to lean her butt out in order not to lean against him. She'd made that mistake once and felt him moving beneath the cloth, trying to feel her up. He'd acted innocent enough, pulling out a Kleenex to wipe his nose, but he was a real player. Tawny smiled. He was incorrigible. She pulled the comb through his thinning crown. Well, let him have his fun now. He'd need a hairpiece later if he was going to stay in the race.

As Tawny took her clippers out of the drawer, she thought of hers and Rad's life together. It was okay. They had their own place, friends, each other, everything they needed. But the mention of Vince's new place at Clear Lake loosened up feelings of dissatisfaction in Tawny. She thought of all her hard work to get her license to style hair, one thousand and six hundred hours of classroom instruction, driving up to Sacramento to take the test. She wanted her own salon someday. And she wanted her and Rad to own their own place too. Maybe a condo, but definitely not a rental like where they were now. And she'd like to go on weekend trips too. She and Rad hadn't been anywhere in a long time, not since that time two winters ago when they went to

Lake Tahoe. She smiled at the memory of it. She and Rad had come out of a nightclub, flush from the glow of a bottle of champagne consumed slowly in front of an aromatic wood fire. They were walking back to their cabin along a small road when it started snowing. It came down all of a sudden, thick and heavy as if some heavenly stagehand had opened up a valve high above to highlight their love scene, to make it like one of those Currier and Ives scenes in Christmas cards. They'd had a little snowball fight and then had gone into the cabin and made crazy, passionate love. Rad had a good heart. He was kind and funny. And once he figured out what he wanted in life he'd go after it. She knew that for sure. His zeal for boarding was proof. But what about her?

Every now and then Tawny had a sense of time slipping by. She thought again about opening up her own shop. She pictured it—polished mirrors, leather and chrome waiting chairs, a carafe of coffee—a modern, professional place with one chair, appointments only. There would be a nice stereo, no TV. It would be the kind of place her dad would never have gone to. He had been more the *Joe the barber* type. But he would have come in and sat in the chair anyway because it was her place and he would have been proud of her. Thoughts of her dad got her to thinking of her mother. Her mother hadn't called, of course. Tawny thought she should make the call. It was hard to sometimes. Her mother didn't approve of Rad, didn't approve of what he did for a living. She didn't approve of Tawny's piercings, her hair, and her nail color, and never let up on any of it. It had been that way since Tawny turned fifteen. Sometimes she thought her dad had had his heart attack just to get the hell out of the house and away from the shrew his wife had become. *Thanks Dad, for leaving me alone with mom.* Tawny winced involuntarily. *Sorry, Dad. Didn't mean that.*

Tawny finished with Vince and went back to Grace. Grace smiled up at Tawny with her little wrinkled face. Despite Grace's negativity, she was a nice old lady. She just needed someone to talk to. Tawny wondered briefly what it would have been like having her as her mother. Who could say? Maybe she'd been an over-lording bitch to her own children. Maybe right now Tawny's own mother was having her hair done in a chair somewhere, and some other stylist was wondering the same thing.

A half-hour later Tawny was on the SamTrans bus headed up El Camino Real to home. As she passed the National Cemetery she said a silent hello to her dad who was buried there. Although he'd been in Vietnam, he'd come home in once piece, having, as he often said, lucked out and fought the war behind a typewriter as a clerk in Battalion Headquarters. He died fifty years after returning, but his status as a war vet got him a place at the National Cemetery.

Tawny got off the bus at Chestnut and walked the six or so blocks to their place. Rad was not home and she took some ground beef from the freezer for spaghetti. As she straightened up the living room she picked up a *Thrasher* magazine that had ended up under the couch. For skaters, it was full of pictures of guys schussing down half pipes and along handrails. She hadn't seen Rad looking at one in over a month. She remembered when he'd told her about not being chosen for the X Games and she marveled at how well he'd taken his disappointment, turning his zeal for skateboarding into something else. She warmed at the thought of him; he was her steady man.

Tawny thought she heard voices in front of the house and parted the curtains. A car was double parked, a girl at the wheel. There was another big, blonde girl in the passenger seat who was kind of 'country' looking. The back door opened and Rad got out. The driver was pretty, Asian. Rad started toward the house and the driver said something. He turned and walked back, leaning into the car to talk to her. Frowning, Tawny let the curtain close.

"Hey, Tawn," Rad called when he came inside.
She looked over at him. "Hey, Babe. Who're the chicks?"

"Oh. They volunteer at The Mountain too. They were going this way and offered me a ride."

Tawny nodded as she smoothed a cushion on the couch. "Spaghetti tonight. How's that?"

"Cool. How was your day, Babe?"

Tawny nodded. "Good. Thirty in tips." She sensed something in Rad that bothered her. It had something to do with those two girls. She forced herself to smile.

CHAPTER 14

ALLEN COLLINS half-listened to the talk radio station as he kept up with the flow of traffic on the 280 freeway. He had missed work the day before, taking Reynaldo to the doctor's. Today he'd dropped him off at daycare and he would soon be in his cubical at work. On Allen's right, ghostly gobs of morning fog hung over the canyons of the verdant Santa Cruz Mountains, dripping cold condensation onto the pines and redwoods beneath. As Allen returned his gaze to the road ahead he could not stop thinking about things at home. Poor Reynaldo! He was not a bad kid. But Tina had been in a foul temper lately and Reynaldo seemed to come in for more than his share of the blame. Allen wondered how and when she had started to feel so sad and angry, and what he could do to make things right again. He thought longingly of their early, childless days. They had been married for five years before they'd adopted, and most of that period had been good, at least for him. In the beginning he had assumed that Tina had been okay with their inability to conceive, but eventually it became apparent that she was not. Her concerns morphed into increasing bouts of moodiness and irritability. There had been several trips to the doctor's office. Allen remembered staring in awe at the wild thrashing of his own sperm under a microscope. The doctor smiled at him when he looked up. "They're in great shape, frisky and raring to go." The doctor's tone became serious and he said that he suspected the reason they couldn't have a child was inside Tina's uterus. Evidently an earlier surgery had left a lot of scar tissue there. And so Tina and Allen had stopped hoping and given up. A grieving period followed. After that passed, Tina was still unhappy so Allen had suggested adoption. At first Tina was not interested and so he stopped discussing it. But after a while she brought the subject up. The more they looked into it, the more interested she seemed to become. They signed up for the County's 6-month Foster Adoption program. Her mood brightened and things got better. They would adopt.

Allen remembered the telephone call. Robert, the social worker for the county, said there was a boy available for adoption. He was what they called special needs, because he'd been born premature and spent much of his first year in a hospital. The mother, an illegal immigrant, had given birth to him and then inexplicably walked away, never even going back into the hospital to hold him or look at him. "We're calling you and Tina," Robert had explained to Allen, "because the boy is Hispanic and so is Tina." Allen had had to smile. Tina was Hispanic, but almost in name only. Her parents had emigrated from Mexico when she was a young child, and there was a lot of Castilian or Celtic blood in the family. With Tina's straw colored hair, she looked more Northern Italian than she did Mexican. And other than an occasional taste for Mexican food, she had almost nothing to do with her parents' culture. Robert, the social worker, had gone on to explain that most of the couples looking to adopt were holding out for Caucasian kids and were not interested in this one.

Allen remembered the look of interest on Tina's face the night the call came. She had listened eagerly to Robert's description of Reynaldo, and Allen hadn't had to coax her to go down to the agency to see him. Those were exciting and happy times.

Getting Reynaldo had been not unlike courtship. There were three visits to the foster home where he lived. Lorry, the foster mom who ran the place, was a nurse, and an angel too. On the first visit Allen watched Reynaldo crawl around the playroom floor, pushing a little car, trailing behind a clear plastic tube which delivered the oxygen he needed to his little button nose via a cannula secured around his head. In the corner, the six-year-old twins, both retarded, leaned into a toy box as they dug out brightly colored plastic building blocks. Against the far wall, a severely disabled fourteen-year-old boy lay moaning in his crib, waiting to have his diaper changed.

Reynaldo was a nice brown color, with handsome features. He was a little smaller than usual, but the doctor's report indicated that he was developing normally, except for some pulmonary problems that were common among preemies. Allen had attempted to bond with Reynaldo in the beginning. He remembered sitting down on the floor with him and being flattered by Reynaldo's little acknowledgments of his presence.

They had simply visited with Reynaldo that first day, playing on the floor with him, periodically chatting with Lorry about his medical history. On the next visit they had taken Reynaldo to a nearby park where he played in the sandbox. Then they took him out for lunch. Allen remembered marveling at how light the little guy was as he hoisted him up and lowered him into his highchair, as if his bones were hollow like a bird's. They ate their meal of burgers and fries, amazed by Reynaldo's smiles and his appetite.

A couple months later they met Reynaldo's mother. An Indian from Guatemala, she was very young, only eighteen. She had cinnamon skin and a round birth mark like a coin, high on her cheek. Allen had had to consciously keep himself from staring at her; she was that beautiful.

The mother's caseworker, an older woman named Doris, said when they entered her office and saw the mother sitting demurely in her chair, "This is Maria. She doesn't speak English."

"Oh, Spanish," said Allen.

Doris shook her head. "No. She speaks only her native language, Cakchiquel. We have only one interpreter in all of Northern California, and he's out of town."

Allen raised his eyebrows and allowed himself a look at the brown Madonna.

"But," Doris went on, "the interpreter spoke to her before he left. He said she agrees to everything, but she wanted to meet you both."

Allen and Tina looked over at the mother.

"Well," said Doris, "she won't understand a word you're saying, but why don't you just tell her you'll take good care of Reynaldo. We'll just have to hope that she gets something out of that."

Allen spoke to the mother and told her that he would treat Reynaldo as if he were his own son, and to not worry. As the words were leaving his mouth, he realized that probably every other soon-to-adopt parent in the state said the same sort of thing. Nevertheless, he felt sincere as he said it and he believed the woman picked up on that. Tina said the same thing, more or less, as the mother watched her mutely.

When Tina finished, the woman said something softly in her own language, seemingly a question, to Doris.

Doris smiled in response.

"Any idea what she said?" Allen asked.

Doris shook her head. "I'm afraid I don't have a clue."

Maria looked down demurely at her feet, saying nothing further, and the meeting concluded.

Despite the mother's physical beauty, Allen had suspected that there was something broken inside her, something that was not right, as if she'd suffered some great loss. Or perhaps, more likely, she'd been terribly traumatized by something. There were all those guerrilla wars going on down there. How else could you account for how she treated her own kid, abandoning him at birth, as if there was something wrong with him?

After the meeting, there had been visits from the social workers to make sure the house was okay. Sharp edges on furniture were pointed out and Allen covered these with wadded-up paper towels and tape. The water temperature was measured and Allen was instructed to adjust it lower, which he did. The paint in the house was scraped and tested but no lead was found.

The pristine beautiful blue of Crystal Springs Reservoir came into view as Allen rounded a curve in 280. Running parallel to the little peaks of the Santa Cruz Mountains, the long, narrow lake was one of a half dozen, all in a straight line if seen from high overhead, like the perforations in fanfold computer paper, all of them part of the San Andreas Fault line. A large bright white splotch appeared in the center of the lake. Allen noted that it was not in the water, but rather, sitting on the surface, like white Styrofoam packing peanuts floating on a puddle. Allen returned his eyes to the road. A moment later he glanced again at the lake as the white spot rose up suddenly to become a whirling cloud of seagulls.

Allen and Tina had a second picnic in the park visit with Reynaldo and then they were allowed to bring him back to their own home for a visit. Allen remembered the proud smile on Tina's face as she carried Reynaldo up the driveway. Their neighbors at that time, Gloria and Phil Thomas, an older, retired couple, were sitting on their porch and came over to the railing to see the boy.

"Is that him?" asked Gloria.

Tina nodded without pausing as she carried the boy

straight into the house. Allen had stopped for a few minutes to chat with them, answering some of their questions. Thinking back, Allen was not sure if it had been because of the fog that was starting to come off the mountain that day and her fear of Reynaldo possibly catching a cold, or if it had been out of possessiveness, born out of such a long-held desire to hold a child in her arms, a child that was hers, or soon would be, and not a friend's or relative's that would have to be given back as soon as it began to fuss and cry. Either way, Tina's haste to get Reynaldo inside their house that day had surprised and heartened him. Two weeks later Reynaldo came to live with them permanently. They were no longer just a couple. They had become a family.

Allen took the Mathilda exit and was soon walking through the FMC facility corridors. Allen's immediate boss, Larry Childers, and Paul Kerr were in Larry's little office, arguing as usual, this time over Paul's proposed changes to the budget. In the next little office, Jim, the systems analyst, was shooting the bull with Helen, the new temp. Allen looked in the office of Ron Nadler, the department manager. He wanted to give him a few details on why he'd missed the previous day.

Ron looked up and nodded as Allen came in. "You're back."

Ron was a light-skinned African-American engineer who had been promoted to supervisor three years earlier. Ron was very supportive of his people, something the last supervisor had not been, and most of the people in the department, Allen among them, liked him a lot.

Allen closed the door and sat down. "Yeah, sorry I couldn't come in yesterday. I'll make up the time. Tina and I had a big fight the night before, and Reynaldo wasn't feeling good."

Ron nodded, waiting for Allen to go on.

"Tina just started a new job," Allen lied, "and she can't take any time off right now. So I had to take Reynaldo to the doctor and stay with him."

Ron chuckled. "Well, these things happen sometimes. It'll straighten out."

Allen nodded.

"I have some news for you," said Ron.

Allen leaned forward with interest.

"Was Childers out there?" Ron asked.

Allen nodded.

Ron softened his voice and said conspiratorially, "Childers has…" Ron looked off to the left as he sought the right words. "… let's just say he's stepped on too many toes around here and more than a couple people have gone to Human Resources about it."

Allen nodded, knowing how tempting that option had seemed to him at times. But, believing that it would have hurt his own career more, he had put up with Childers' excesses.

"They're gonna bench him," said Ron.

"Really?"

"Yeah," said Ron, "and when they do I gotta put a new man in there. I want that to be you."

Allen nodded appreciatively as he considered what it would mean.

"Childers has four people, including you, to supervise. But Linda has been doing his budget for him, in addition to her other duties, so she would continue to do that with you in charge. It'll be a good opportunity for you, Allen. But you will have to put in a little more time."

Allen frowned as he nodded. He had already been thinking about that, how much he could do without stressing his already-stressed marriage. Maybe with the increase in pay he could get a nanny for the kids. "What kind of increase would come with the promotion?"

"It would be about twenty five percent," said Ron.

Allen's mind raced. That might be enough to get a nanny for the kids. If you were going to rise up the corporate ladder you had to be available, had to put in long hours... and with Tina demanding that he take care of Reynaldo... that wouldn't work. But now...

"Well," said Allen, "I'm definitely interested."

"Good," said Ron. "This has to go through Human Resources, and these things can take time. So, be thinking about it and I'll let you know the minute I hear something from HR."

Allen nodded.

"So," said Ron, "how's the kid doing today?"

"He's pretty much back to normal," said Allen. "But my wife was a little bit angry with him."

Ron frowned with concern. "Why?"

Allen nodded. "She thinks he took his coat off and that's why he got sick."

Ron folded his hands over his stomach and shook his head. Allen marveled at how large Ron's hands were. He had been a boxer in his younger days.

"Maybe she's going through the change," said Ron.

Allen nodded. "I thought of that too, but she's only forty three."

Ron raised his eyebrows thoughtfully. "Some of 'em start younger than that. You ever talk to her about going to the doctor? Or about counseling?"

Allen nodded. "She won't hear of it. She insists that there's nothing wrong with her."

"What about a priest? She's Catholic, right?"

"Yeah. Same thing. She won't go." Allen shook his head. "It's kind of a challenge."

Ron nodded as he looked at Allen thoughtfully. "Does she have any history of violence?"

For some reason Allen suddenly thought of the cat. He couldn't even remember what they'd named it. He had gotten it for Tina a couple of years before they'd adopted Reynaldo, in the hopes that it would help ease her pain over not being able to get pregnant. A tabby, it was only about two months old, still a kitten. She had loved it in the beginning, holding it, letting it sit in her lap. Then she discovered that it had been crapping behind the refrigerator. She went into a rage and kicked it clear across the kitchen. He took it back to the Humane Society the next day and told them that they had to move and could not have pets in their new apartment.

"Not that I know of," he said.

CHAPTER 15

FATIGUE AND A VAGUE SENSE of worry weighed Allen down as he took his exit off the freeway and drove down from Daly City on Westborough Boulevard. As he drew nearer to home his mood darkened with the long gathering shadows of day's end. He thought about Don's offer and how it might help. Allen's friend, Larry Fong, had gotten his MBA and gone into business. Now Larry and his wife Cecilia had a nanny for their two kids. Allen wondered what life would be like with a nanny for the kids. It would certainly take the pressure off Tina. And him too, because then he could stop worrying about the kids when he was away.

Allen pulled up to the house. Everything looked okay. So far so good, he thought, his mood brightening a bit. He let himself in.

Christine watched TV on the couch. She didn't turn her head or greet him.

"Hello, Christine," he said

Entranced by the cartoon characters on the screen, she didn't hear him. Allen wondered why Reynaldo wasn't watching too and he grew apprehensive. As he hung up his jacket, he heard Tina let one of the cupboard doors slam shut in the kitchen. When she did not greet him he knew something had happened.

"Hi, Honey," he called in to her. "I'm home."

She said nothing, continuing her preparations for dinner.

Allen walked down the hall to Reynaldo's door. The little guy sat at his desk, pencil in hand. Allen went in. Reynaldo's eyes were reddened from crying. "What's the matter, Reynaldo?"

Reynaldo held out his hand. "Mommy hit me."

A reddened welt was visible on Reynaldo's knuckle. Tears welled up in his eyes and Allen realized that Tina was standing behind him, looking down angrily at Reynaldo.

"Now you're going to lie to Daddy, aren't you?" said Tina.

Reynaldo said nothing as tears ran down his cheeks.

The boy's obvious pain upset Allen but he kept his tone calm. "What happened, Honey?"

Tina glared at Reynaldo. "He kept making the same sloppy mistakes on his work so I smacked his hands, that's all."

Allen frowned. "Honey, if you're hitting him hard enough to bruise him, that's too hard."

Tina began to grow agitated and moved into the room closer to Reynaldo. Allen put his body between her and the boy. He felt awkward and dramatic doing it, but some instinct told him to.

Tina peered suspiciously down at Reynaldo's hands. "He did that to himself! I didn't hit him that hard.

He must have been in here rubbing and scratching his hand. That's why it's so red."

Allen wanted to believe her, but couldn't. It strained credulity to think that Reynaldo was devious enough to do that. "Really?" he said flatly, stalling for time.

"Really?" said Tina in a mocking tone. "Really? Why do you always fall for his tricks? Huh? He's going to break up this family. Don't you see it?"

"I'm not falling for anything, Tina," said Allen, "I'm just..."

"I'm just... I'm just..." said Tina, mocking him. She walked out of the room.

Tina would not say another word to Allen and after dinner he left the house. He got in the van, slammed the door, and drove up to Hillside, turning toward downtown. On his left, the gentle slopes of San Bruno Mountain had turned tan in the heat of early summer. The sight of the little mountain range had always soothed him, especially from the air whenever he flew into the Bay Area. Then the mountains appeared to be covered with velour—green in winter, tan in summer. God, if there really was a God, had given reign to his artistic side when he created them. But now the colors and textures held nothing for him.

Allen stepped down hard on the gas pedal and the smooth power of the van's V-6 calmed him slightly. He thought about how the van could deliver him from all of his pain and strife. All he had to do was head out on the highway. He had everything he needed—two credit cards, the clothes on his back. It was like that song by Bruce Springsteen, something about having a wife and kids and going out for a walk and never returning. Could he leave his kids like that? How could any man do that? But Tina was beginning to bring him to an understanding of how. She was refusing to listen to any of his concerns, closing all the doors. He'd asked her if she would go with him to see the therapist the next time and she had flatly refused, telling him mockingly, "There's nothing wrong with me! You're the one with a problem." Maybe he could find someone who could help her, could help them, a woman therapist, a priest. But, if not... Allen couldn't finish the thought.

Allen turned the radio on, finding some blues-y jazz that suited his mood. He turned it up loud as the van ate up the rode hungrily. It was a good vehicle. They'd had it for a long time and gotten good service out of it. Allen remembered buying it just weeks after getting Reynaldo. It was a Saturday. The local Ford dealer was having a sale. Tina suggested they go look at minivans. They did and one thing led to another. He didn't care that they'd decided to buy it on a whim on a Saturday afternoon. Vans were for families and that's what they had become. The fact that it was Tina's idea made it even nicer. She wanted it for them, the family, so they could take drives in the country in a vehicle that had room in the back for Reynaldo to nap if he wanted, or so she could have room to change his diaper—at two he still hadn't been completely potty trained.

At the bottom of Hillside, Allen turned south. Something clanged metallically and started rolling around in the back. He pulled over on Chestnut, got out and opened the sliding door to the back. The shiny aluminum tube support for the camp table had come loose. The table was about as big as a large pizza, but the three of them had used it on their first camping trip together. That had been his idea—to celebrate getting Reynaldo by going camping. Tina's contribution had been to insist that they have the van outfitted with a nice convertible camp bed and a table. They had used the bed and table twice in five years. But that first trip was beautiful, at least the beginning and the end, but not the middle. He would never have suggested it if they had known how frail Reynaldo still was. The social workers hadn't made that clear enough to them. He didn't blame them though. Finding homes for kids that nobody else wanted required a bit of salesmanship.

They had gone to Grizzly Creek State Park up near Eureka. The weather had been terrible. It rained for three days and nights. Reynaldo didn't mind; he spent his time pushing his little car around on the rollout bed, or looking at the pictures in his books, or watching as the raindrops on the windows formed rivulets and ran down. And Tina and he didn't mind either, at least not at first. In fact, they later calculated that that trip was when and where Christine had been conceived. But after three days of rain they'd had enough. Allen got the map out of the glove compartment and decided to take Route 130, a twisting hairline scratch on the map, compared to the bolded and red lines of freeways and highways. The road would take them up over the mountains and down the other side into the valley to

Redding where, he excitedly told Tina, the weather was always hot and for sure there would be several good, Mexican restaurants. They could also check into a motel for a few days and dry out. So they packed everything up and started up the mountain.

Allen figured it would take them an hour to cross; it took over three. The weather was miserable most of the way, either pouring or drizzling, and cold and clammy, and the road was challenging, one lane in many places, and winding, very winding. But it wasn't oncoming traffic that held them up—there wasn't any to speak of—it was Reynaldo. The many twists and turns in the road made him nauseous and he started throwing up. Tina looked frightened as she cradled him in her arms on the side of the road where they had stopped to rest. Allen wasn't worried, at least not at first. A lot of kids got carsick. He had as a kid. But it soon became apparent that they couldn't drive a hundred feet without Reynaldo throwing up, poor little guy. He didn't cry; he just grew weaker. And Tina grew angrier with Allen, and Allen felt like a fool and a punching bag. It had been a bad idea, he agreed with Tina, but how could he have known it would turn out this way? And now they had no choice but to push on or they would never get down the mountain and into Redding. They drove on for another few minutes and again had to stop as Reynaldo vomited. Bile hung from his mouth in thick gelatinous threads. Tina angrily harangued Allen for his stupidity, for the lack of traffic, for the rain, for the cold, for suggesting the camping trip in the first place, as she worriedly fretted over Reynaldo.

Allen didn't have the heart to argue with her. He felt like crap. But Reynaldo felt a lot worse and Allen was very concerned.

Allen drove the van slowly, cursing the road, hoping stupidly that some other car would arrive from the other direction driven by someone who could help them with Reynaldo, maybe a police car or a car driven by a doctor or nurse. But no one came and Reynaldo grew weaker. Allen prayed silently. He apologized to God for abandoning Him and begged Him to deliver them from their nightmare. Finally the road straightened out and Allen drove faster, leaving the cold wet gloom behind as they raced down the mountain toward the dry flatlands and Redding.

Allen got them a room in the first decent motel they came to. Tina gave little Reynaldo some glucose drink and Tylenol. His temperature disappeared and he was soon scooting his little car across the bedspread. They showered, then napped, then left the motel room to buy a delicious meal in a nice, family-run Mexican restaurant. That night they watched a mindless old Laurel and Hardy comedy on the motel room TV, laughing uproariously with relief. They had made it. They had been lost in the wilderness, but they had finally made it out. Now they were dry and warm and happy. And they had "bonded" as the expression went.

Now what the hell had happened to them? He put the van in gear and slowly edged its nose out into the street. He wished he could go back in time to that day. A horn blared as a beat-up old Toyota passed. The driver, a young man about twenty who was the same brown color as Reynaldo, yelled something in Spanish. His muscled chest was bared aggressively as he flipped Allen the bird. Allen clenched his jaw as he stomped on the gas and sped down the street after him. His pulse raced. It seemed like everybody in the whole goddamned fucking world was on his case or in his face, 'dissin' him, as the kids said. He had to fight back. He wanted to catch this guy and hit him—hard.

Allen held the accelerator to the floor and the van shot forward. The kid was only two cars ahead. The car in front of Allen slowed for a couple that had started to walk across the street. Allen cursed and beeped the horn, going around them, ignoring their looks of angry incredulity. His breathing was rapid, his heart thumping as he attempted to close the gap. The Toyota was about five car lengths ahead. It glided through the light at Grand Avenue just before it turned red. The car disappeared around the bend.

"Christ," said Allen, braking hard for the light. The pursuit at an end, his senses began returning to him and he saw an old Hispanic man on the curb glaring at him angrily. On the sidewalk, a couple of teens were laughing as they discussed something excitedly, probably his failed pursuit.

"Jesus Christ!" he said under his breath. "What the fuck am I doing?"

He drove slowly back toward home.

CHAPTER 16

RAD GOT OFF THE SAMTRANS bus on El Camino and started up the hill to Wayne Spencer's apartment on F Street. Wayne was about twenty years older than Rad and lived in Colma next to the Woodlawn Cemetery. Wayne drove a limousine for a living and wrote novels in his spare time. He had driven Rad and his date and one other couple to their El Camino High School senior graduation party eight years earlier. As Rad walked up the hill, he remembered that night, some of it anyway, the parts before he and the others had started drinking heavily. In the early part of the evening he hadn't paid much attention to Wayne. He was just a pair of uninterested eyes occasionally noticed in the limo's rearview mirror as they passed the bottle around in the back and laughed and talked. On the way back from the party they stopped at a bar in Daly City. Rad had been mildly drunk by then and didn't remember some of what happened next. They were sitting at a table when Jim, the male half of the other couple, got into an altercation with some Mexican gang banger. Jim probably would have gotten his ass kicked if Wayne hadn't come in and smoothed things out. They left the bar and drove to a stretch of beach over in Pescadero, hanging out till dawn.

After the cold and damp of the sea air and sand began to wear on them, Rad and his date slowly walked back up from the beach. After she fell asleep in the back, Rad got out of the limo. Wayne was sitting with the door open, writing in a notepad. Rad assumed at the time that it was some kind of log or report that Wayne was required to keep, but Wayne told him it was a novel he'd been working on for a long time. That intrigued Rad. Not that he wanted to write anything himself, but he had never known anyone with any such inclination. And he'd always assumed that writers worked in more professional settings—puffing on a pipe meditatively in a quiet office, reference books open on a polished mahogany desk. Certainly not dressed in a black tux with ruffled shirt front and loosened bow tie, sitting in the front seat of a limo with the overhead light on, writing in a legal notepad while babysitting four high school seniors who were drinking and screwing in the sand in the dim light of an early summer morning.

Rad met Wayne the second time at a filling station about five years later. The years had taken a toll on Wayne. He and his wife were divorced and he'd lost his house and most of his hair, managing only to retain half custody of his young son. He'd finally published the book he'd been working on that night on the beach, a novel about early contact between the Chinese and the Indians along the West Coast. But the book had not sold well and now he was working sixty hour weeks with the limo company. As Wayne put the hose back on the pump, he told Rad he was going off duty and invited him to have a beer with him. They went to a bar in Daly City and drank beer and shot pool, talking for a couple of hours.

Rad was breathing heavily from the climb and he felt apprehensive. He thought about the fact that the reason he was visiting Wayne was to get something from him. He used to stop by just to bullshit with him, maybe every couple of months, but he hadn't seen him in almost a year. And now Rad was on a mission. He remembered trying to sell chocolate bars as a kid for his football team uniform. Discouraged, he had eaten them all instead. He remembered his dad yelling at him. The experience had soured him on selling. Still, this was for a good cause.

Rad looked at his clipboard. He'd collected only a half-dozen signatures. But Wayne would sign. Then Rad would force himself to walk down to the El Camino near the Kmart and try and get some of the people going in there to sign. Rad wondered vaguely if Wayne knew about the effort to save the mountain from the developers. Probably not. He worked a lot of hours driving and more than likely spent his spare time working on his writing.

Rad heard a noise from the cemetery across the street. A Mexican groundskeeper wearing a broad sombrero hat to keep the sun off himself, trimmed the weeds around the monuments with a gas powered weed whacker. The noisy machine spat out a succession of tiny puffs of oily blue smoke as the man swept it back and forth.

Rad rang the bell to number 7.

Wayne's voice rattled out of the little metallic speaker. "Who is it?"

"It's Rad."

The door lock buzzed and Rad pushed it open. He walked down the hall to number 7 and Wayne let him in. Wayne sat in a chrome and leather swivel chair before his computer. The TV was off. The little apartment was furnished with old and worn furniture, the kind of stuff you'd buy at the Salvation Army. But, Rad noted, it was clean, cleaner than his and Tawny's place.

"I'll be with you in a minute," said Wayne. "I just want to close this out." Wayne turned back to his computer.

Rad nodded and sat on the couch. He looked at his reflection in the darkened TV. That was another thing about Wayne, he realized. Any other guy would have the TV on to a game or something. But Wayne hardly ever had it on. He was one hella serious guy.

"Nice day, huh?" said Rad.

"Yeah," said Wayne absently.

"Tight," said Rad. "That something you're writing?"

"Yeah." Wayne closed the program on his computer and pulled the floppy disc out of the drive. He swiveled around in his chair. "So, long time no see! How's everything going with you and your girlfriend?"

"Tight," said Rad. The muted sound of the weed whacker came through the window glass. "We're getting along. How do you like living in Colma?"

"It's the greatest. You know there are a lot of people dying to get in here."

Rad laughed with Wayne at his little joke. "How's the writing going?" he said.

"You know who else resides here?" said Wayne, ignoring the question.

"No."

"Wyatt Earp and Ishi."

"I know who Wyatt Earp is. Who's Ishi?"

"He was the last wild Yahi Indian in California."

"Awesome," said Rad. "You writing a book about him?" Rad felt a little guilty. He had meant to buy Wayne's first book and have him sign it, but he had never gotten around to it.

"Nah! I don't know what this is. I'm just writing, that's all." Wayne got up and walked into the kitchen area and opened the refrigerator, taking out a can of Bud. "Want one?"

Rad nodded. "Sure."

"You know," said Wayne, "about eight or nine years ago they had the big funeral for Harry the Horse right over there." He pointed to his front window.

"Who's that?"

"Some Hells Angel biker. Supposedly they buried him sitting on his Harley."

"Really?"

"Oh, yeah." Wayne grew serious. "There must've been a thousand bikers on the road out there. You couldn't get anywhere for hours... and the fuckin' noise..."

Rad nodded.

Wayne brought a beer over to Rad, going back to get himself one. "Writing doesn't pay. I'm still messing around with it because I can't stop. It's an obsession.

But I really should be figuring out how to make money, maybe learning web page construction or TV repair, real estate, dental technician and auto body repairer." Wayne laughed and sat down across from Rad. "So, what brings you by, stud?"

Rad laughed nervously. "I just wanted to talk to you about something." Rad was nervous about the petition. He hoped that Wayne wouldn't look down on him the way people did the zealots who stopped you at the airport to ask you if you wanted to be saved or if you wanted to find out about Hari Krishna. "You hear about San Bruno Mountain? You know, the development?"

Wayne nodded solemnly. "Yeah. The City Council seems really hot to do it. Someone must have offered them a lot of money."

Rad knew that if he didn't ask now he never would. "Maybe so," he said quickly, "but, I mean, we might be able to stop them."

"Oh yeah?" Wayne looked genuinely interested. "How?"

"Well, there's this petition. If they get enough signatures we can get something put on the ballot. And I'm collecting money too, for the outfit that's trying to save the mountain. They're working with lawyers, you know, environmentalist types, and that costs money."

Wayne nodded. "You're becoming quite the crusader, huh?"

Rad smiled and shrugged. "I'm just trying to help. I wrote three letters to the *San Francisco Chronicle* but they didn't print them." Rad shook his head. "Maybe I should've had you look at them first. I haven't written a letter in years."

Wayne shook his head. "It probably wouldn't have mattered. They don't care about South City. This is just a place that people drive through on their way to..." Wayne made quote marks with his fingers, "'The City,' after they land at SFO. We're too blue collar for them. They could give a shit about what happens in South Screwdriver, The Industrial City."

Rad smiled and Wayne shrugged and took a pull at his beer. "You want me to sign it?"

Rad nodded, glad Wayne hadn't asked him any more questions. Rad realized that he could never run for political office or anything. He just wasn't comfortable asking people questions and trying to get them to do things. He took the petition out of his back pocket.

Holding his beer can in his fist, Wayne pointed a finger out the window at the cemetery. "That is the only open space that's going to be left on this peninsula in twenty years. And then they'll change the City charter and move all the graves out. Then it's going to be wall-to-wall condos, from bay to shining sea."

Rad frowned. "I don't know. If people get organized and fight back, maybe not."

"Whatever floats your boat. Give me the petition." Wayne signed the petition and handed it back. He opened his wallet and handed Rad a five. "That's all I can spare, stud." Wayne sat back down.

"Well, you're young, Rad," he continued. "You got the natural optimism of youth going for you."

Rad nodded, noting with a little sadness that Wayne looked older and was slowly going to fat. Wayne started talking about how he had briefly interned with Greenpeace in his younger days, but Rad wasn't listening. His mind was already moving on, going through the phone book, figuring out who else he could call and visit to get to sign. He thought of a friendly teacher who lived in South San Francisco, Mister Campbell. He decided to visit him next.

Wayne finished talking and Rad realized guiltily that he hadn't heard anything Wayne had said. "So," said Rad, trying to bluster his way through, "tell me more about this Ishi dude."

"Well," Wayne said, smiling slightly, "Ishi, the last wild Yahi Indian wandered out of the forests up by Mount Lassen. He was almost naked and half starved and hid in a barn. When the farmer found him, they took him to San Francisco where he ended up at the University of California. The academics there took care of him and nursed him back to health. He became almost a walking exhibit until he died. It's a sad, but fascinating story."

Rad nodded. "So," he said, pointing out the window, "next you're gonna tell me he's right out there, fourth plot from the curb."

Wayne frowned, imparting an air of seriousness to the discussion. "No. I think his ashes are in the Olivet Columbarium."

"Columbarium?"

"Olivet is the faux Greek Temple style building where they have these beautiful urns full of the ashes of deceased people. It's down El Camino Real a half mile. You know where Kmart is?"

"Well," said Rad, "one of these days I'll get over there."

"Yeah," said Wayne.

They lapsed into silence for a minute or so and then Wayne said, "You still got that snake in the garage?"

"Yeah. When Gabriel split, he just abandoned it."

"That the guy that's into black candles and Wicca, stuff like that, right?"

Rad frowned. "Yeah. Who knows what he's into now, probably Buddha or Jesus."

Wayne chuckled. "That snake must be pretty big by now."

Rad shrugged. "I don't know. Maybe fifteen feet. Maybe longer."

"Don't you want to know? I mean, how big can those things get?"

"Twenty feet max, I think, maybe a couple hundred pounds. But Gabriel never feeds it enough for that. He just comes by once in a while. He was supposed to have taken it by now, but he still hasn't."

Wayne shook his head in wonder. "And your girlfriend's okay with it in the house?"

"Not really. She wants me to give it to the zoo. But I'm not sure they'd take it. Anyway, I just want Gabriel to come and get it. It's his responsibility."

Wayne nodded. "If I had ever brought something like that home my wife would have freaked."

"Really?" Rad smiled. "Well you don't have to worry about that now. If Gabriel doesn't come and get it would you like to buy it? I'll give you a good price."

Wayne laughed. "Yeah, right. By the way, I'm putting together a new business on the side."

"What's that?"

"I'm gonna start giving tours of the cemeteries of Colma."

"I thought they already had a cemetery tour out of the Colma museum," said Rad.

Wayne nodded. "Yeah, but this is different. It's going to be a private luxury tour, starting this Halloween. I'm going to dress in costume, like Dracula maybe, and provide a couple bottles of Champagne and hors d'oeuvres. I'll charge about forty or fifty bucks a head. I could knock that in half if you wanted to take your girl."

Rad smiled. "Wow. Sounds cool, but money's a little tight right now. Let me think about it."

CHAPTER 17

1015 Skyview Drive

REYNALDO SAT AT HIS DESK looking over at the poster of the Power Rangers. He looked back down at the paper before him. He was tired of copying the words and definitions from the dictionary. He had filled up a whole page like Mommy wanted, but she had found some mistakes. She yelled at him, ripped up his paper, and told him that he had to do it all over again. He thought about the time she had gotten so mad at him that she broke the ruler on his hand. And when he had cried she had screamed at him to stop crying.

Reynaldo chewed on the pencil eraser absently, listening to the sounds of the TV coming from the living room where Christine was watching cartoons. He had been in his room a long, long time now. His face darkened into a frown. He couldn't wait until next year when Christine would go to first grade. Then Mommy would make her sit in her room and do work all day too. Reynaldo drilled a hole into the soft wood of his desk with his pencil point. He wished he were in the park with Daddy or at the toy store. He heard Mommy coming and began writing on the piece of lined paper.

Mommy ducked her head into the room. "How much have you done?"

Reynaldo held up the paper.

"Why is it taking you so long?"

"Sorry, Mommy."

Mommy scowled at him. She shook her head. "No break for you today!" She went out and he heard her talking softly with Christine.

Tears filled Reynaldo's eyes and he went back to work copying the definitions. After a while he forgot Mommy and the sun grew faint on the curtains. His backside started to hurt from sitting on the hard wooden chair. Finally Mommy came in and told him to go out and play with his sister. He knew that this meant that Daddy would soon come home. Sure enough, a little while later the key turned scratchily in the lock. Daddy winked playfully at Reynaldo and Christine as he came in the door and set his briefcase down.

"Hello, Christine."

"Hi, Daddy."

"Hello, Reynaldo."

"Hi, Daddy."

"Were you a good boy today?"

"Yes, Daddy."

Mommy said something from the kitchen but Reynaldo couldn't hear it. Daddy went into the kitchen and closed the door. Mommy's and Daddy's voices grew loud and Reynaldo and Christine stopped playing and watched the TV quietly.

At dinner Daddy tried to be happy, but Mommy was angry and didn't talk. After Reynaldo finished eating, Mommy told him to return to his room, put on his pajamas, and continue writing down the words and their definitions. As Reynaldo went into his room, Christine went back into the living room to watch TV. Mommy and Daddy started fighting in the kitchen. Reynaldo heard their voices rising. He heard Christine turn off the TV. She went into her room to play with her Barbie doll.

"You care more about him than you do me!" Mommy shouted.

"That's ridiculous," Daddy said. "If you treated him better I wouldn't always have to take his side."

Mommy broke into sobs. "Take him back!" she screamed. "Take him back!"

"Five years, Tina," said Daddy. "That's how long it's been. You can't just take him back like some puppy to the pound!"

"You do it or I will!"

"That's crazy! We can't do that!"

A plate crashed and Mommy came out of the kitchen and went into Christine's room. The door slammed and Reynaldo could hear Mommy and Christine crying in there. Reynaldo wondered what the pound was.

Later Reynaldo heard Daddy come out of the kitchen and turn the TV on. He came down the hall as far as Reynaldo's open door and paused. Reynaldo watched him stare at Christine's closed door. Daddy turned and seemed surprised to see Reynaldo watching him. He smiled sadly. "How are you doing, Reynaldo?"

"Okay, Daddy. I love you Daddy."

"I love you too, Reynaldo. You had better get ready for bed."

"Okay, Daddy." Reynaldo got down off his chair and flipped down the covers on his bed. "What's a pound, Daddy?"

"Ah, nothing. I'll tell you when you're older."

"Is Mommy gonna take me back?"

"Nobody's taking you anywhere. Don't worry. Mommy's just upset. She needs to talk to somebody, that's all. Now you better get to bed."

Allen took a beer from the fridge. He went into the living room and sat in front of the TV. He popped the can and took a long pull. He picked up the TV remote and surfed the channels. He stopped at the cartoon network, seeing Wile E. Coyote tying himself to a rocket. The Road Runner blasted by him and he lit the fuse, that look of smug superiority on his face. The fuse burned down but instead of hurtling him down the highway to catch the Road Runner, the rocket blew up.

Allen stared, not laughing. How pathetic is that? he thought. Even a stupid cartoon seemed to mirror his life. Wasn't he every bit as ineffective? Hadn't everything he tried to save his family, to repair it and keep it together, blown up? He'd tried to get himself and Tina into counseling; she wouldn't hear of it. He'd tried to get her to go with him to see a priest; she wouldn't go. He'd even recruited her brother, Tomas, to make his case to her. That was a bust. Allen had been in the next room, listening. He remembered Tina's voice slowly rising to anger until she was shouting at Tomas, "Don't tell me how to raise my kids! This is my house! This is none of your business!"

Allen took another sip of the beer. He'd written the lawyer, but hadn't heard anything back. He'd even included a self-addressed, stamped envelope, for crying out loud. Everything he tried was checkmated. It was hopeless. He glanced up at where the family pictures used to sit on the mantle. Reynaldo wasn't the only one who would be hurt by this. There was Christine too. What was all this anger and fighting doing to her? She seemed to have already found her escape into the TV. When she watched it she seemed willfully oblivious to everything around her.

And, Allen thought, what was *he* doing to cope? He became suddenly aware of the cold can in his hand. Other than drinking more and more? A kind of paralysis seemed to be slowly taking him over. Whenever he sat down and tried to think logically about their problems, the specter of a breakup loomed out of the gloomy fog like a shoal of rocks spotted by the tillerman at the last moment, too late to steer the ship to safety. Then his mind would grow numb and shut down.

"Wait a minute," a little voice in his head seemed to say. "If one thing doesn't work, you go on to the next. You don't give up!"

Allen blinked dully. Had he given up? He drained the beer can, washing away the discussion. "I don't know," he said aloud. He went into the kitchen and returned with another beer. He sat and popped the top.

"Jesus Christ!" he muttered. His life was turning to shit. Pure shit. He put his feet on the coffee table and surfed the channels, settling on the Nature channel. The camera slowly panned across a jungle river bank. The announcer was droning on in a thick British accent about the giant snake, the anaconda.

Reynaldo couldn't sleep. He got out of bed and went out into the hallway. He saw Daddy sitting in front of the TV. Reynaldo looked back down the hallway at Christine's door. He knew Mommy would not come out tonight. She would sleep in Christine's room. Reynaldo crept down to the living room. Daddy didn't hear him approach as he watched the TV with his back to him. On the TV, an animal that looked like a large rat hurriedly crossed a jungle clearing. It came to a swamp and stood on its hind legs, quickly looking around, its little black animal eyes full of worry. It jumped into the water, making a splash, and started swimming. Somewhere else, a big snake raised its head at the sound. It slithered down the mud bank and entered the waters of the swamp. The rat thing looked around suddenly, sensing danger, then swam forward in a fury. The snake went under the water. Reynaldo watched open-mouthed as the water erupted and the coils of the snake engulfed the rat thing like huge thick ropes. The rat thing struggled frantically and the snake encircled it with more coils. Reynaldo saw the rat thing's eyes full of fear and pleading. He imagined Mommy's face on the rat thing as more coils encircled it, the look of fear freezing into a look of motionless nothingness. He watched, enthralled.

Daddy turned and saw Reynaldo. "Reynaldo! What are you doing out of bed?"

"Sorry, Daddy. I wanted a hug."

Daddy quickly changed the channel to the news. He got up and came around the couch.

"Daddy," said Reynaldo. "Are there really big snakes like that outside?"

Daddy smiled sadly. "Nah. In the jungle, maybe. There are people who have boas as pets, but they don't get that big."

"Why not, Daddy?"

"Oh, they probably don't get enough food to grow that big... and being kept in a cage, they can't grow that much."

"Really?"

"Really," Daddy said. He knelt to Reynaldo. "Now, you go to sleep, okay?"

"Okay, Daddy."

Reynaldo got into bed and Daddy turned out the light. Reynaldo thought about the snake on the TV. He wished he had a giant snake for a pet. He could keep it under his bed. If Mommy hit him again he could send it out at night to squeeze her neck like it did the rat thing.

Reynaldo heard Daddy turn the TV on out in the living room to some people laughing. A beer can popped. Reynaldo remembered the other place he'd lived at before Mommy and Daddy took him. The lady there smelled like flowers. She never hugged him and he couldn't remember her face. But she never yelled at him and she never hit him. There were two other kids there and the sick man who was always in the bed, and a friendly cat, and a shade tree in the yard. There was a sandbox too, and a little pool. Reynaldo wished he could go back. He would miss Daddy. And he would miss Christine too. Maybe Daddy could go with him. No. Daddy would not leave Christine. Daddy loved Reynaldo, but he loved Christine too.

Reynaldo sighed sleepily. He wished he could go to work with Daddy in the mornings. He fell asleep.

Allen sat in the darkened van across from the closed Olympic gas station. Tina had locked herself in Christine's room and he had been too upset to sleep, so he had taken a ride. Five, six years, how long had it been since his mother had died? Sometimes it seemed like she was still alive and that the phone might ring and she would be on the other end. When she was alive she would never identify herself when she called, never say hello, just launch into a discussion, asking him about this or that. She was a little odd, had been for the last ten years of her life, but harmless and always warm and kind. What would she think of all of this craziness?

Allen grew tired of sitting. He started the van and drove to McCoy's. Four big Harley Davidson hogs sat in the parking lot. Inside, the old bartender sat in front of the taps again, the TV on. As Allen entered, rough laughter and cursing came from the back room. He sat a few stools down from the old man and nodded a greeting.

"The same?" the old man asked.

"Yeah. My name's Allen, by the way. What's yours?"

"They call me Lou."

Lou set the tall pint of beer on the bar and slid it down toward Allen. Allen was about to say something when raucous laughter echoed from the back room. A man came out carrying a pool cue menacingly, like a weapon. He had a full beard and long hair and wore a cutoff dungaree jacket, like a Hells Angel biker. The old man, Lou, raised his head inquisitively.

"Tar come by yet?" the biker asked him.

Lou shook his head and the biker went back into the other room without a glance at Allen. Allen looked away from Lou to the TV where a basketball game was in progress. He drank half the beer down and felt better. He stared at the bottles on the bar. "Lou," he called. "Give me a shot of bourbon whiskey, will you?"

Lou took a bottle from under the bar and wordlessly poured a double into a tumbler, sliding it down to Allen. Allen took a sip. He felt the heat of it course down into his belly and he felt lighter, serene. Why did everything in his life have to be so fucked up? He watched the game for a while. He took another large gulp of the whiskey and seemed to ascend up into the blackness of the night sky. Looking down, he followed the darkened roads back the way he had come until he came to his house. He passed effortlessly through the locked door and floated down the hall. He hovered over his wife and then his two children in turn as they slept in the darkened house. He longed to reach down and touch them, but he could not.

CHAPTER 18

TAWNY SWEPT THE HAIR FROM her station and thought again of the Mexican woman. She wondered if she'd see her this evening. The week before, when Tawny had been sitting on the steps, the woman had walked past and her belly had looked empty and she didn't have her kids with her. The woman had also seemed troubled and hadn't looked over to smile a greeting at Tawny the way she usually did. Tawny had watched her walk slowly up the hill and wondered if she was all right. Had she had her baby? Or had she lost it? The woman had not shown up the rest of the week and now Tawny worried about her.

Vince Rinaldi came in the shop and took off his jacket. Tawny smiled and waved him into her chair, glad to have someone to talk with to take her mind off of things. Vince looked great, as usual, and Tawny enjoyed the attention he gave her. The last time he was in he'd complemented her choice of shoes and her slacks. "They show off your figure nicely," he'd said.

"When are you and skater boy gonna drop by my cabin?" Vince asked.

Tawny's smile faded at the reference to Rad. Since

he'd gotten involved with the Save the Mountain people he had seemed a little distracted and distant. And there had been that chick that drove him home. Despite her telling herself that it was nothing, it worried her a little.

"One of these days," she said. "Rad's schedule is really hectic now. He's involved with an environmental group."

Vince's hand had snaked from under the part in the cloth she'd covered him with and he touched her on the back of the hand that held the comb. An electric tingle went through her.

"You could come by yourself, you know."

Tawny smiled and pulled her hand away. "How much are houses going for up at the lake now?" she said.

After Vince left, Tawny again swept her station. As she put the broom away it was close to four and quiet. Outside in the mall there was a fair amount of foot traffic—mostly teens just let out of school; they moved along in pairs or small crowds, checking each other out slyly. Across the corridor in front of the toy store, a Hispanic couple talked heatedly. Dressed in a peasant gown, the woman was small, slender and beautiful, despite the penny-sized birthmark on her cheek. She seemed to be pleading with the man. He was about twenty years older than her, a head taller, and reminded Tawny of a picture she had seen in one of her textbooks in school of an Inca Indian. The hat he wore was certainly from that part of the world—a woven woolen job with earflaps hanging down. Looking like a couple from a visiting ethnic dance troupe, they would have drawn stares a dozen years earlier, Tawny realized, but not now, and not here on the San Francisco Peninsula. Wishing a customer would come in, Tawny looked over at the empty chairs. She looked back out at the corridor. The woman was now walking off, her head down, a worried look on her face. Tawny looked back to where the man had been and was surprised to see him still standing there, staring straight at her. She looked away, fussing with the combs on the Formica topped counter. She looked back. He was still staring at her. He smiled, evidently enjoying her discomfort.

Tawny felt a chill. She acted as if she'd heard the phone ringing and went over and picked it up. As she brought it to her ear and said hello, she looked back at the man, but he had gone and she sighed with relief. "Well, thank goodness for that," she said to the dial tone, then hung up.

Tawny took the magazines off the seats and returned them to the rack. She thought again of the Mexican cleaning woman around the corner from her house and wondered if she'd be walking up the hill today. She really should speak to her. How long had she been saying hello and watching her make the climb up the hill to the bus? Three or four months? Four or five? Six or seven?

Tawny looked out the plate glass window. In the toy store across the corridor, a boy who couldn't have been more than seventeen, carried a sleeping baby in a baby carrier on his chest. They were having them younger and younger. And where the hell was the mother? She must be in another store, Tawny decided. The boy took the baby off his chest and lay the carrier on its back on a stack of cardboard cartons. Tawny didn't think that was safe. If she was the mom, she'd give him a good talking to. The boy moved off a little and another teen came down the aisle. He started tugging at one of the neighboring stacks of cartons, trying to get a toy down to look at. Tawny watched in amazed horror as the baby's carrier rocked back and forth. She was starting for the door when, to her horror, the cartons tumbled and the baby went down.

"Oh my God!" she cried, "Jesus Christ!" She threw down her apron and opened the door just as the original boy returned and picked up the baby—upside down by one of its legs! It was a toy, Tawny realized, a very lifelike toy, but a toy just the same. "You goddamned brat," Tawny said under her breath. "That's it," she declared to no one as she retrieved her apron from the floor. "It's time to go home."

Tawny began closing up. As she readied to leave, she remembered that tonight was the City Council meeting about the road and houses they wanted to put on San Bruno Mountain. Rad was scheduled to speak, along with some other local people, to try and convince the Council members to spare the trees, his big beautiful medicine trees, as he called them. Tawny felt a glow as she imagined him addressing the local powers that be. She was proud of him already.

CHAPTER 19

TWO DAYS AFTER ALLEN'S FIGHT with Tina, things still had not gotten back to normal. Tina and Christine ate their dinners alone. After they finished and vacated the kitchen, Allen would take Reynaldo in and feed him. This evening after they finished, Allen decided to go see Tina's brother and sister-in-law. Maybe he could again enlist them to talk to her. He didn't feel good about constantly bothering Tina's family with their problem, and it seemed disrespectful of Tina, but he felt that he had no choice any more. He cleaned the dishes and took Reynaldo to his room, putting him to bed.

Allen had always liked Tina's brother, Tomas. Tomas's large, sad eyes hinted that he had seen more than his share of life's sufferings in his almost-sixty years. And he seemed to have turned his life's observations into an earthy wisdom that many native-born Americans lacked. Tomas was only about two or three years away from retiring from his job at the fire department. Allen calculated that Tomas, as a fire fighter with thirty years under his belt, probably made as much money as Allen did working as a engineer at FMC—not bad for an immigrant with only a high school education. Tomas's wife Susan was Anglo, and worked as a secretary for the school board. They had worked hard, saved, and done well. They owned a house in Millbrae, a nice suburb of San Francisco, and together they had raised a son, Hector, who was now an undergrad at UC Berkeley, majoring in political science. When last Allen had talked to him, Hector said that he intended to go on to study law at Boalt Hall. Allen marveled at how well Hector had turned out so far. Obviously, Tomas and Susan knew a thing or two about child rearing. This realization buoyed up Allen's hopes as he rang their bell.

Tomas opened the door, smiled and let Allen in.

"Who is it?" Susan called from the kitchen.

"Allen."

"Oh," said Susan, coming into the hall. "Are you guys fighting again?"

"Yeah," said Allen. "Tina's angry with Reynaldo again. She hit him across the knuckles for messing up on his writing."

"Come on in the kitchen," said Tomas.

Allen followed them and sat down at the kitchen table. Tomas took a can of beer from the fridge and popped the top, handing it to Allen. Susan busied herself washing some dishes in the sink. Tomas frowned in concentration as he sliced an onion on a cutting board on the table. Some kind of sauce was simmering on the stove.

"What's so bad about a rap across the knuckles?" Tomas said, pausing in his slicing. "I got my share of them when I was growing up."

"Yes," said Susan, "and you probably deserved it." She smiled at Allen. "And so did our son, Hector. But not from me."

"Yeah," said Tomas slowly, "I'm the enforcer." He winked at Allen. "Every kid can use a good smack once in a while."

"Yeah," said Allen, "but she hit him so hard he's got a bruise."

"What?" said Tomas wryly. "Did he need to go to the hospital?"

Allen smiled a sad smile. "Of course not. It's not that bad, Tomas. But it seems like Tina never lets up on him. Why can't she let him play more? Why does she insist he sit in his room all the time writing and memorizing definitions?"

"Allen," said Tomas in a brotherly tone. "My father had a good job with the Government in Mexico City. We had a big house, servants... But he wanted his kids to grow up in America. When he came up from Mexico, he spoke hardly any English, and he had a wife and two children to support. He taught himself the language. He used to study words from the dictionary every night."

Tomas sighed. "Tina just wants Reynaldo to have something in this world. A man is nothing without an education. You want him mowing other peoples' lawns when he grows up?"

Allen blushed guiltily as the image of illegal Mexican immigrants mowing lawns and wielding noisy leaf blowers filled his head. "Of course not," he said, "but..." Allen looked around the kitchen. "Her discipline is too harsh. He's just a little kid."

Susan shook her head as she dried her hands on a towel. "Allen, has she ever hurt him badly?"

Allen frowned. "No... but it just seems to be too much."

Susan smiled kindly. "Why don't you just take a walk when Tina's disciplining Reynaldo? Just take a walk around the block."

Allen didn't say anything as he considered her advice. The idea was appealing. Maybe he was overreacting. But why couldn't Tina try talking to Reynaldo instead of hitting him? And why didn't she ever give him a hug when it was all over and forgive him? That's what his parents had done when he was a child. Sometimes she really seemed to have it in for Reynaldo.

Susan turned to Tomas. "I'm going up to get dressed." Tomas nodded without looking up from his chopping. Susan turned to Allen. "I have a class tonight." She smiled. "Don't worry, Allen. It'll work out. I'll stop by tomorrow and talk to her."

Allen nodded. "Thanks." He turned back to watch Tomas at his cooking. Allen looked up at a picture of Hector on the wall. It was your standard football photo. Hector held his helmet by the strap with one hand. The kid looked massive in his shoulder pads and jersey, and wore a big warm smile. He was handsome, with mostly Anglo features. In three or four years he'd finish college, get his law degree. In California, with those looks and a Hispanic surname, the world would be his oyster. Allen realized that he could be staring at a picture of a future governor or senator, maybe even president. Allen took quick stock of his own assets. He had two children, a wife, a house in a decent neighborhood, a good job. His world should have been bright and hopeful too. But instead he felt like it was growing darker, shrinking and shutting down.

Tomas scraped a white mound of chopped onions off the cutting board and into a bowl. He began slicing one of three lemons sitting on the table. The fresh smell quickly filled the room. "You guys fight too much, you know that?" he said.

Allen felt a coldness inside. He knew Tomas was right. The fights were corroding their marriage. It would fall apart if they kept it up. "Maybe," he said.

Tomas stopped his cutting and looked at Allen, his face full of concern. "Not maybe. You two fight too much." He smiled slightly. "Want another beer?"

Allen nodded as Tomas popped another one open and placed it before him.

"We didn't fight much in the beginning," said Allen "It's just been the last couple of years. I think maybe Tina's going through the change."

Tomas shrugged. "Kind of early, but, maybe, maybe not. It doesn't matter though. You're going to have to choose, Allen."

Allen frowned in confusion. "Huh? What do you mean?"

Tomas's big sad eyes looked into Allen's. "You're going to have to choose either your wife or your adopted son." Tomas squeezed the lemons into the bowl and went over to the stove to stir the sauce.

Allen stared down at the beer can, not believing

what he'd just heard. He laughed as if Tomas was kidding. "How's Hector's knee coming along?" he asked, changing the subject. "He going to play ball this year?"

CHAPTER 20

RAD AND TAWNY WALKED ALONG Grand Avenue on their way to the City Council meeting. Rad thought of the fact that despite having lived all of his life in South City, he had never been to City Hall. Hell, he'd never even climbed San Bruno Mountain until Pygmy's turned him down for the X Games.

They walked past the double glass doors of the police station and down to the next set of doors that went inside. A crowd of about fifty people milled about amid a half dozen folding tables set up on the tile floor. Some people sat on folding chairs as they talked and sipped coffee from paper cups purchased from the lone vending machine in the corner. Others stood, talking intently in small groups. Tawny held Rad's hand as they paused to look around.

Rad scanned the faces in the crowd, seeing no familiar ones. He was pleased that Jenny and Cait were evidently not there because he did not want to deal with any discomfort Tawny might feel about them at this time. He was already feeling a growing discomfort within himself and wished that he had not volunteered to speak at the meeting.

David Hunsicker walked past—intelligent bright blue eyes, apple red cheeks and white beard and pony tail—the picture of middle-age, organic-fed, Hippie health. Rad called out a greeting. David nodded.

"Who's that?" said Tawny.

"David Hunsicker, the guy who started the whole Save the Mountain movement."

A young woman with a tape recorder, obviously a reporter, had attached herself to David and was questioning him as they passed into the crowd. Rad and Tawny watched them for a moment and then returned their attention to the floor-to-ceiling plate glass windows and the hearing chamber on the other side. That room was full of folding chairs, an aisle up the center leading to a table, upon which a microphone had been set up. A dozen or so people had already taken seats as two men in business suits walked up to the dais and sat, looking down at the chamber. People began going into the chamber and Rad and Tawny followed them. Rad felt his pulse pick up as they took two seats toward the rear of the chamber. Tawny seemed to sense his unease and smiled at him, squeezing his hand.

Four more Council members, two men and two women, ascended the dais. A recording clerk took her seat at a table upon which a computer sat. David Hunsicker appeared at Rad's side. He handed him a card.

"You're speaker number seven," he said. "The luck of the draw. Lucky seven."

Rad felt himself smile instinctively, then looked down at the card in his hand.

The meeting began with the pledge of allegiance. Then a summary of the status of the last month's minutes was read by the clerk. There was a pause in the proceedings and people started talking amongst themselves. The Mayor banged the gavel sharply and looked at the audience over his reading glasses. He cast a look at the clerk and she rose and read the itinerary. The meeting progressed smoothly and soon Rad and the others in the chamber were looking at a map of San Bruno Mountain projected onto the white screen off to the side. David Hunsicker rose first to speak. Looking sincere and somber, he made an informed and passionate case for preserving the mountain. Then others rose to speak. Rad's heart seemed to pick up a few beats after each speaker.

"Number seven!" an amplified voice called out from far away.

For a moment the significance of this particular number didn't register with Rad and he looked around with the others.

"Number seven," the voice repeated and then Tawny was shaking his arm and smiling at him. "That's you, Babe."

Rad nodded, getting shakily to his feet. He stood still, his throat constricting, and he was surprised at the changes taking place in his body. His heart was pounding, his breathing rapid and heavy, and his legs weak. He was frightened, he realized, as he looked at all the faces watching him, more frightened than he'd ever been in his life. More frightened than the first time he'd stood poised above a half-pipe, his board in his hand. Why was he so frightened, he wondered vaguely? What was the big deal about just speaking his mind? What was happening to him?

As if from a great distance he heard the secretary say again, "speaker number seven, Rad Anderson."

Rad approached the microphone. He'd been introduced and identified. Now all the faces in the room focused on him expectantly, probably wondering what the hell was wrong with him and why he was standing there like a moron. When Rad got to the podium, his heart flopped about in his chest like a landed fish in the bottom of a boat. He cleared his throat as he pulled the mike closer, his breath rattling like the engine of a car starved for gas. As his face flushed beet red, anger filled him. What the hell was he doing, he wondered? Why was he being such a wuss? Get a hold of yourself he begged, then demanded of himself. Stop shaking. Stop the goddamned, chickenshit coward routine. Just stop it!

"Stop it!" The microphone screeched with feedback as the shocked faces looked up into his. Rad realized that he had said it out loud. He pulled the mike from its holder and shouted 'stop it' again.

The faces in the hall stared at him, wearing looks of awe, amusement and alarm.

Realizing that he'd overcome something, that he'd got his voice to work, Rad continued, "Stop the greed!"

The crowd erupted with applause, laughter and raised fists. "Stop it!" some of them echoed him.

"Order!" the secretary called.

"Stop the development," Rad barked into the mike.

"Stop it!" the crowd shouted back.

The din died a bit and Rad continued, "Save the mountain! We have enough houses, but not enough open space. Save the mountain! We have enough development in South City, but not enough parks. Save the mountain! I grew up looking up at that mountain. As a boy I rode my bike on its slopes, breathing in its clean fresh air. Will other South City children be able to enjoy its green pleasures?" Rad glared briefly at the Council members and then looked back at the audience. Tawny's face beamed at him. "The Indians worshipped that mountain," he said to the crowd, "and now the money-worshipers want to pave it over and build roads and houses on it!"

"Nooo!" the crowd shouted.

"Tell it like it is!" said someone.

"Save the mountain!" said another.

"That's right," said Rad. "Stop it... and save the mountain!"

When Rad finally took his seat he was exhausted, sweat pouring off his face. Tawny squeezed his hand as the people in the room slowly quieted and the next speaker approached the table.

Later that evening as Rad and Tawny recounted the day's highlights, Tawny felt touched and moved by Rad. She had seen a side of him she'd never known was there, a side she suspected Rad hadn't known was there either. The suspicion caused by the two Save the Mountain girls that had begun to taint her love for him slowly sloughed off. There was nothing to that. It was just her and him. That night their lovemaking was the best she'd ever known; Rad was strong and tender at the same time, and it seemed to go on forever.

CHAPTER 21

T AWNY SPENT OVER AN HOUR getting dressed and made up for their trip downtown to the SOMA district. She hadn't gone clothes shopping in over a month, but luckily she had one last decent top to wear. Rad was taking her to a new club called the Kat's Dawg. Tawny'd heard about it from one of her girlfriends, but never thought they'd go. There was a ten-dollar per person cover charge and the drinks were very expensive. But Rad's friend, Chaz, another skater, tended bar there and was getting them in for free. And, Rad had told her, when the boss wasn't around, Chaz would score them free drinks. Rad was amazing. He had so many friends and he always made things happen.

Just after the sun set, Chaz and his girlfriend Jane arrived in an ancient Mustang that Chaz was rebuilding. The thing was painted a mottled gray, had unfinished bodywork, holes and rough patches on the rear flanks. Jane was already stoned on grass and slept in the back. Tawny got in the back beside her as Rad sat in the front next to Chaz. As they rolled over the dips and bumps of the elevated freeway, the springs in the back of the car squeaked loudly like the sound of a couple making love on a old spring mattress.

Tawny watched the pastel-colored buildings of the Mission District flow past. Warm air, perfumed by the purple and pink oleanders that lined the freeway, rushed through the open windows of the car and Tawny felt happy. Money was tight now and they did not go out often. So this was a real treat. Leave it to Rad to get them a night of dancing and drinking without spending hardly any of their own loot. Tawny knew she was going to have a good time.

They exited the freeway and pulled to a stop at the light at the bottom of the ramp. An emaciated, wretched-looking baby-boomer street person stood on the divider holding a "will work for food" sign. Tawny knew it was a ruse, knew he didn't want anything to do with work and that he would drink away whatever money he was given. But she reached into her purse anyway and took out two one-dollar bills, holding them out the window. The old dude hurried over with what was probably a fake limp, and grabbed them before the light changed, calling out, "God bless you."

"Yeah," said Rad, "like he believes in God."

"Bacchus is his god," said Chaz, adding something else that Tawny couldn't hear as the words and laughter were lost in the roar of the Mustang's V-8 engine and the rush of air into the car. They raced down Mission Street. In the growing dark, they passed abandoned warehouses, neon-lighted gay leather bars, laundromats, groceries, Mexican restaurants, a Thai restaurant. Chaz took a sharp right, waking Jane, who looked out the window and exclaimed, "Wow! We're here already?" Chaz and Rad laughed as Chaz turned down a small side street and pulled up onto the curb in front of a garage door marked, "No Parking."

"It's cool," Chaz announced, as they began getting out of the car, "my boss told me I could park here."

Chaz led them wordlessly past the line of club-goers and the bouncer at the main entrance who gave him a nod of recognition. They turned a corner and went in a side door. They passed a few shabby black-painted doors labeled Dressing Room and entered the main hall. The dance floor was still empty. Later it would be jammed with sweating bodies, Tawny knew, based on what Rad had told her. Rad steered Tawny over to the bar and ordered her a Bloody Mary. Someone turned on the music. As Tawny took a sip of the earthy, biting concoction, the sounds washed over her in waves, more a visceral experience than a musical one. The electronic drumming and computer-generated notes seemed to knead her skin like a million rubber-coated metal fingers.

After Rad got Tawny set up at the bar, he left to go into the back office to check out the long board that Chaz had just bought. When he returned twenty minutes later the crowd had doubled and the dance floor was already full. He sat beside Tawny and ordered a shot of vodka. He downed half of it, then turned around, leaned back, and watched the dancers. Tawny got to her feet, pulling him toward the dance floor. "Wait, wait" he said, drinking down the rest of his vodka.

As Rad danced opposite Tawny, he smiled at the pleasure he saw in her face. She was really enjoying this night out and that made him feel like a man. The techno-trance number thrummed like a great machine and the patrons jerked and spun like marionettes. Finally it was over and Rad took Tawny's arm and led her back to the bar. He ordered another vodka. Talking over the music was impossible and so he and Tawny necked and drank, looking into each other's eyes. The bartender's hand appeared before Rad, offering him another vodka. He took a sip and floated on the waves of music, watching the bodies swirl and writhe under the flashing colored lights. Tawny nodded toward the dance floor; Rad shook his head no. She tried to pull him off the stool by his arm. He smiled, shouting, "I'm too stoned." She playfully scowled at him and said loudly into his ear, "I'm going to the ladies' room." Rad nodded and watched her walk off. He turned back to the dancers in the flashing lights, then closed his eyes and enjoyed the sensation of movement that came over him. After a few moments he grew dizzy and opened his eyes. A pretty Asian face was looking into his—Jenny Chin. Her friend, Cait stood a few feet away, watching the dancers on the floor with a look of wry amusement.

Jenny leaned close. "Wow," she shouted in his ear, then something that sounded like, "do you come here often?"

She laughed at her own joke, if that's what it had

been, and Rad smiled, unable to take his eyes off her. She leaned closer to him and again he felt the warm glow of attraction and had to resist the urge to pull her to him. Despite his dulled senses, he recalled the sight of Tawny disappearing in the direction of the ladies' room; he fought for self-control. Yes, he thought to himself, he would give almost anything to hook up with this girl. But he already had a girl, a good one. He looked toward the hallway, looking for Tawny. Jenny said something. He caught only the word, mountain, and he indicated with a jerk of his head that they should go to the hallway that led back to the offices. They would be able to hear each other back there. He led her away.

The movement seemed to sober Rad a bit and he wondered vaguely where in the crowd Tawny was. Could she see him now? No matter, he told himself, he was just talking to Jenny; nothing sinister about that. He paused under a naked red light bulb where he could see her better. As he leaned closer and looked into her eyes he got a hard on. "What were you saying back there?" he said. "I couldn't hear a word."

Tawny marveled at the music and dancing as she skirted the dance floor. A tall spike-haired man bumped into her as she made her way back toward the bar. Rad wasn't there. She scanned the room slowly and noticed a woman who looked familiar—tall, big-boned, blonde. She was standing and watching the dancers. Tawny suddenly realized where she had seen her before; she was one of the two that had driven Rad home from the Save the Mountain meeting.

Tawny looked over toward the offices. She frowned when she saw Rad talking to the Chinese chick. "What the…" she mouthed silently. He was standing a little too close to her, and the chick's eyes were all gaga as she listened to him.

She started toward them. But before they saw her, the chick took Rad's arm and led him onto the dance floor. Tawny moved closer but the sea of undulating bodies enveloped them.

Tawny went back to the bar and her Bloody Mary. The music went on for a long time and she grew more irritated. Rad hadn't wanted to dance with her and now he was out there with that chick. She put her drink down, deciding to go out and cut in on her. Why not, she thought, as she threaded her way through the dancers, all was fair in love and war, wasn't it?

The dancers shifted, opening up, and she saw them. The alcohol in her brain could not insulate her from the icy shock she got; the two of them were freak dancing! Freakin' for God's sake, the chick looking back over her shoulder as she rubbed her little ass in Rad's crotch. Rad saw Tawny and his face turned guilty, then slowly morphed into a stupid, 'I'm not doing nothin' smile.

"Thanks, Rad," Tawny shouted, her voice swallowed by the raging music. He and that little bitch must have been doing more than just stapling posters to telephone poles. There was obviously more. She turned and started away, pushing through the bodies.

Tawny left through the front door, the chill night

air hitting her like a bucket of water. She pushed her way through the crowd of people hoping to get in the club as she headed for the street.

"That damn bitch!" she cursed under her breath, "...and Rad!" When the two girls had dropped him off, her suspicion had been a tiny itch in the back of her brain. Then there had been his off-putting manner whenever she'd bring up her wants and dreams for the two of them. And the calls too. Three times she had picked up the receiver and said hello and there had been no one on the other end, at least no one that wanted to talk to *her*. Obviously Rad and this chick had something going on. But for how long? And how deep? And all this time she had thought she'd known him. What the hell did she know? Really?

Tawny reached Mission Street and looked at the traffic streaming by. A yellow cab turned onto the street two blocks down, heading in her direction. She stepped out in the street and flagged him. He saw her and put his signal on, moving into the right lane. She crossed when the traffic opened and the cab stopped. Just then someone ran up behind her. It was Rad. She ignored him.

"Where to?" the cab driver asked Tawny.

"South City. Take 101."

"Tawny," said Rad, "what are you doing? We were just dancing? What's with you?"

Tawny ignored him, looking out the opposite window. Rad opened the door and got in the back. The cab driver looked back at them, raised his eyebrows, then moved out into the traffic. Neither Rad nor Tawny said anything as the driver picked up his microphone and told the dispatcher he had a fare to South City.

"Give us a call when you get there," the voice rasped over the speaker.

Rad's stomach slowly turned to ice as the traffic rushed by. The big leather rear bench seat seemed like a mile-wide river, with Tawny on the other side. Outside, the night looked darker than it had in a long time, autumn dark. Rad felt rain in the air. Soon a few drops splashed across the windshield. Then gust-driven splatterings smeared the night lights crazily. The driver turned on the windshield wipers and the rain became a steady downpour. The air chilled as they rode through the gentle rain in silence. When the cab finally pulled up in front of the house, Tawny got out. Rad followed her.

Tawny ignored him as she said to the driver, "Don't go anywhere. I'll be right back."

"Tawny," Rad said, "listen, I was just talking…"

Tawny ignored him as she walked up the steps.

Rad started pacing in the rain. "Shit!" he said.

"Don't worry about it, pal," said the driver. "She'll get over it."

The rain soaked into Rad's hair and ran down his face and neck, chilling him. Tawny exited the house with a suitcase and a plastic-covered dress on a hanger. She looked right through him as she got into the cab. He went over to the driver's window and handed him a twenty. The driver spoke into his handset as he drove off. The rain picked up and Rad watched the cab make a U-turn at the bottom of the street. It headed back up the hill and turned onto Hillside.

Rad went into the house and sat on the couch. His head had cleared somewhat, but he still felt in shock. He tried to put the evening's events in their proper sequence and figure out how to explain things to Tawny. The house was quiet enough to hear the wind-driven rain lashing the windows. Why the hell did she get so angry? All he'd done was talk to Jenny. And then she'd wanted to dance, and so he had taken her out onto the dance floor. Fuck! What was the big deal? It wasn't like he was hooking up with her or anything.

Oh! He remembered the freak dance thing that Jen had done. Shit, that was just for a minute or so. And they had just been fooling around, making fun of the whole freak dance thing. But that must have been the very moment that Tawny had spotted them. Shit! It was all just a lousy coincidence.

Rad got up and went to the window. In the glow of the street light overhead, the rain came down like a veil, occasionally ruffled by gusts of wind. It was the season's first Pacific storm. The sight soothed him a little and he went into the bedroom. The top drawer in Tawny's dresser was still pulled out. Rad sat down on the bed. The thought of sleeping alone depressed him and he went back out into the living room. The digital clock read 12:18. The Dawg would still be full of thumping electronic music and gyrating people. The image enticed him. He could sit around here alone and feel sorry for himself or he could go back to the crazy, noisy humanity of The Dawg. But how could he get there?

He picked up the phone and dialed his old friend, Buddy Romero. Buddy's mother's voice came on. The Romeros lived two blocks away.

"Hello, Mrs. Romero. This is Rad. Is Buddy home?"

"Hello, Rad. Yes, I'll get him. Hold on."

Rad knew he didn't really have to ask. Buddy was always home at his mom's by bedtime. Rad had gone to the same grade school as Buddy, the same middle school, and the same high school. They should have been real good friends. But Buddy had turned out to be a real loser, a big fat momma's boy masquerading as a bad ass. He was way too into grunge and looked it, with his black T-shirts and black jeans. And with his weight problem, he had a hard time getting a girl. But he was also into motorcycles and had a Harley hog and four or five Japanese bikes, some of which he sometimes rode on the trails of San Bruno Mountain. Rad had an open invitation to ride with him any time he wanted.

"Dude!" said Buddy, coming on the line, "what the fuck's up?"

"I need to borrow one of your bikes."

"Not my hog, man."

"No, one of the other ones."

"Okay, dude. The Yamaha's runnin' smooth as shit. I just changed the plugs and tuned it up."

"Good. I'll be there in five minutes."

"Okay. What the fuck are you goin' out in this shit for, man?"

"I don't know. Bored, I guess. I'll be right over."

Rad hung up and went into the basement. He spied Ketsel on the other side of the chicken wire enclosure, snuggled up next to the water heater on the mound of dirty laundry. He felt guilty about neglecting him. Screw it. He'd check on him later. He grabbed his slicker off of its nail in the wall and went out the back door, locking it behind him.

The rain came down steady and thick as Rad leaned into the turns of 101, the car lights smearing the oily asphalt with red and white glare. He exited on Geoff and was soon pulling into the alley behind The Dawg. The bouncer remembered him and let him pass. It was just past one and the place was packed, stifling with body heat and throbbing with music. Rad immediately went into the men's room and dried his face and hair with paper towels. He combed his hair and went out to the bar and ordered a vodka. Chaz showed up a few minutes later and sat beside him, asking him where Tawny was. Rad shook his head, yelling into Chaz's ear, "She went home."

"What happened?" said Chaz.

Rad shrugged, not caring to elaborate. Chaz nodded slowly and knowingly and moved on. After a while Rad saw Jenny's friend Cait separate from the wall of bodies on the dance floor. Another young woman dressed in studded leather followed her to the bar. Rad looked at Cait but she gave no indication of knowing who he was. Perhaps she was too high, Rad reasoned. The movement of the bodies to the music, the mix of expressions on the dancers' faces—all of it took the edge off Rad's anxiety. What the hell had he done? he asked himself. He'd only been dancing with Jen, for crissakes! Maybe it was Tawny's time of the month. He tried to remember when she'd had her period last. She usually got a little sad, but not crazy angry like this. As he watched the dancers he hoped she would come to her senses in a day or so. After all, he'd only been being friendly to somebody. What was the big deal?

Somebody grabbed Rad's knee. It was Jenny.

Rad smiled.

"What happened?" she shouted to him over the noise. "Your pants are wet?"

"It's raining outside," he shouted over the music.

She looked at him in confusion, not having heard, then asked, "Where did you go?"

He shrugged. "Tawny wanted to go home."

Jenny nodded and looked over at the dancers. She leaned close. "You want to dance?"

Rad slid off the barstool and led her to the dance floor. After a few minutes of dancing the DJ suddenly shifted to a sultry slow number. Most of the other dancers drew their partners closer and it was obvious that they had chosen someone for the night. Jenny moved against Rad and he pulled her closer. They moved slowly, exploring each other's bodies. After a few seconds or a few minutes something deep and animal took over them and they began deep kissing. Suddenly the music stopped. Rad and Jen parted but continued to hold hands as they pushed through the crowd.

"You want to go to my place?" Jenny said.

Rad nodded. "What about your roommate?"

"She won't be there."

Rad nodded again, a lump forming in his throat. "Cool."

"Do you have a car?" Jenny asked. "Cait drove us here."

Rad smiled. "A motorcycle."

Jenny's eyes widened. "Oh... that's why you're so wet. Is it safe to ride when it's like that?"

Rad nodded, not saying anything.

"I'll be right back." Jenny went and found Cait. They talked for a moment and Jenny came back and took Rad's hand.

The vibration of the motorcycle's engine seemed to weld them together on the bike. Rain fell steadily, soaking into Rad's clothing, but he felt warm. Jenny pressed up tightly against him, her hands locked around his abdomen. He felt as if they were flying as he guided the bike along the blackened freeway. Soon they were on 19th Avenue, and rolling smoothly down dark, quiet streets past apartment-style dormitories.

Rad held their helmets as she opened the door. As soon as it closed he dropped them and she came into his arms. They kissed as they quickly pulled off their wet clothing. Rad carried Jenny over to the couch and she laughed as he lay her down in the dark, kneeling beside her. "We better go in my room just in case Cait changes her mind and comes back," she said.

"Why? You and her aren't, you know..."

Jenny laughed. "She is. But we're just roommates. She doesn't hit on me or anything. Come on."

Rad followed her. She quickly lit an aromatic candle and turned the lights off, climbing into the little twin bed. Rad lay beside her. As they made love, he marveled at her slender beauty, her strength and her passion.

After she'd fallen asleep, Rad quietly got out of bed and went into the bathroom. Finishing, he went into the front room to the kitchenette and ran a glass of water. Before he'd finished drinking it she had come out.

"Oh, here you are."

He smiled as he put down the glass. She took his erection in her hand. "Come on back to bed," she said with a smile as she slowly pulled him back toward the bedroom.

CHAPTER 22

1015 Skyview Drive

ON SATURDAY MORNING THEY DROVE into the city as a family. Allen was amazed at the turn things had taken. Earlier it had seemed as if he and Tina were at an impasse that would cost them their marriage. But something had changed. He suspected that Tina's sister-in-law had called her. Tina had come to her senses. And last night after watching a movie together, they had made love lustily like two strangers in a hotel room.

Allen listened to the radio. He was determined that they would all have a good day. Especially the kids. He wanted them to enjoy the park. The sun was shining. There wasn't a cloud in the sky. On such a beautiful day he wanted to enjoy his wife again too, just like in the old days.

Allen pulled into the green shade of Golden Gate Park. The cool pine and eucalyptus-scented air seemed to promise a new beginning. He drove toward Stowe Lake, picturing the paddle boats and canoes slowly cruising the green, algae-filled water, the ducks that would rush to the shore whenever someone threw down crusts of bread, and the seagulls that would swoop in at steep angles, making bold, splashing landings as they aggressively stole what had been intended for the ducks. Elderly retired Russian immigrants crowded the benches that circled the lake, chatting animatedly in their native language. Allen and Tina and the kids usually walked the circumference of the lake on the paved footpath and then got back in the car for the short ride to Clement Street where they would go shopping and have dinner at one of the many Chinese restaurants.

"Park there." Tina pointed to a space under the shade of some pines. Allen parked and helped the kids out of the back. Tina fussed over Christine as Allen took Reynaldo by the hand and walked ahead in the direction of the boathouse. They used the restroom in the back and by the time they finished, Tina and Christine were approaching. Allen moved close to take Tina's hand but she took Christine's instead.

They started off at their usual leisurely pace. The fresh air made Allen frisky and he wanted to walk faster so as to get more exercise out of it, but Tina did not like the children getting sweaty. She thought it would cause them to catch a cold. Allen forgot about Reynaldo for a few moments and he ran ahead like a puppy let off its leash. Allen called after him to slow him down and ensure he did not get into trouble with Tina, but Reynaldo ran on.

Allen caught up with Reynaldo where the path passed through some tall flowering bushes, obscuring the view of the lake. When Reynaldo saw Allen, he laughed and darted away. Allen quickened his pace. When he came out of the bushes he could see across the lake clear to the other shore. He spotted two men in a rowboat headed for the promontory where Reynaldo was headed and he had one of those, 'what's wrong with this picture?' moments. The men were seated in the boat like lovers, one rowing, and the other facing the rower, chatting pleasantly. Allen felt awkward about that, remembering the time on the train when the two men across from him and Reynaldo had started deep French kissing. Reynaldo had asked him about that, but before he could say anything a train had passed in the opposite direction with a thunderous rattle and Reynaldo's attention was once again out the window. The men got off at the next stop.

Allen caught up with Reynaldo on the shore of the little promontory. There were rocks there that the turtles liked to sun themselves on. Sure enough, three turtles had crawled up onto a rock and they too seemed to be watching the approach of the rowboat as the sun warmed their shells.

"Daddy," said Reynaldo, "can I catch a turtle?"

The sun glinted brightly off the water. A mass of water lilies extended out about ten feet from the bank. It was a beautiful day. The rowboat drew closer. Allen could hear the slap of the oars. They were not men but, rather, two mannish-looking women, lesbians.

"Daddy?" said Reynaldo.

"No. They have to go home."

The boaters were within earshot. The woman who

was rowing smiled at Reynaldo's question. Allen smiled in her direction.

"Why, Daddy?"

"Their mommy and daddy would be sad if they didn't come home."

"Really?"

"Sure," said Allen. He turned to see where Tina and Christine were. They were still about twenty five yards away. A man with a black lab on a leash jogged by. Allen saw movement near his feet. A groundhog stuck its head out of its hole. Allen turned back around and saw that Reynaldo had climbed out onto the first of the three rocks leading out to the turtles. He hurried towards him but he was too late. As Reynaldo stepped onto the second rock, it turned beneath his feet, throwing him off balance. Allen grabbed Reynaldo by the shirt as he foundered around in the shallow water. Fortunately he didn't fall down and get completely wet, but his shoes and socks were soaked. Allen helped Reynaldo up onto the bank as Tina came up. Christine held back, worry darkening her features.

Tina grabbed Reynaldo by his shirt and spun him around. "Look at you! I told you not to go on the rocks, didn't I?"

Allen realized with some discomfort that the women in the rowboat were listening to Tina and watching them.

"Didn't I?" demanded Tina.

"Yes, Mommy. I'm sorry."

"Take off your shoes."

"Okay, Mommy." Reynaldo started to sit down.

Allen grabbed him and steadied him as he took his shoes off.

"And the socks too" said Tina.

Reynaldo peeled off the wet white socks. Tina took the shoes and socks over to the trashcan and shoved them inside. She walked back. Allen was in a sort-of shock. He hadn't expected that. The women in the boat were still watching and seemed to be quietly discussing what had just happened.

"You're not getting any new shoes and socks," Tina said to Reynaldo. "You'll just have to go barefoot for the rest of the summer."

"Sorry, Mommy," said Reynaldo, "I didn't mean it."

Allen's face reddened. "Tina, c'mon. It was an accident."

Tina's face flushed red as she grabbed Christine's hand. She walked off.

Allen watched her go as Reynaldo held his hand. The women in the rowboat talked softly as the rower put the oars back in the water and moved their boat back out into the lake. Allen went over to the trash can and retrieved the shoes, wringing them and the socks out as best he could and shoving them into his back pockets. He picked up Reynaldo, carrying him piggyback style and started slowly back along the path, following Tina and Christine at a good distance. Allen looked at his watch. It was only two. The day was ruined, the weekend ruined. Tina would be on a tear for the next three or four days. From behind him, Reynaldo said, "I'm sorry, Daddy. The rock moved. It wasn't my fault." Allen tried to sound as upbeat as he could. "Ah, don't worry about it. It'll be all right in a day or so." He shook his head in disgust.

The ride back was unpleasant. Tina had settled into an angry, irritable mood and her neurotic, backseat driving was almost too much for Allen to bear. Several times she wanted him to beep at the other drivers when they violated the rules or were rude. He ignored her. "Why do you stay in this lane?" she demanded at one point when the traffic in his lane had slowed. He sighed inaudibly and said nothing.

He could feel his heart pounding in his chest. He thought it would burst; he was so angry and tense. Reynaldo sat next to him, uncharacteristically quiet. Christine leaned against her mother in the back seat, dozing in the afternoon heat. Allen turned on the radio. He glanced in the rear view. Tina's face remained stony, her eyes refusing to meet his. On the radio, some rock band played. Guitars rang out, the drummer pounding hypnotically as the singers crooned in soothing harmonies. He slowly tuned out and went with them to their special place. In his fantasy he was dancing. Tina did not dance and was indifferent to music. Now he, like a man in a wheelchair who dreams of running on the beach, was on the dance floor, colored lights flashing as his feet moved deftly, moon walking, spinning, watched by several pretty young women—all while the recently-vacated husk of him sat in the driver's seat, its primitive yet capable brain stem scanning the road ahead through auto-pilot eyes, directing the hands on the wheel and the feet on the pedals in performing the very simple task that driving had become for the modern male Homo Sapiens.

On Saturday morning Allen went again to see his therapist Joel Beckett. Entering the old Victorian house, he closed the heavy door, shutting out the street noise. He sat in the waiting room, the hiss of the white noise generators making him sleepy. Moments after he closed his eyes the door opened. Joel's girlfriend Sheila looked out at him. Allen had met her once before when he was leaving Joel's office.

"Come in," Sheila said.

Allen felt odd sitting in the office when Joel wasn't there. Sheila took Joel's chair and sat down. "I've had to meet with most of Joel's clients today," she said. "You're the fifth."

Allen nodded and smiled slightly, wondering what it was all about.

"Joel is dying," Sheila said.

"Huh?" said Allen dumbly.

"He has inoperable liver cancer. He has two, maybe three weeks left."

"Oh," said Allen, aghast. He looked at her, searching her face for the pain he knew she must have been feeling. But it was hidden from him, perhaps by medication. "I'm sorry," he said.

Sheila nodded grimly and took a calling card from the desk and handed it to him. "Joel is referring all his patients to Karen Pendleton. He has a very high regard for her."

Allen took the card she gave him and looked at it.

She looked at him, waiting for him to say something.

"I'm sorry," he said. He got to his feet. "Tell him I said hello." Allen felt stupid as the words left his mouth.

Sheila nodded. Again he tried to read her face and could not. He turned and quickly left the office.

On Sunday morning after Mommy had gone to the grocery store, Reynaldo was playing with his cars on the rug. He looked up and saw Daddy watching him. He smiled. Daddy didn't smile back. Daddy seemed sad.

Daddy blinked the way he did when he was thinking and walked over. "Reynaldo, have they told you about earthquakes at school yet?"

Reynaldo shook his head. "Earthquakes?"

Daddy nodded. "Yes. Sometimes the earth shakes very hard, hard enough to make some houses fall down."

Reynaldo smiled. "Is an earthquake coming, Daddy?"

Daddy's smile was sad. "Maybe, maybe not. I hope not. But we have to be prepared. I will show you what I want you to do if there is an earthquake."

Reynaldo nodded. "Okay, Daddy."

Daddy led Reynaldo into Reynaldo's room. "If the house starts shaking, you must get out right away. And if you cannot get out of the front door, you must go out the window." Daddy pointed to the window in Reynaldo's room.

Reynaldo frowned. "Mommy says I can't open the curtains. She says that if the curtains are open I'll just look out my window all day and not do my work."

Daddy nodded. "I know. But if an earthquake comes you must open the curtains and the window too."

"How, Daddy?"

Daddy nodded. "I will show you. But there is one more thing. You must take your sister with you. Do you understand?"

"Yes."

Daddy walked over to the window and drew the curtain back. "Here," he said, "put your hand here." Daddy placed Reynaldo's hand over a moving part on the window.

"This is the latch. Push down and then slide the window open. Like this."

Daddy moved Reynaldo's hand and the window slid open. A cool breeze washed into the room and Reynaldo grew excited. He had never had his window open before. Outside, the tree was doing its happy dance and the big yard beckoned invitingly.

"Bring over your chair," said Daddy.

Reynaldo brought over his little yellow plastic chair and placed it under the window. Daddy gently placed Reynaldo's hand on the screen. "To get out, you must push the screen out. Then you can climb out. Do you understand?"

Reynaldo frowned with concentration. He began to push against the screen and Daddy pulled his hand away. "Not now, Reynaldo. When the time comes. Now, remember, you must help your sister out first. Then, when she is outside, you can climb out the window. Do you understand?"

Reynaldo smiled. He was happy Daddy had told him these things. He hoped an earthquake would come soon so he could leave the house through the window.

"Yes, Daddy."

They heard the front door slam and Daddy quickly closed the window and pulled the curtain closed. He knelt to Reynaldo. "Secret," he said, holding a finger to his lips. "If ever you have to get out of the house fast, that is how you do it. Okay?"

Reynaldo nodded happily. "Yes, Daddy."

"Put your chair back," said Daddy. He quickly left the room.

Reynaldo put his chair back in its place by his bed and went out into the hallway. Daddy was carrying plastic bags of groceries into the kitchen. Mommy came in carrying two bags. She closed the door and saw him. She frowned. "Get the dictionary and get to work. Start on the page we left off on. I'll check your work later."

"Yes, Mommy," Reynaldo said. He looked over at Christine where she played with her Barbies on the floor by the fireplace. She hadn't even noticed Mommy's arrival, so intent was she on her Barbie dolls.

Mommy came back out of the kitchen and saw Reynaldo watching Christine. "What are you waiting for? I told you to get to work."

"Sorry, Mommy," said Reynaldo.

CHAPTER 23

RAD AWOKE TO THE SMELL of a woman who was not Tawny. The bedroom was still dark but he could clearly see the glowing red numbers of the digital clock across the room: 7:17. He looked up at the ceiling as he thought about dancing with Jenny the night before. A dark guilt crept over him. He wondered where Tawny was. He remembered her cold anger as she got in the cab. It was an over-reaction. All he had done was dance with another girl. Then, as he became aware of Jenny's warmth beside him, the guilt returned. He tried to recapture the feeling of righteous vindication for what he had done, but he couldn't.

Jenny stirred and came awake beside him.

"When did you wake up," she said.

"A few minutes ago."

Jenny pressed herself up against him. "I know a nice place in Pacifica for coffee. You can get it to go and sit on the dunes and watch the waves come in. Would you like to go?"

Rad turned to her. "Sure. But I gotta get the bike back to my friend."

"Okay. I'll follow you in my car."

"Yeah. That'll work," said Rad, his thoughts returning to Tawny guiltily.

Jenny rolled over on top of him. She kissed him slowly. "Let's not go just yet," she said.

"Nam myo-ho ren-gay kyo, nam myo-ho ren-gay kyo." Tawny tried not to listen to the chanting filtering through the flimsy bedroom door of the flat Terri rented in Ingleside. The second floor of an old three story Victorian, the place was creaky and drafty, but it had character, with lots of woodworking flourishes— grapevine-framed polished panels, bas relief vases, and a deliciously musty redwood scent.

Tawny sat on the couch as she sipped her coffee and thought about the previous day. Fortunately Terri had been home when Tawny arrived in the taxi. Terri stood out in front of her place, her smile like a torch atop her tiny four foot, ten inch frame. She gave Tawny a quick hug and a kiss and helped her carry her things up the stairs. At Terri's urging, Tawny had chanted for about a half hour with her to her Gohonzon, a sort-of sacred scroll enshrined inside a black lacquer box that sat atop an old mahogany sewing machine table with a still-attached foot treadle at the bottom—Terri's altar. Afterward, Tawny cried while she told Terri what had happened the night before. Terri listened intently the whole time, saying nothing. When Tawny had finished Terri had gently suggested that maybe it wasn't as bad as it seemed and that perhaps it was just a friendly thing and maybe Rad had had a little too much to drink. "You know," Terry had cooed, "the most important thing is for you to develop a strong, unassailable life force so you won't be so easily affected." Terri's confident reassuring words and a hot cup of chamomile tea had soothed Tawny, allowing her to step back from her emotions and get some sleep on Terri's couch.

"Ting! Ting! Ting!" On the other side of the door Terri struck the bell three times and solemnly and slowly chanted her mantra. A moment later she exited her room, smiling brightly. "Ready to go?" she said.

They got into Terri's car. Twenty minutes later Terri took the South San Francisco exit off the freeway. As she and Tawny drove down Hillside Boulevard they saw a young man sitting astride a motorcycle in a driveway. He got off and walked over to lean into the window of a blue Toyota parked at the curb.

"That's Rad, isn't it?" Terri asked.

Tawny couldn't keep the emotion out of her voice. "Yeah. Don't slow down… just drive past. Please!"

CHAPTER 24

1015 Skyview Drive

REYNALDO OPENED HIS EYES WHEN the birds began chirping. Daddy had already left for work; Reynaldo could tell by the dim light. He wondered what he would do today. Then he grew sad because he knew he would spend much of the day in his room. He wished the summer would be over so he could go back to school. Then he would get homework, but the teacher would let him play more.

The birds were making quite a racket now. It sounded like there were two gangs of them, like the Power Rangers on one side and the putty men on the other, and they were shouting and taunting each other. He wanted to open the curtains and look at them, but he dared not, for Mommy might catch him. Water ran somewhere in the house and soon the outside light was bright enough for him to make out the familiar masks of the Power Rangers on his poster.

Mommy knocked brusquely on his door without opening it. "Get up and get yourself ready."

"Okay, Mommy."

Later Reynaldo went out to the kitchen.

"What took you so long," said Mommy. "Were you playing with the water again?"

"No, Mommy. Sorry, Mommy." Reynaldo held back from the table as Mommy glared at him from where she stood at the sink.

"The next time you're late you won't eat. Do you hear me?"

"Yes, Mommy."

"I love you, Mommy," said Christine.

Mommy ignored Christine as she continued to glare at Reynaldo. Finally she turned away and Reynaldo took his seat. Christine's place was across from Reynaldo. She chewed on a piece of toast as she watched TV. Reynaldo turned around to look at the TV. Christine's chair faced the TV and she could see it good, but Reynaldo's back was to it. The roadrunner streaked through a trap the coyote had set for him and the coyote was smashed flat by a rock, which then shattered into a million pieces. Reynaldo laughed. He heard Mommy approaching and turned back to his plate. Mommy tossed a piece of buttered toast onto Reynaldo's plate and it slipped off and landed on the table. "It's okay, Mommy," he said, but she had already turned away and was on her way back to the counter. Mommy returned with the milk carton and filled his glass.

"Thank you, Mommy," he said, but again she had turned away. Reynaldo knew Mommy was angrier than usual, so he tried to be a good boy. He picked up his toast and ate it slowly, the way Mommy liked. He was ready to drink the glass of milk when Christine's eyes grew large at something she saw on the TV. He turned around in his chair to see what it was. He heard a clunking sound and turned back to see that his outstretched hand had knocked over his glass of milk. The milk raced across the table in a white wave toward Christine, finally dripping down onto the floor next to her chair. Christine began crying. "I didn't do it, Mommy," she said. "I didn't do it."

Mommy came over quickly, yanking Christine's chair back out of the way. "God damn it!" she said. Her face was bright red as she looked at Reynaldo. "God damn you!"

"Sorry, Mommy," Reynaldo said. He repeated the phrase a couple more times in the hope that it would placate her.

"I didn't do it," Christine cried.

"I know you didn't," said Mommy. "Go to your room."

Christine ran crying to her room.

Mommy grabbed a roll of paper towels from the counter and threw it at Reynaldo. "Clean it up, damn you!"

Reynaldo leapt off his chair, hurriedly mopping the floor with the towels. He held a sopping towel toward Mommy, looking at her. Mommy yanked the trashcan from beneath the sink and threw it across the room.

"Sorry, Mommy," Reynaldo said as he continued soaking up the mess with towels and dropping them in the trash can. When he finished Mommy yelled at him, "Go to your room! I don't want to see your face for the rest of the day. Do you hear?"

"Yes, Mommy," he said as he backed out of the room. "Sorry, Mommy."

All day, with only a quick lunch break, Reynaldo worked at writing down the words and definitions. Late in the afternoon, a breeze started up. Outside, the the tree branches clicked and clattered as they banged up against his window. He quietly got down from his chair and opened his door. He went to the bathroom. He could go to the bathroom to pee as long as he didn't go too many times. He flushed and came out as Mommy hurried down the hall with a laundry basket. She brushed past him on her way to the garage to do the laundry. Reynaldo went back to his room and looked at the window. Unable to stop himself, he parted the curtains and looked out. The sun shone on the tall fence and the tree moved in the breeze, doing its happy dance. He remembered how Daddy had opened the window and placed Reynaldo's hand on the latch. Maybe he could go out and play, then come back before Mommy found out. He heard the lid of the washing machine clang closed and he pulled the curtains closed. He quickly got back onto his chair. Mommy's familiar footsteps trod by in the hall. Out in the living room, Christine's cartoons droned from the TV. As Reynaldo worked, he thought about the snake he had seen on the TV. He thought about it squeezing Mommy's neck. The thought made him feel good.

CHAPTER 25

In the living room of the old Victorian house, Tawny heard the now-familiar 'ting, ting, ting,' as Terri rang the little brass bell on her altar. After staying with Terri for the past two weeks, Tawny knew that the three sharp rings meant that Terri was about to begin *Gongyo*, a vigorous, rapid-fire recitation of certain portions of the Lotus Sutra.

Tawny smiled slightly as she began folding up the wonderfully-warm blue woolen blanket that Terri had provided her with for sleeping on the couch in this delightful but chilly old house. Tawny carefully placed the blanket along with the folded sheets in a plastic bin. She snugged the top onto the bin, closing it tight with a snap, and slid it under the couch. Going out into the kitchen, she poured the cup of coffee that Terri had left her in the Mister Coffee carafe. She turned on the radio to get the weather report. As she listened she wondered about Rad. He'd called twice the first week she'd been here, but she had refused to take his calls. This week he had called once, and she talked to him briefly, telling him that today, Monday, her day off, she was coming by the place to get some of her things and she didn't want him to be there. Despite the anger she still felt for him and the sadness that constantly fatigued her, she still thought tenderly of him. But she did not want him to know that. Not yet.

Ting, ting, ting! The sharp ringing of the little bell was followed by Terri's drawn-out intonation of the Buddhist chant, nam myo-ho ren-gay kyo three times, which meant that she was concluding her morning's meditation. Tawny had started chanting at Terri's urging. Terri had told her that it would give her the strength to get out of her funk and give her the insight to know what to do. Tawny chanted about fifteen minutes each day, which seemed like an eternity, but was nothing compared to Terri's two hours a day. Tawny did not get much out of it yet. Joy, or more correctly, Buddhahood, was, according to Terri, supposed to come to a person slowly as they chanted each day. Tawny certainly did not feel joyful. But whether or not it was logical or reasonable, or had anything at all to do with the chanting, she *was* beginning to feel a bit more hopeful about her situation. It was not a bright multicolored hope, but rather a vague black and white hope, born mostly out of the growing determination she felt to get on with her life—with or without Rad, whichever *she* decided in a month or so when she was ready to decide.

The bedroom door opened and Terri came out beaming, evidently having gotten her ration of joy or Buddhahood from the chanting. Tawny smiled back at her diminutive friend.

"Did you have your coffee yet?" Terri asked.

"Yes, thank you."

Terri went back to her room and quickly reappeared with her bag. "Well, I have to get going. Oh!" Terri dug down into her bag and took out a little key chain with two keys on it, handing them to Tawny. Tawny had asked to borrow Terri's car to go back to her and Rad's place. Terri worked only three blocks away at City College and walked to work.

"The gas gage says it's empty," said Terri, "but I put five dollars in it last night before I parked."

"Thanks," said Tawny. "I'll gas up when I come back."

"Okay. Don't forget about the meeting tonight."

"I won't." Tawny had given up on trying to dampen Terri's hope that Tawny would officially join the Buddhist organization. Tawny had agreed to go to the big introductory meeting tonight, but she didn't think she was going to be joining.

Terri gave Tawny a hug and went quickly out the door.

Tawny wondered briefly what the meeting would be like. Terri had been trying to get her to go to one for the last four years. And now, out of a sense of gratitude to Terri for having taking her in, Tawny had finally agreed. Terri went to meetings every other night, it seemed. Tawny could never see herself getting that involved, but she would go just this one time to make her friend happy.

Cool fog swirled around Tawny as she walked the street but she could see the pale image of the sun above through the moving river of milky whiteness and knew that it would burn off by two or three in the afternoon. Despite the chill, the air had that autumnal feel of short days and hibernation. Tawny found the little beat-up Ford Escort on Benicia Street and put the key in the door. She drove down Ocean Avenue toward the freeway, past the City College campus and the many students getting on and off the buses and trolleys, and her mood improved a little. She estimated that she could get most of what she needed out of the house and loaded into the car in less than an hour. As she took the South San Francisco exit off the freeway, she hoped that Rad would honor her request and not be there. No matter, she told herself. Even if he was there when she showed up, wanting some face-to-face reckoning, she would simply not speak to him.

Tawny pulled up in front of the house and turned the engine off. She suddenly thought of the box of old vinyl records she had stored down in the garage what now seemed like a long time ago, after their record turntable had broken. At that time all the big music corporations had been shifting over to CDs. But there were still record turntables for sale and she wanted her records. A vague coldness went up her spine as she thought about going down there. She couldn't recall if the box was on the snake's side of the garage or not. Maybe she should just leave them.

Tawny got out of the car. It had rained in South City the night before and the ground was still wet, the air fecund with musk and spores. Tawny's nose flared involuntarily and began running. She could taste the air and earth of South San Francisco on her tongue although she had yet to open her mouth. She felt as if some tiny physical thing had invaded her body and was clawing at the sensitive mucus membrane of her throat. Then her mouth turned metallically bitter, sickening her. She put her head down and spat out a small amount of bile. Wiping her mouth with a Kleenex, she felt better. She decided that she probably should start having more for breakfast than just black coffee. Straightening up, she surveyed her surroundings. The truck was still up on blocks and the yard that had been a hard packed patch of earth, now sported a foot high, thick green growth of grasses, the same native grasses, Tawny was sure, as grew on San Bruno Mountain, which loomed at the top of the street.

Tawny went into the house and was relieved to find it cold and empty. A sleeping bag lay half-open on the couch; Rad was not sleeping in their bed. A pizza box sat on the coffee table. He'd probably stayed up late last night watching a movie. She went into their bedroom and found it much as she had left it—the top two drawers, hers, still slightly open, the bed made, with, she'd be willing to bet a week's tips, the same sheets and blanket that had been on it when she'd left. Shaking her head sadly, she threw the rest of her cosmetics and loose ends from the top drawer into a box. She then grabbed her hair dryer and went out to the car. As she put her things in the trunk she noticed Mister Peepers coming up the hill in his van, the cute little, brown-skinned boy sitting in his child booster seat beside him. The boy smiled at her and she remembered her vinyl records in the garage. She decided to go in through the back door, rather than through the door in the kitchen. Walking beside the house, she marveled at the luxuriant proliferation of weeds and moss which now sprouted from every crevice underfoot. Swallowing, she put the key in the door and slowly opened it. She peered in, waiting for her eyes to adjust to the dimness inside. After a few moments she could make out most of the garage and its contents. She scanned the enclosure side but didn't see Ketsel. She reached in and turned on the light switch. The snake's mottled length, most of it anyway, became visible at the far end of the enclosure coiled in and around Rad's stack of old tires.

Tawny went inside. She walked over to the washing machine and checked the bulge in the enclosure. It was bigger, and the chicken wire had now been pulled off two of the nails, instead of just one. She frowned. She would call Rad and remind him to take care of that. And why the hell hadn't Gabriel come and taken back his goddamned snake? Tawny sighed. Guys were such procrastinators. She quickly looked around and located her box of records. As she knelt to it, she saw that the one on top was Kenny G, the album she had bought when she and Rad had first met. It seemed as if those mellifluous clarinet notes were always hovering in the air whenever they made love. Tears welled in her eyes and she was about to give full vent to the deep sadness that had now taken hold of her when she detected movement out of the side of her eye—the snake's thick body was slowly pouring down the stack of tires, disappearing behind some of the storage boxes. Tawny slowly turned away from the records and ran to the door, turning to slam it closed with a loud bang.

Tawny's breathing was labored and her back pained her sharply as she slid into the front seat of the car. She heard somebody chanting nam myo-ho ren-gay kyo and realized it was herself. After a while her fear subsided and she decided to go back into the house. Leaning into the closet, she quickly yanked the rest of her clothes off the hangers and hurried out the front door, slamming it behind her. As she sat in the car and looked back at the house, her sadness seemed complete. It was like an achy flu now, painfully swelling every muscle in her body. As she stared at this house where she had known happiness and love, she realized that her pain was now coupled with an unshakable determination to move on and take her life to the next level, whatever that might be. The determination made her want to shout out, to thrust her fist into the air like the jocks did when they dunked a basket or scored a touchdown. She backed the car out of the driveway and drove off.

Rad walked down the hill from the bus stop. He loathed the thought of spending another quiet evening in the house, but he was too tired to go out to the club and he wouldn't see Jenny till the end of the week. He vaguely fantasized about finding Tawny in the house when he went inside—her laying across the bed, having fallen asleep as she waited for him, then the two of them making love. As he approached the door the fantasy faded. Inside, she had left little evidence of having been there, just an emptied closet and two hangers lying on the floor. Rad looked around, hoping to find something, a note or some indication of her wanting to communicate with him, but there was nothing. He picked up the mail in front of the door— some junk mailers and a letter with an official-looking, but unfamiliar, return address, neatly printed on the envelope. It was addressed to him. He opened it up, scanning the legal sounding words, stopping at, 'your vehicle, evidently in non-working order, abandoned on the property in violation of your lease…Etc. etc., forty five days to rectify the situation.'

"Shit," said Rad aloud, "the guy down the block, I'll bet."

Rad went to the refrigerator and took out a can of beer, popping the top and swallowing half the can, the effervescence burning his throat. He went into the living room and sat on the couch. Picking up the TV remote, he scanned the channels, finally settling on a wrestling match. Frowning at the obviously faked throws, kicks and slams, he watched out of boredom. A commercial came on and he reached over to hit the play button on the message machine. There was nothing. "Shit!" he mouthed silently and sullenly, getting up to go back into the kitchen for another beer. He brought the beer and the bottle of vodka back to the couch and sat down again. He drank a shot and chased it with a swallow of beer. After a while he began to feel guilty, knowing his parents would never approve of him sitting around getting drunk. He thought of maybe going to his parents'. He wanted to reestablish a relationship with his dad but he didn't know how to start. He thought about going over to his sister's place, maybe showing little Jay some moves on the board. A quick glance at the curtains behind him ruled that out; the sun was already setting and it would be dark before he could get there. And he had probably had too much to drink already.

Fuck it! He poured another shot. Just fuck it! "You could work on your board," a voice seemed to whisper in his head, "and give it to little Jay." He went down into the garage. The smell of something rotting got his attention and he realized it came from the green trash bag that he had forgotten to put out on the curb the week before. For a moment he considered putting it out in the yard. "Fuck it!" he said, grabbing his board instead. He went back upstairs and sat on the couch. He spun the wheels as he stared at the TV. The smooth sound of the wheels and their bearings soothed him and he lay back on the couch. Soon the chill of early evening penetrated his clothing and he pulled the board close to his chest to warm himself. He fell asleep.

"Nam myo-ho ren-gay kyo, nam myo-ho ren-gay kyo." The women in the hall, and there must have been a couple hundred of them, chanted the words in determined unison and the sound was like the throbbing of a great engine. Tawny looked around surreptitiously and was amazed at the variety of faces in the room. White, Hispanic, Asian, black. The only men in the room were the two who acted as ushers, stationed at the entrances. Tawny tried to concentrate on the chanting, thinking hard about what she wanted to get out of it, about what she wanted to overcome or accomplish, but her mind wandered. She imagined Rad seated next to her, smiling in wonder about all the chanting women, and she immediately grew angry with herself. She thought of what Terri had said about how she shouldn't look to him for her happiness, how her happiness had to come from within. Next to Tawny, Terri held her beads in her hands as she stared sternly at the altar and chanted loudly. Every now and then she leaned over to try and help Tawny repeat the words with the group. Just when Tawny seemed to become one with it, the chanting concluded with the ringing of a heavy iron bell. A woman at the front stood and faced them. She took the microphone from its stand, sending a squawk of feedback through the hall.

"Good evening ladies of Golden Lotus Chapter… and welcome to our annual young woman's division meeting!"

Exuberant cheering and clapping burst from the assembled women. Tawny could not help but be caught up in the enthusiasm of the other women. Next, a rather shy woman got to her feet to explain the Buddhist practice, "a tripod," she said, "of chanting, studying the writings of the Japanese Buddha, Nichiren, and propagation, or telling others." She was followed by three women giving testimonials to the religion's power. Although Tawny was moved by the sincerity of the women who got up to testify, she was inclined to attribute their achievements and personal triumphs to wishful thinking, probably coupled with a little good luck. She still had no intention of joining up. But the women's division leader, a black woman named Dorothy Stokes, changed her mind. Mrs. Stokes' words effused strength and love, Tawny realized, for all the women in the room. Tawny had never experienced anything like it before. No relative or teacher, no nun from her days in catechism class, no one had ever awakened in her such feelings of hope and determination to change her life. "I challenge you," Mrs. Stokes concluded, "chant nam myo-ho ren-gay kyo for ninety days and you will change your problems into benefit and joy."

Tawny decided to give it the requisite ninety-day try.

CHAPTER 26

As Tina Collins drove north on 101 she couldn't get out of her mind the image of her manager's fat pink face. "Tina," Elizabeth had said, smiling as if Tina were an idiot, "don't you see it? This is better. It says it all." Elizabeth held the red-lined letter in front of her that she had dictated first thing in the morning, and that Tina had later edited and made grammatically correct. Elizabeth might be the new manager, but Tina knew the English language better than most native-born Americans.

Tina had kept her tongue because she'd always liked this job, had loved it, in fact, back when David Wu had been the manager. But now this big fat stupid Anglo woman was making her life miserable. Every day Elizabeth closely scrutinized her work and always wanted changes, all of them clumsy and ungrammatical, and Tina had to comply!

Tina fumed as she came up on a slowly-moving car full of old white folks that had just come off the exit from the airport. What did Allen call them, 'silver-headed snails.' Tourists, no doubt, they were all talking at once and looking around, instead of driving and doing the speed limit.

"Sixty-five!" Tina said aloud as she leaned on the horn. She swerved left and went around their car, turning to glare angrily at them.

Three miles up the highway Tina took her exit, pulling into the parking lot of Hillview Daycare Center. Across the street, the tall eucalyptus trees of the little grove on San Bruno Mountain moved gently in a freshening breeze.

Tina went inside the office. Patty, one of the younger girls working there, was at the counter. She smiled and said, "I'll get them for you, Mrs. Collins." Tina nodded and scanned the sign-out sheet on the counter for Reynaldo's and Christine's names. Christine came out from the playroom. She was a beautiful vision in her yellow playsuit. Tina's heart lifted. "Hi Honey," she said. "Did you have fun today?"

"Yes, Mommy," said Christine.

Patty came out a moment later with Reynaldo. His face was filthy and he looked a mess. "Reynaldo and another boy were throwing sand," said Patty with a kindly smile. "He had a timeout and he told me he wouldn't do it again. Isn't that right, Reynaldo?"

"Yes, Miss Patty," Reynaldo said.

Tina frowned and leaned down to Reynaldo. "Never do that again, Reynaldo. Do you hear?"

"Yes, Mommy."

Tina took Reynaldo by the sleeve. His hands were dirty. She led the children outside and unlocked the doors. "Get in the car," she said to Reynaldo as she helped Christine into the child seat up front.

Tina said nothing on the short drive from the

daycare to their house. She glanced back at Reynaldo and he looked out the window guiltily.

As Tina passed another slower moving car she thought again about how she had taken a leave of absence when she'd adopted Reynaldo. The adoption people had told her she needed time to bond with him. She glanced back at Reynaldo and thought again how unfair it all was. He had been more trouble than she'd ever imagined a kid could be. Much more... despite everything she'd given up for him!

Tina drove quickly down Skyview and pulled into the driveway. Inside the house, she immediately had Reynaldo take his sweatshirt off. Holding it with her fingertips as if it were infected with plague, she told him to go to the bathroom and take off his clothes for a bath. She dumped his sweat shirt in the hamper and washed her hands in the sink. Then she turned on the TV for Christine and went into the bathroom. Reynaldo stood naked, his clothes in a pile on the tile floor. Tina frowned. His skin seemed to be growing more brown as he grew older. She wondered how much of it was skin color and how much the dirt he picked up at daycare.

"You make so much work for me," she said.

"Sorry, Mommy."

"Get in the tub."

"Yes, Mommy."

Tina turned on the shower and soaked him thoroughly. She poured shampoo on his mop of black hair. As she massaged the gel into his hair she could feel the grit beneath her fingers. "Reynaldo! You got sand all in your hair!"

"Sorry, Mommy," he said, annoying her further.

"Sorry? Is that all you can say? Sorry?"

"Sorry, Mommy."

"Shut up," she said angrily, starting Reynaldo to sniffling.

Tina finished scrubbing Reynaldo and rinsed the soap off him. As he began drying himself, She took his dirty clothes to the basement. She passed Christine watching the TV in the living room. Tina went into Reynaldo's room to get fresh clothes from his bureau drawer. Her nose crinkled at a musty odor in the room. She pulled the underwear drawer open. Taking a pair of undershorts and a shirt, she noticed something silvery beneath the pile of undershirts. She picked it up—the shiny silver foil wrapper of a chocolate kiss. She rushed out to the bathroom. Reynaldo's eyes grew large as he stood naked, the towel over his little shoulders.

"Have you been taking candy from the dish in the living room?" she demanded.

"No, Mommy."

"Liar!" Tina held the silver foil before his face.

"Sorry, Mommy."

"Sorry mommy, sorry mommy!" Tina shouted. "You make me sick!" She put his clothes on the table. "Get dressed and go work on your definitions in your room." She closed the door as she left.

Tina took the fish out of the freezer to defrost for dinner and then she bathed Christine. She felt as if she never had a moment to herself and Christine anymore. If only they hadn't adopted. They'd tried to have children and had had no luck. Out of desperation she'd gone along with Allen's idea about adoption. And then, nine months after they'd brought Reynaldo home she got pregnant with Christine. If only they'd held off on the adoption. Tina found herself growing more angry as she thought about it.

Tina got Christine dressed and went out into the living room. She looked at the clock. It was almost five and she still hadn't vacuumed the living room rug. She got the vacuum out of the closet and plugged it in. She turned it on and the drone calmed her a little. She began running it back and forth, enjoying the way the brushes lifted the nap of the carpet, like brushed cotton or suede, leaving clean swaths behind in the gray of the rug. She worked quick and determinedly, increasing the clean expanse of smooth swaths. The vacuum clattered and spat something out. Tina looked closely—one of Reynaldo's tiny toy men, a soldier. She angrily ran the vacuum over it several times until the machine broke it up and swallowed it. Reynaldo! Tina continued to roll the vacuum back and forth. She kept a clean house, an orderly house, and she didn't need this brat always making work for her. She was a good, hard worker. She didn't need Elizabeth scrutinizing everything she did with a magnifying glass. The woman's house was probably a dump. Soon Tina was breathing heavily, sweat beading on her brow. She had most of the living room done. She left the vacuum running while she leaned her back into the back of the couch, sliding it over. She went back to the vacuum and stopped. A half dozen silvery chocolate kiss wrappers lay on the rug where the couch had hidden them.

Reynaldo! That little imp! He was always making work for her, lying, stealing.

"Reynaldo! Come out here."

Tina's was breathing heavily when Reynaldo ran out of his room. He saw the papers on the rug and stopped short, his eyes growing big. Tina knew he was guilty and it was all she could do not to rush at him and hit him with her fists.

"Reynaldo," she demanded, "did you put those papers there?"

"No, Mommy," he said.

His obvious lie ratcheted up her anger a few notches. "What do you mean, 'no, Mommy'? Daddy didn't do it. Christine certainly wouldn't do that; she's not devious enough. The only person around here that would have done it is you."

Reynaldo's eyes pooled with tears but they only made Tina more angry. "Bastard," she spat. "Little bastard!" She rushed into the kitchen and took the one foot ruler from the drawer. She came back out. "Hold out your hands."

Reynaldo kept his hands at his sides. "Sorry, Mommy," he said. "I won't do it again."

"Put your hands out, damn it!"

Tina brought the ruler down, shouting with each blow, "Don't, Take, Any, More, Candy!" On the last word the ruler snapped in half and Reynaldo shrieked with pain.

"Don't go crying to Daddy about this, do you hear? Do you hear me?"

"Yes, Mommy."

"You deserved this, didn't you?"

"Yes, Mommy."

Although Reynaldo had admitted his guilt, Tina was shocked to see defiance in his face. "Now go to your room," she said, "and don't come out until I tell you!"

Reynaldo howled like a little animal as he angrily scurried back to his room. Tina's breathing was labored as she gathered up the pieces of the ruler and put them down in the garage. She went back to her vacuuming.

Her mind raged. That little imp! He made her so upset! He was no good. Just trouble, trouble, trouble. And he was smarter than he let on. He was deliberately coming between her and Allen, trying to break the family up. He was alien, an intruder and usurper. She had to do something. But what?

Twenty minutes later the carpet was a mesmerizing pattern of swaths, not unlike the raked pebble gardens of the Zen priests of Japan. The drone of the vacuum waxed and waned with each push, the sound soothing and calming. Tina stopped. She knew what she must do. She had to get him out of her house. It was the only way. She went down into the garage to get things ready.

Allen knew that something had happened as soon as he walked in the door. Christine sat in front of the TV, her face an unmoving mask. Tina was in the kitchen with the door closed. Allen walked back to Reynaldo's bedroom. He looked in. Reynaldo's eyes were a little red but he wasn't crying. He was seated at his desk, pencil in hand. Allen went in his own bedroom and got changed into his casual clothes. His anger and frustration returned. Why did things always have to be so upsetting and dramatic in his house?

He walked back out into the hall and looked in at Reynaldo.

"Hi, Daddy."

"Hi, Reynaldo. Were you good today?"

Reynaldo looked in the direction of the kitchen, but said nothing.

Allen went into the room and pulled the door closed.

"I took candy, Daddy."

"Oh," said Allen. "I'm sure you didn't take too much."

"Mommy's really mad. She hit me."

They heard Tina coming down the hall and Reynaldo immediately turned back to his writing. Allen came out of the room as Tina went by. She said nothing to him and he knew they were all in for another depressing evening.

They ate their dinner in silence. Allen decided it was better to not say anything until the kids were in bed and then he would try and talk some sense to Tina. After they ate, Tina and Christine sat on the couch together, watching the TV. Reynaldo sat alone in his room at his desk, writing his definitions. Allen washed the dishes. Finishing, he went into the bedroom and got a book and read. About nine he heard Tina putting Christine and Reynaldo to bed. He read until it grew quiet and then went out into the living room. Tina watched the Spanish channel on the TV. A beautiful, bathing suit-clad couple argued beside a pool at a mansion. Tina laughed at their repartee. Allen sat down beside her. She said nothing to him.

"Do you want to talk about it?" he said.

Tina continued to ignore him, laughing at something the couple argued about.

"What happened here today, Tina?" he said calmly.

She continued to ignore him.

Allen felt himself growing angrier. "Look," he said, surprised at the coldness in his voice, "you can't keep treating him like this. We're going to end up with Child Protective Services on our backs. We need counseling or something. If you won't go with us I'll take Reynaldo and we'll go without you. But something has to change here!"

She turned from the TV and looked at him. "After he leaves this house things will change."

Allen felt like he'd been gut punched. "What are you talking about?"

Tina glared at him. "I want him out of my house. You call the adoption agency and tell them to take him back, or I will." Tina returned her attention to the TV, smiling at something the actors said.

"What are you talking about?" said Allen as panic quickly grew inside of him. He couldn't believe what he had just heard. "Take him back?"

"I'm through with talking about it," said Tina, turning round to him. "I don't want him in my house anymore."

Tina got to her feet and went into the kitchen. Allen followed her, wondering if Reynaldo was asleep yet, hoping he could not hear them out here. Tina was opening the door to the garage. He followed her down.

Tina pointed to a bundle. Shaped like the sarcophagi of an Egyptian boy Pharaoh, it was about three feet long, tapered, and wrapped in black plastic trash bags and tied with yellow cord.

"Those are the things he came with, his pillow, blanket, his clothes and his toys. He can take them with him."

Allen stared at the bundle. It was about the same size as Reynaldo. Allen recoiled as if Reynaldo himself were wrapped up in it.

Tina went over to the shelves and lifted down the big yellow Tonka truck Reynaldo had brought with him from the foster home. Tina had taken it from Reynaldo a couple of years before for some infraction or other and never given it back. She put it next to the plastic bag. "He can take his truck with him." She pointed to the bike by the closet. Allen had bought it for Reynaldo three years ago. Tina had only allowed Reynaldo to ride it twice in that time and it still had the training wheels on it. "The bike stays," said Tina, "and don't take any of the clothes or toys in his room. Just the things he came here with."

Allen felt a mixture of coldness and fear inside that threatened to overwhelm him. "I can't do that."

"You call them or I will," Tina said flatly. "I'll give you till next Friday." She walked back up the stairs.

Allen stood alone for a few minutes, not believing it. Nobody returned a child they'd adopted. It was crazy! They'd end up on the nightly news. Allen could see the feigned looks of shock on the faces of the TV news talking heads as they set up the video footage—"Today in South San Francisco... a married couple returned the beautiful child they had adopted four years earlier..." He thought of the looks of his coworkers. His boss. Forget about any pay raises or new positions. He thought about the looks of the neighbors. Even the nipple ring skateboard punks up the street would look at them like they were freaks.

Allen went up the steps and back into the living room. Tina was again seated before the TV, laughing at the Spanish sit-com humor, none of which he could decipher. Even if he could understand what they were saying, He realized he was no longer capable of laughter. He went into the guest room and tried to read. He stared at the same page for ten, twenty minutes. Closing the book, he went back out into the living room. Tina kept her eyes on the TV.

"Tina," he said, not sure what he was going to tell her.

She ignored him and he left the house.

Allen wasn't sure what time he got to McCoy's. Lou was behind the bar, as usual. Allen could hear the rough laughter of the biker types playing pool in the back room.

He sat down and Lou drew a tall lager and wordlessly set it before him. There was a soccer game on the TV and they both watched. As usual, Lou was closemouthed.

Allen thought about the mess he had just left behind him at home and said, "Your parents must be gone by now, huh?"

"Not the old man," said Lou.

"God," said Allen, "he must be as old as Methuselah."

"Older," Lou scowled.

An angry curse came from the Hells Angel biker types in the back room, followed by low conversation, then a burst of raucous bawdy laughter.

"Did you have a good relationship with your father?" asked Allen.

"Hell no! My old man kicked me out."

Allen nodded and said almost into his beer, "I try and be a good dad, but..."

Lou was watching the game on the TV and didn't respond.

Allen recalled Tina's matter-of-fact tone as she told him of her decision to kick Reynaldo out of the house. Allen saw again the little bundle wrapped in trash bags and tied with yellow cord. There was no way he could do what she wanted. Later, he got unsteadily off the stool and went out to the van. He was about to get in when he thought of calling Tomas and Susan. Maybe he could get them to talk some sense to Tina.

He left the van and went over to the pay phone. He let it ring for four rings and was about to hang up when Tomas's voice came on.

"Yeah?"

"Tomas, this is Allen. I have to talk to you and Susan."

"Allen, do you know what time it is?"

"No." Allen looked at his watch. It was after twelve. "Sorry."

"Are you and Tina fighting again?" asked Tomas

tiredly.

"Yeah. She wants me to put him back, you know, take him back to the adoption agency. I can't do that, Tomas. It's crazy."

Allen heard Tomas's hand slide over the mouthpiece.

Susan came on the line. "What happened, Allen? What did she say?"

Allen told her the whole story, everything that had happened from the moment he came home to when he left. When he was finished Susan promised to talk to Tina.

"Can you call her tomorrow?" he asked.

"Yeah. I'll go over there. You better go home and get some sleep."

Allen drove home slowly and let himself into the darkened house. He slept in the guest room.

CHAPTER 27

WHEN I GROW UP, BY Garbage, played softly on the PA at the board shop. Rad's boss Larry was in and Rad didn't want him to complain about the music and so Rad was careful to keep the volume low. Rad begrudgingly divided his attention between the music and the kid on the other side of the counter who was complaining about his problem. The board wasn't doing what it was supposed to, the kid said. It wasn't responsive. Would better bearings help? Better trucks? What about wheels?

Rad nodded, a serious demeanor to his face. The kid wanted new, more expensive bearings, new trucks and wheels, and the kid would get them. It wouldn't do to have it get back to Larry that he, Rad, had told some poor little rich kid from St. Francis Wood with ten grand worth of silver wirework on his teeth, that bearings and trucks weren't his problem, but rather it was his lack of experience and skill. And he certainly couldn't tell this kid that he, Rad, could jump on any piece-of-shit Target or Kmart board and outskate ninety nine point nine percent of all the guys that came in here, despite what those jerks at Pygmy's thought.

Rad's mind still railed at the injustice of having not been chosen to skate for Pygmy's. The guy had even said he was the best skater, but he didn't have the 'right look.' What the fuck was up with that? It was a business decision, Rad knew. It had nothing to do with his skill on the board. But that didn't help. Fuck!

Rad looked at the kid's face which seemed to say, hey, I'm good; it's the board that's fucked up! Rad forced himself to nod pleasantly. This was his gig, but it was Larry's business.

"I'll have it ready in a couple hours."

The kid's face lit with a smile as he imagined himself outskating all of his buds. "Cool," he said, without asking how much it all would cost.

Rad secured the board in the vise. As he worked, he thought of his troubles. His thing with Jen was still hot. He wanted more of her time to get to know her better, but she was always too busy with her schoolwork. And people kept bugging him about Tawny. His mom had called the day before. "Rad," she'd said in that slow, slightly dramatic way that meant he should listen up to what would follow, "you're not going to find another girl like her."

"I know, Mom," he'd said. "Tawny's great. But I don't know. I think it's really over between us."

His mom ignored what he'd said. "Those piercings and that hair really bothered me when you first brought her over, but now that I've gotten to know her, she's a very sweet girl, and loyal to boot!" She paused and he'd imagined her looking at him sternly. "Rad, you're never going to find a better girl to marry."

And the week before he had been at Wayne's place talking about his situation. Wayne had fixed his big blue eyes on him and said of Tawny, "She seems to be the kind of woman to make a family with. You know, to have a lot of kids with. Don't you want someone to grow old and fat with?"

"I guess I don't think that far ahead," Rad had said at the time, laughing. But the more he thought about it the more likely it seemed, and that scared him. Yeah, Tawny had been his completely. But was that the life he wanted? Jen was beautiful and all, but he didn't really fit into her world. Yet... But if he went back to college that could change.

Tawny had finally returned one of his calls. He realized he still missed her. It wasn't right the way things had ended. She should have at least agreed to talk, then he could have told her his side.

Rad was removing the trucks from the board when the phone rang. As he picked up the receiver he was sure it would be Tawny. Jen's voice tickled into his ear. "Hey, lover boy."

"Baby! What's up?"

"Would you like to come to a party tonight?"

Rad could hear voices in the background. Jen said something softly to one of the people she was with and Rad heard a girl laugh. "Sure," he said, "but I have to pick up my nephew after work and take him home. When and where?"

"At the dorm. Seven o'clock."

"I'll be there." Rad felt himself becoming excited. "Where exactly?"

"Building T, number eleven."

"See you there…"

Rad heard another burst of laughter, girls and guys, and then Jen said bye and hung up.

When Rad walked into the church gymnasium, the practice was already in session. He took a seat in the stands and watched. On the court, Father Mike towered over the boys as he supervised. Rad remembered the priest from when he'd been a boy. Father Mike was tall, maybe six feet six, and stocky. When he'd occasionally walk into the classroom, his physical presence was intimidating and everyone would grow quiet. But he was kind and engaging. All the kids liked him. Despite that, Rad had avoided him, not wanting to have anything to do with him. At the time he hadn't thought about why. Now he realized that it was because he'd been afraid Father Mike would try and pressure him into joining one of the teams or clubs. He'd always been a loner, never a joiner, staying well away from team sports and Scouts, despite his dad's admonitions to the contrary.

As Rad watched the little kids running around on the court he wished that that had not been the case and he'd gotten more involved. He realized now, begrudgingly, that it probably would have been good for him.

Rad picked little Jay out of the crowd.

"Where's the ball?" Father Mike was asking the boys. "Keep your eye on the ball!"

Rad smiled as he watched the boys running around on the court, confused or questioning looks on their faces.

"Where does the center go?" Father Mike asked Jay.

Jay looked at him dumbly.

Father Mike turned to another boy. "Where should he be, Tommy?"

The boy pointed.

The whistle still between his lips, Father Mike gestured for Jay to get in position. Some of the boys looked at Father Mike blankly, some in awe. Father Mike tossed the ball in, the whistle dropping from his lips. The kids stayed in place. "Go! Go!" Father Mike shouted, breaking the spell. "He's not going to shoot from there... And if he did he'd probably miss."

Rad watched Jay and the other boys bouncing and running, their arms held up at 10 and 2 o'clock positions. Some of them, too immature to get seriously into the competition, mugged for each other whenever Father Mike looked away. A few were totally *not* into it, standing still and lost as the other boys played around them, then casting earnest cherubic faces at Father Mike whenever he looked their way or explained something to them, then totally ignoring or forgetting what he said a moment later and remaining rooted on the court. Rad watched it all in fascination, forgetting his tiredness, his hunger, and his pending date with Jen. The practice game was suddenly over, the kids high fiving each other as they looked around for their parents or guardians waiting to take them home.

Rad waved at Jay, then walked over to him slowly.

"You got some good moves there, little guy,"

said Rad.

Jay smiled self-consciously.

Father Mike saw Rad and nodded a greeting. Rad went over to him and shook his hand.

"How's it going?" the big priest said.

Rad nodded. "Goin' good."

"Liar," said Father Mike. "I was talking to your mom."

Rad laughed sheepishly. "That's my mom."

"She thinks you're lost and too much the loner these days. Is that right?"

"I wouldn't go that far," said Rad. "I have a job..."

"C'mon, Rad. Your mom told me all about it. That's not exactly a career path... working in retail."

"It's not retail," said Rad.

Father Mike went on as if Rad hadn't spoken, "Why don't you come by and we'll talk. I promise I won't lecture you. We'll just talk."

"I don't know," said Rad. "I don't have a lot of extra time."

Father Mike laughed.

Rad blushed, momentarily dumbfounded. "Okay," he said. "Can I call you?"

Father Mike nodded. "Sure. Anytime. Call the rectory. If I'm not there they'll take a message."

"Cool," said Rad. He took Jay by the hand and they headed for the door.

Rad drove his mother's car down 19th Avenue and turned into the dorm complex. He found Building T easily and soon stood before the door of number eleven, surprised at how quiet it was—no music, loud laughter or talk emanated from the place. It didn't sound like a party was going on in there. Maybe Jen had gotten the address wrong. He rang the bell.

A woman in her late twenties with her blonde hair coiled in a bun atop her head answered the door. She wore a cocktail dress and a string of pearls about her neck. Rad felt a little self-conscious at his own clothing: jeans and a tie-dyed tee shirt; he hadn't had time to go home and change. This had never been a problem when he went to Jen's; they didn't stay dressed very long anyway.

"Hello," said the woman, her blue eyes widening as she smiled. "You must be Rad."

"Yes," said Rad.

"I'm Polly." She extended her hand. "I'm an old friend of Jen's. I'm so glad you came."

"Nice to meet you," said Rad as he followed her into the apartment.

"I invited two other couples," Polly said, "but they couldn't make it."

"Oh," said Rad, nodding as he spied Jen seated on the couch. A young man, prematurely balding, sat in a chair across from her. The man was nattily dressed in slacks and a Polo shirt. For some reason he didn't fathom, Rad took an immediate dislike to him.

Polly indicated the man as she and Rad approached. "This is my fiancée, Harold. We're flying out of SFO tonight to see my parents."

Harold got to his feet and extended his hand.

"Hello. You must be Rad, right?"

Rad shook his hand. "Yeah. Nice to meet you."

Harold nodded as he sank back into his chair. Rad sat next to Jen on the couch.

"Would you like a beer?" Polly asked Rad.

"Yeah. Thanks."

Harold, Jen and Rad were silent for a minute as Polly left the room, smiling at each other. Polly brought back a green bottle of Heineken. She pried the top off and handed it to Rad, then pushed a chair over next to Harold.

Harold smiled at Rad. "Yours is an interesting name, Rad."

Polly smiled broadly and focused on Rad. "Yes, it is."

Rad felt his initial distaste for Harold, which he knew was unfair, grow. "It's a Viking name, actually," said Rad.

"Ooh," crooned Polly, "how interesting."

Jen began rubbing Rad's shoulder. "I never knew that," she said. She laughed a little self-consciously. "But I never wondered about it, actually."

"It has a nice sound," said Harold, "you know, as in the shortened version of radical." He turned to Rad. "I thought perhaps it was a nickname."

Rad forced himself to smile.

"Do you go to class with Jennifer?" Harold asked.

"No." Rad felt a little twinge of embarrassment. "I work at the mall, building boards."

"Boards?" asked Harold.

"Skateboards," interjected Jennifer. "Rad is quite a

skater. He almost made it to the X Games."

"Oh," said Harold, nodding as he sucked his upper lip downward. "You know, I did a little skateboarding myself when I was a kid."

Polly leaned forward, ignoring Harold's comment. "I think it's amazing what those kids do on skateboards. It's a wonder they don't break every bone in their bodies."

Jennifer nodded.

Rad smiled at Polly. "If they keep at it long enough, they will."

They all laughed. Rad took advantage of the lull to try and change the subject of the conversation from himself. "Where's Cait?" he asked Jen.

Jen smiled. "Back at my place. She has a date."

"Oh," said Rad.

Polly nodded pleasantly, without adding anything. Rad mostly listened as the conversation meandered from soccer to politics, to music.

"Last month we went to see Don Giovanni," said Polly.

"Is he some kind of European pop singer?" Rad asked.

Polly and Jen laughed. Harold said nothing, but he was unable to hide the smile on his face.

"Don Giovanni," Jen explained to Rad, whose face was beginning to redden, "is a classic opera."

Rad laughed, trying to be gracious, but his ignorance of such things stung him inside like a slap. The loud peal of the doorbell took everyone's attention momentarily off Rad's faux pas and they waited expectantly as Polly went to answer it.

"Well," said Polly when she returned, "the cab

is here."

Harold brought two bags from the bedroom and he and Polly said their goodbyes at the doorway. The door clicked closed.

Jen got to her feet and bolted it. She turned to Rad. "I thought they'd never leave."

Rad shrugged.

Jen looked deep into his eyes. "You okay?"

"Yeah, I'm okay." Now, in the quiet absence of the other couple, Rad felt calm returning to him.

Jen put her hand on his arm. "Let's go into the bedroom."

Rad got very turned on by everything—Jen, the differentness of the place, the decor. Polly had some kind of modernist painting of a couple sixty-nining on the wall above the bed, and the bed was firm and smelled of exotic herbs. As he was looking around, Jen rubbed his chest and said, "It's always exciting to fuck in new places."

They made love in the cool quiet, finally falling asleep. In the morning they made love again, then showered together. Later, over coffee and bagels, Jen told Rad she had a lecture to attend.

"What's it about?"

"Classical Rome."

"Cool. Can I go."

"Sure," said Jen, surprising Rad. He picked up the phone and dialed the shop, getting Larry's message machine. Rad put a rough, phlegmy edge to his voice, "Larry, I'm feeling kinda sick today. I won't be coming in."

The classroom was a huge amphitheater capable of seating over a hundred and fifty students. Rad and Jen took a seat about midway up in the back. After the place had slowly filled to about two-thirds capacity, a student assistant came onto the stage and did some sound checks on the mike at the podium. Five minutes later the lights dimmed slowly and Rad smiled. Neither high school nor his classes at Ridgeline had ever been like this. A short, sixty-something year old man with sparse gray hair, dressed stylishly in a tailored blue suit and red tie walked purposefully out to the podium carrying a manila folder of papers. He opened the folder, cleared his throat and began.

"My lecture today will correspond with the chapter 22 outline handout you received the first day of class. Staff will be recording it, so if you don't have your own machine and you want to get a copy, they'll have them available at the book store."

Professor Howard Katz then proceeded to give a general overview of the Romans and their history. Rad was intrigued by it all. He smiled over at Jen but she was looking down at her notes and did not make eye contact. Professor Katz talked about how the Romans were practical and "problem solvers." He talked about the 'Rubicon' in the south, Gaul on their northern border and how the Romans borrowed much from the Greeks. Most of the students looked bored and tired and the only one in the room seemingly more interested in the subject than Rad was the professor, who gestured excitedly, sometimes pacing out a few steps to the right or left of the podium, then, pausing, then turning away, then back to face the room dramatically. Katz pointed out that the American Founding Fathers had modeled much of their new republic on Classical Rome. Rad was astounded by how much, and the similar-sounding governmental functions—the Senate, from the Roman word, Senex, meaning old men, the Consuls, the "Assembly" of all citizens, like the U.S. Congress. The thing that struck Rad the deepest was the timeline. All of this creative thinking, this emergence of the civilization upon which modern Western societies were based, took place before the birth of Christ, maybe 800 to 400 BC. When men in many other parts of the world were trekking across the savannas to follow the wild game and ripening fruits, or hunting their enemies down and clubbing them to death like animals, the Romans were building aqueducts, roads and temples, and refining and participating in their own government, debating and defining the rights of all their citizens and slaves, expanding their republic. By the time the lecture had come to an end, Rad had decided to go back to school. When the lights came up he told Jen of his decision.

Her smile did not seem genuine to him. "Really?" she said. "That's nice, Rad. Well, I have to get to my macro class now. I'll call you later."

CHAPTER 28

1015 Skyview Drive

REYNALDO KNEW SOMETHING DIFFERENT WOULD happen today. Mommy had spent all morning cleaning, and she had let him play with Christine instead of working in his room. When the doorbell rang he realized it was because company was coming. Whenever company was coming he was allowed to watch TV with Christine.

The door opened and Aunt Susan came in. Her mouth opened in astonishment as she looked at Reynaldo and Christine. "They're getting so big now!" she said to Mommy. "So grown up!" Aunt Susan knelt. "Come and give me a hug."

Christine went over shyly and Aunt Susan pulled her close. Reynaldo looked at Mommy and held back. "C'mon, Reynaldo," said Aunt Susan, "you're not too big to give your aunt a hug and a kiss." Reynaldo smiled and went to her.

"How was school this year?" Aunt Susan asked him.

"Okay."

"Okay?" said Mommy sharply. She shook her

head as she frowned at Reynaldo. "Is getting out of your chair okay? Is taking candy from someone's coat pocket okay?"

"No, Mommy," said Reynaldo.

"He wants to be a good boy," said Aunt Susan. "Tell Mommy you'll be a good boy at school next year."

"I'll be a good boy, Mommy."

"Yeah," said Mommy. "That's what you say."

Aunt Susan got to her feet. Mommy turned on the TV to Power Rangers. Reynaldo's eyes immediately locked onto the screen. A moment later Mommy was jabbing her finger roughly into Reynaldo's back. "Did you hear what I just said?"

"No, Mommy. Sorry, Mommy."

"I said, 'Don't fight with Christine.'"

"Okay, Mommy." Reynaldo was suddenly filled with love for Mommy. She hadn't hit him, despite being angry with him, and she was letting him watch Power Rangers. "I love you, Mommy," he said as she turned away.

The kitchen door closed and Reynaldo watched the drama unfold on the TV screen. Christine sat beside him, her Barbie on her lap. The Power Rangers fought off an attack by the putty men. The action stopped for a commercial and Reynaldo turned to look at the closed kitchen door. He could barely hear their voices, but he knew they were talking about him. He didn't care though. He wasn't sitting at his desk writing down definitions. And Power Rangers was on, his favorite show. But soon Aunt Susan would leave. The realization made him sad again. He wished he could leave with her. What if Mommy gave him to Aunt Susan to take home? He imagined himself happily and hurriedly packing his suitcase before Mommy changed her mind. Then he would say goodbye to Mommy and Christine, and take Aunt Susan's hand and leave. He wondered if Aunt Susan had any toys at her house. He could take some of his. But what about Daddy? He would miss Daddy. Aunt Susan would let him call Daddy though. He was sure of that. She was nice. And Daddy would come and visit. He really would.

The Power Rangers came back on and Reynaldo watched in awe as the Rangers simply disappeared when the number of putty men surrounding them became too many to fight. Reynaldo thought about how wonderful it would be to be able to do that. He could disappear whenever Mommy got really mad at him.

For a week Allen had gone about his business, worrying about Tina's ultimatum. He didn't know if Susan had come over to talk to Tina or not. And he didn't want to badger her about it. At work, he threw himself into his tasks, dreading the free times when worry over the looming threat would fill him. Would she really do it? And if she did call them to come and get Reynaldo, would they? Could they? What about him? What were his rights in all of this? At work he'd been checking his in-basket every time he got up from his desk. When was the God-damned lawyer going to respond? Maybe his case really was hopeless and she wasn't interested?

Friday came and during the drive home, Allen

wondered what he'd find when he got there. As he let himself into the house he immediately knew something was different, but what? It was quiet; the TV was off. He guessed that they were all in the back of the house. He went into the kitchen and noticed little faint squares and rectangles of white where their pictures had hung. Every photo with either him or Reynaldo or both of them in it, had been purged. Only a couple of pictures of Tina and Christine remained. With a sense of dread he went quickly into Reynaldo's room. Relief flooded through him when he found Reynaldo at his desk, working on his definitions. Allen decided to call Susan later and thank her.

Tina walked by in the corridor. Allen heard her go in the kitchen. He turned to Reynaldo. "There's my boy. . . working hard!"

"I love you, Daddy," Reynaldo said.

"Love you too, Reynaldo," he said.

Allen went into the kitchen. Tina busied herself at the sink, not turning around to acknowledge him.

"You took down our pictures," he said.

Tina didn't answer as she continued to rinse some vegetables in a colander under the faucet. She set them on the counter and turned to him. "From now on you will take care of him. You will bathe him, do his laundry, take him to school, feed him; you will have to do everything."

"How can I do all that and get to work on time? You know how early I have to leave."

"That's not my problem. Tonight is the last night I cook for the two of you. Dinner will be ready in a half hour. You set his place." She turned away.

Allen shook his head in disbelief and left the kitchen. Christine had come out of her room and now played with her Barbies on the couch. He sat down next to her.

"Hi, Daddy," said Christine.

"Hi, Christine."

Allen heard the toilet flush. A moment later Reynaldo was standing in the hallway looking at them.

"Hi, Reynaldo," said Allen.

"Hi, Daddy."

The kitchen door began to open and Reynaldo ran back into his room as quiet and swift as a mouse.

Tina was busy with something in the back of the house. Allen's head hurt. One crisis had passed. Susan had evidently talked to her. But things were still not right. Things were still crazy. He wondered if they would be that way forever. Things had to change, had to get better, didn't they? Jesus Christ! They needed help in this family. Joel was dead. Talk about a door slammed in your face. There would be no help from that quarter. Where is my guru? My priest? My rabbi? Who do I have to help me with this? The lawyer had never bothered to respond. Why? What the hell should I do? If I take Reynaldo and leave I'll lose my daughter for sure. The courts will leave her with her mother. If I let Tina send Reynaldo back into the adoption system, there'll be a scandal for sure; these things just didn't happen. Who can I talk to about this? No one! The image of Lou came to Allen and he sighed. "Yeah," he said aloud, "right!" Close-mouthed Lou the bartender, what a joke! You could hardly get three words out of the guy. But the more Allen thought about it the more he realized that McCoy's had become the only place he could go. He could go there and, while he would find no answers, at least he would have warmth, relative peace, comfort from the booze, and maybe, just maybe, a little conversation. It was all he had at the moment.

"Daddy!" Christine demanded, breaking into Allen's thoughts. "You're not helping me."

Christine held up her Barbie doll, its long skinny legs bent at odd angles. Allen helped her dress her Barbie. He then set a place in the kitchen for Reynaldo and went out the front door to water the lawn. He put some chemical fertilizer into the lawn feeder and ran it across the lawn. Nick, his neighbor from across the street, was trimming his hedges with a pair of electric shears. Nick waved and turned the shears off. "How's the family?" he called over.

Allen cringed, but said, "Fine." He forced himself to smile and nod his head. What the hell could he say? He continued pushing the spreader back and forth. He looked at the sky. Soon the days would grow shorter and the rains come. The thought of thick grey woolen clouds overhead, muted daylight, short days, long nights, was strangely soothing. And he would no longer need to water the damn lawn.

CHAPTER 29

IMAGES OF THE BUDDHIST WOMEN'S meeting played out in Tawny's mind as she drove Terri's car up the ramp in the Tanforan Mall parking garage. She was going in to KoolKuts just to pick up her check—she wanted to give Terri something for allowing her to stay on her couch—then she was off to the old place to get more of her things. Exiting on the second floor, she drove carefully down the parking lot, the fog-dimmed South City daylight and occasional overhead neon lights barely illuminating the cars parked in their spaces. She spotted a slot close to the other end. She put on her signal, resisting the impulse to speed up to get there, afraid someone might back out into her path. She was only about six spaces away when a van rounded the turn ahead. Despite Tawny's blinking turn signal indicating her intention to park there, the van made a sharp awkward turn into the space. The van immediately began backing up, its tires squealing on the concrete as Tawny rolled up to it. Tawny was incredulous, wanting to see who this fool was. She saw a little boy sitting in a booster seat; it was the little boy from down the block. He was all smiles.

The mother leaned across him and rolled the window down, calling out, "I was here first!"

Tawny rolled her window down. "You didn't see my signal?"

"That doesn't matter. I got here first."

Tawny was shocked by the woman's brazenness. The woman waited, continuing to lean over the little brown boy and glare at her. Then Tawny noticed the tiny girl in the child's seat behind the woman. With a pixie-ish face framed in golden ringlets, the girl looked scared out of her wits by her mother's aggressive behavior. Tawny shook her head in astonishment as she drove slowly around the van. Tawny had been in fights before, not a lot of them, but she'd traded a few punches with some of the Mexican gang girls at South City High—and this woman looked like she wanted to get physical. Tawny was glad she saw that frightened little face before it got to that. She slowly drove up the ramp to the next level, marveling at the experience, wondering if the strange way it played out had anything to do with the Buddhism and the chanting. They were always saying that your whole environment would change for the better when you started chanting. Tawny spotted a parking place just before the ramp to the next level and parked.

Later that day Tawny turned onto Hillside and started up the hill to Skyview Drive. She wondered if Rad would be at the house. She had called the night before and hadn't gotten an answer. It didn't matter. This was her decision and she had decided. She was getting the last of her things, and her box of records out of the garage, and that was it. When she finished she would give him the key or leave it under the door with a note. She would not need it any more.

As she crested the hill she saw a lot of activity at the bottom. Crowds of people had collected where Skyview intersected with Hillside and a line of people were walking along the side of the road. It was some kind of organized march, she realized as she drew closer. Men, women and children, some of them shouting, were chanting something in unison. A few of the people were crying. Many of them held signs, the nearest one reading, SAVE SAN BRUNO MOUNTAIN! Near the eucalyptus grove, half a dozen huge, yellow, earthmoving machines were parked here and there. Hard-hat workers were everywhere and four police cruisers, red and yellow lights flashing, had pulled over on the side of the road. Tawny turned onto Skyview and parked. She got out and hurried up the hill.

The ringing of the phone woke Rad. For a moment he lay still, lazily expecting Tawny to pick it up. Then he remembered she was gone. His head ached as if his brain had swollen and was now throbbing and chafing against the sharp bony confines of his skull. He leaned over and grabbed the phone. "Hey, man," said a voice that was vaguely familiar, "your trees are going down."

"Huh?" said Rad.

"The trees, man!"

"Who is this?" Then Rad recognized the voice as Wayne's. "Oh, Wayne. What trees? What are you talking about?"

"I just drove by Hillside in the limo. The place is crawling with dozers and hardhats, police and protestors. It's like the beginning of a fucking war out there, man. They got the howitzers and tanks and they're getting ready to assault your trees!"

"Shit!" said Rad. "Thanks."

"No problem," said Wayne. "Sorry, man." He hung up.

Rad threw the covers off. "Shit!"

When Rad got to the top of the hill he was amazed at all the activity. He had never seen so many people in one place in South City in all his life. They lined the road, many of them neighbors he had seen on occasion. There were a lot of children among them, kids he had seen in the playground or playing ball or skate boarding or riding bikes. All of them were agitated; some cried. Some of the adults seemed to be in shock and watched the hardhats with mouths agape. Others shouted at the army of workers. Cries of, "Go home," and, "Save the mountain," filled the air. Rad saw a man in a hardhat that appeared to be in charge, talking with a couple of policemen on the side of the road. The other hardhats stood about talking nonchalantly as they waited. Every now and then one of them would turn to cast indifferent looks at the protestors.

Rad scanned the crowd and was shocked to see Tawny fifty feet down the road, talking to two preteen girls who were crying. He walked down to her.

"Oh, hi," she said. Her eyes were big.

Rad's confusion and the excited talk and shouting overwhelmed his awkwardness at suddenly being confronted with the presence of Tawny. He frowned and looked back up at the police cars.

Tawny said something to the girls and they walked off. She turned to Rad and shook her head. "I didn't know they had won in court."

"Neither did I," said Rad. He pointed to the man talking to the two policemen. "Maybe it's still not over."

She nodded and they turned to watch awkwardly. After a few moments the hard-hat man walked away from the policemen and waved his hand in signal. A roar came from the eucalyptus stand as the engines of the bulldozers started up. Black sooty columns of exhaust gushed skyward from the gleaming stainless-steel exhaust stacks. The bulldozers began rumbling about, raising clouds of dust and gushing thick columnar clouds of black diesel smoke. A huge yellow dozer with a large circular saw attached to its front lumbered over to a giant eucalyptus on the edge of the grove and began ripping into its base. "Oh, God," said Tawny, grabbing Rad's arm unconsciously. A rooster tail of sawdust flew from the saw as it quickly ate through the trunk. The last bit of trunk snapped like a rifle shot and the tree started to fall. The crowd cried out collectively as the big tree hit the ground with a sound like thunder. Several nearby women began crying.

"Oh, my God!" said Tawny again. Rad put his arm protectively around her as he watched incredulously. Shouting, curses and threats filled the morning air and Rad felt like he was witnessing some kind of massacre. His heart thumped in his chest as anger filled him. He held Tawny closer as they watched. Several of the dozer drivers and hardhats smiled broadly, enjoying the peoples' impotent outrage. Rad turned and saw a nearby hardhat holding a red STOP sign. The man smiled at him.

"What the fuck are you smiling at, you son of a bitch!" Rad shouted.

Tawny pulled on Rad, trying to turn him away.

The man nodded aggressively, giving Rad a "do something about it" look.

Tawny put both of her arms around him to hold him back.

Rad turned to her and saw that her face was wet with tears. He shook his head again, not knowing what to say.

"C'mon," Tawny said. "There isn't anything we can do anymore. It's over."

For a while Rad couldn't move from where he stood. Men with chainsaws hurried over to the huge downed eucalyptus. Their chain saws roared as they sawed the limbs off the fallen giant. They really were like an army, Rad realized, attacking an enemy. And they were in a hurry, a blitzkrieg, so no last-minute appeals court would be able to undo what they were doing. He shook his head in disgust as Tawny continued to pull at him. He cursed in futile frustration, his words lost in the awful drone of diesel-fueled mechanical destruction. Finally he let Tawny lead him away. He felt numb inside, like he'd lost a fist fight, or like after his first big breakup with a girl. He and Tawny slowly walked down the hill in silence.

After they entered the house and closed the door,

things moved on their own accord. There was no scheming on Rad's part. They didn't talk or negotiate. Things just happened. Tawny began crying and he put his arms around her. A moment later they were in the bedroom. He picked her up and lay her down on the bed. They made love slowly and gently. Before he rolled off of her, he kissed her face gently, tasting the salt in her tears.

"Tawn. I'm sorry."

Tawny shook her head. "Why? You couldn't do anything about it. Nobody could."

"No," said Rad. "Not that. I mean, I'm sorry about us. For screwing things up between us."

"Not now, Rad," she said. "Hand me a Kleenex."

Rad extended the box to her and she pulled one, wiping what remained of her tears away. "You know I ran into the lady down the block today?"

"Which one?"

"Mr. Peepers' wife. She stole my parking place at the mall parking lot."

"No shit," said Rad.

Tawny laughed a little and Rad smiled sadly, both welcoming the change in subject. Tawny shook her head. "I couldn't believe it. I had my signal on and she came around the bend and jumped into my spot."

"What'd you say to her?"

"God," said Tawny, "I wanted to get in her face, but she had her kids with her... the cute little brown boy and a sweet-looking little girl in a child seat behind. I couldn't get into anything with her with those kids looking on."

"Yeah," said Rad, "I can understand. You know that son of a bitch must've contacted the landlord about the truck."

"Mister Peepers?" said Tawny.

"Yeah. I got about forty five days to get it fixed and off the lawn."

"Hmmm," said Tawny, looking up at the ceiling.

The fell quiet for a while.

"Tawny," said Rad. "I want us to try again. Will you try?"

Tawny ran her hand lightly over Rad's arm. "I don't know, Rad. I'm not sure we should." She saw his face fall and quickly added, "I'm sorry. We shouldn't have done this. I don't hate you or anything, Rad. It's just that I'm not sure anymore that we're really right for each other. I need more time to think about it."

"Okay," said Rad sadly. "I understand."

Tawny didn't say anything further. A moment later she started crying softly. They lay together quietly and soon fell asleep in each other's arms.

Rad awoke as Tawny was getting out of bed. He didn't move as she began putting her clothes on.

"Can we at least get together to talk sometime?" he said hopefully. "You know, just as friends."

Tawny's smile looked forced. "Maybe… in a couple of weeks. I'm going down to the garage to get my things, Rad. I'll leave from there."

Rad nodded as Tawny left the room and closed the door. Immediately the cold, quiet emptiness of the house swallowed up the little hope he'd felt since he'd spotted her earlier that day on the hill. He fell back to sleep.

CHAPTER 30

R EYNALDO SAT AT HIS DESK for a long time working on his definitions; he was doing some E words that Mommy had assigned him. *EMBRACE*, he printed out in crisp letters, a. to clasp in the arms: *HUG* b: *CHERISH, LOVE*. The phrase was repeated in a somewhat orderly fashion three quarters of the way down the yellow foolscap page. His hand was tired from writing but he dared not stop. Mommy was madder than he'd ever seen her, her face red and puffy, and he was scared. He wished Daddy would come home but he knew from the light that he would not be home for a long time. He heard vague voices from the TV and grew angry with Christine. She always got to watch TV. Mommy said that she would have to work like him when she went into first grade, but he didn't believe it.

Reynaldo heard Mommy calling him loudly and he got out of his chair and ran to the kitchen. Mommy was down in the garage at the washing machine, looking up at him through the opened door. "Did you take any candy from the candy dish?"

Reynaldo didn't say anything for a moment. Both he and Christine had taken candy, but they had sworn each other to secrecy. He wondered if Christine had told. "No, Mommy," he said.

Mommy held out some shiny green paper. "I found these in the washing machine, Reynaldo, after I washed your clothes."

Reynaldo thought he had hid the papers under his bed, but he couldn't be sure. "They're not mine," he said. Maybe they *were* his. He knew he shouldn't lie, but he was afraid of what Mommy would do if he told the truth.

"Don't lie to me, Reynaldo," Mommy said

"I'm not lying, Mommy."

Mommy slammed the lid of the washing machine down. "Yes you are. Now go to your room, you goddamned liar! You're gonna get it. Go!"

Reynaldo turned and left the kitchen, calling out, "Sorry, Mommy," behind him, knowing that it would do him no good, but not being able to stop. He saw Christine watching the TV fixedly, trying to blot out what was happening and what was about to happen. He went into his room and looked around. What should he do? The sunlight coming in the window flickered as the branches of the tree moved in the breeze outside. He stared worriedly at the window and remembered when Daddy had shown him how to open it if there was an earthquake. He went and got his little yellow chair and brought it over to the window. He climbed up on it. He pulled the curtains aside. He slid the window open, feeling the coolness of the outside air. The air smelled sweet and fresh. He wanted to go outside and run. Mommy could never catch him because he ran fast like the Power Rangers. He could hide outside until Daddy came home. Then Mommy wouldn't hit him. He pushed against the screen like Daddy had shown him and it fell away. As he put his foot up on the window sill, rough hands grabbed his hair, yanking him painfully back inside the room.

Allen hadn't wanted to work late, but he'd had to. Ron had called a last minute meeting and Allen knew that if he wanted to be considered for Childers' lead slot, he had better stick around. The meeting had gone longer than anyone anticipated. When Allen went back to his desk to get his things he saw the letter from the lawyer in his in basket.

> *Dear Allen,*
>
> *I apologize for the delay in responding to you; I've actually been out sick for the last couple of weeks. I have reviewed your letter and understand, and very much sympathize with, your situation. I do have to advise you that the best thing you could do for your children at this point, if at all possible, would be to stay as long as you can in the marriage. I do hear you, however, that you feel that you have stayed as long as you can, and that for the sake of your son, you need to get out.*

Unfortunately, there is no guarantee that even under the conditions you describe, that you would get custody of your son, and if you are not in the house to ameliorate things when the children are with your wife... it is not a pretty thought. There are, however, a few things you can do to strengthen your case.

1. Consider calling the police so that you have police reports for every incident. You will need these in order to get temporary custody.

2. You will need statements from anybody and everybody who has first-hand knowledge of Tina's behavior towards Reynaldo, particularly the more abusive behavior. In other words, there needs to be eyewitnesses. The best statements come from professionals, such as doctors, nurses, teachers, etc.

3. Immediately prior to leaving the house you will want to file a request for temporary custody. In preparation, you should start becoming as much as possible, the primary parent. You should pick up the children from daycare, take them to school, etc.

All of this is to help you set up your case. However, I am sad to report that the biases in the Courts are so deeply ingrained in favor of mothers, and against men, that all of this may only gain you a 'slim chance.' I am sorry that the news could not be more optimistic, but I would be doing you a disservice to tell you what you would like to hear, rather than the reality.

If you still want to proceed, contact me through my secretary and we will schedule an initial consultation.

Sincerely,

Camille Simpson

Attorney at Law

All the way home Allen's mind picked over the details of the lawyer's letter. 'Get police reports,' she'd written. For what? None of it had ever been bad enough that he had had to call the police. It was the sum total of it all, the cumulative effect of all that anger and, yeah, hate, it seemed like, directed at Reynaldo. How do you get that in a police report? And statements from people who know Tina and him and the kids? What were Susan and Tomas likely to say? Would they repeat to the authorities what he had told them about what was going on at home, or close ranks with Tina? Statements from professionals? Who? Reynaldo's pediatrician, Doctor Goldman? He hadn't seen any evidence of abuse. Joel Beckett? He was dead, and even if he weren't, Allen had pulled his punches in his description of Tina's behavior toward Reynaldo out of some screwed-up sense of marital loyalty. And what would the courts do with this? He recalled what the lawyer wrote about the court's bias toward mothers.

Tina would play that up big time. No doubt about it; he was screwed.

The closer Allen got to home the more discouraged he became. Despite that, he resolved to start keeping a journal. But he doubted it would change anything much. He ran into a major traffic jam up on 280 near the airport. While sitting in traffic he thought about the situation again—but what the hell could he do? How could he fix this disaster?

Darkness had already fallen when Allen drove down Skyview. As he parked the van he realized his stomach was empty and he should eat, but he had no appetite. He went in the house. As usual, Christine was sitting on one of the little yellow plastic chairs in front of the TV, playing with her Barbies. Allen didn't see Tina in the kitchen and he moved down the hallway to look in on Reynaldo. As he put his hand on the doorknob to Reynaldo's room, he heard the door to the garage open. He turned the knob, but it wouldn't budge. It was locked.

Tina came out of the kitchen with a loaded up white plastic laundry basket.

"His door is locked," Allen said to her.

"Because he's being punished," Tina said as she brushed past him on her way to their room.

"Goddamn it, Tina," he said. "What..."

She had already closed the door to their room. He went in. She was folding clothes and setting them in neat piles on top of the bedspread.

"Where is he?" Allen said.

She glared at him. "In his room. Where else would he be?"

Allen felt his frustration rising, ready to boil over. "Well, I want to see him."

Tina stopped her folding and looked at him. "Not tonight."

Allen shook his head. "Why the hell not?"

"Because you'll just ruin it like you always do. He has to be punished. If you go in there you'll start commiserating with him, taking his side, ruining things."

"What the hell..." Allen looked at her as she went back to her laundry folding. He got the sense that she was on the verge of one of her violent temper explosions, but he couldn't let her get away with this. She didn't rule here; they were supposed to be a team. He remembered the key ring with all the keys from the bedrooms in the top drawer of the chest of drawers. He went over, slid open the drawer, took the keys and left the bedroom.

Allen put the first key on the ring into the keyhole as Tina came up behind him. She grabbed his hand, trying to wrest the keys from his grasp. He tried the key; it wouldn't turn. He pulled the key out and pushed her away, sticking the second key in. It, too, wouldn't budge. Again she was on him, trying to grab the keys out of his hand. Failing that, she tried to shove him aside. He shoved her back and looked down at the key ring. There were only two keys left to try. He put one in the lock. Just as he was ready to turn it her hands found his face. He flinched at the pain as she dug her long nails into his flesh. He turned away from her, attempting to turn the key. It wouldn't budge. As he was pulling it out she attacked again. "God damn it," he said as he pushed her away. She came right back, grabbing at the keys in his hands; they fell to the floor. She squealed as she reached down and grabbed them. He looked at her and saw triumph in her eyes. He knew he could easily take them from her again, but what was the point? She had won. Not because she had the keys, but because of what she had brought them to. They had crossed the Rubicon; their fighting had become physical now, like two ignorant welfare case losers in some ghetto. The thought sickened him. Things had escalated too far; they were on the precipice. If he forcibly took the keys from her and forced his way into Reynaldo's room, she'd be on the phone to the police in seconds. It would go badly for him. Hadn't the lawyer said as much? He knew it as surely as he knew anything. In any domestic disturbance situation, the cops always asked the husband to leave; it was SOP. So there would be a police report, but it wouldn't be about child abuse, but rather domestic abuse, battery—who knew what she might throw at him? The neighbors would be treated to the sight of a police cruiser, lights flashing, parked outside their house, him handcuffed with some cop's big meaty hand on his head as he was pushed into the back seat. It would become an issue at work too. Then what? Despite the new awful turn their relationship had taken, he would still need a job. Actually, more than ever. He'd heard all the stories from the older men at work that had gotten divorced—spousal support, some of them, child support, court costs, counseling fees, finding and furnishing a new domicile for himself. He turned away from her in disgust.

He went out into the living room, panic rising in him. He was surprised to see Christine sitting rapt before the TV on her little yellow chair. He had forgotten all about her. Did she hear or see what had just happened between him and her mother? She gave no indication and for that he was thankful. He watched her for a moment; nothing existed for her other than what was happening in front of her on the TV. Not him, not Tina or Reynaldo, this house, nothing. All for the better, he realized, poor kid. Had he been doing the same thing, he wondered, blocking out much of what was going on right in his own home?

Allen went out into the night and closed the door. The awful thing that had happened back in that house could never be fixed or made right ever again. The lawyer was right; he was screwed. But he wasn't going down without a fight. All that mattered now was going forward, and the details—who got what, who lived where. It would be hashed out by greedbag lawyers and busybody judges as they pawed through his and Tina's and the kids' lives. It would be somewhat public and ugly.

As Rad worked in the darkness he thought about Tawny, wondering where she was and what she was doing—probably at one of her Buddhist meetings. Rad pulled the last of the wheels from the bed of the truck and leaned it up against the rear fender. He had installed three of the wheels earlier today and had taken a break, intending to do the fourth and last tomorrow.

But after sitting in the house alone for a couple of hours he had started to feel lonely and depressed. And so he'd decided that despite the darkness, he would get them all on tonight. The tires were bald; he couldn't afford new ones, but at least they held air. And he still needed new shoes for the front brakes, but as long as he didn't drive the truck too far he'd be all right. But he had to get it off the blocks and off the front yard.

As Rad began jacking up the left rear he did not notice that the wheel leaning against the truck fender had moved. Each stroke of the jack raised the truck above the wheel further and further until there was nothing holding it. The wheel began rolling down the slope of the yard.

Allen walked up the sidewalk, his breathing becoming rapid. He craved something down to the bone. What? Someone to listen to him. Someone to help him understand what was happening. Was he crazy? Was Tina? He heard a steady clicking sound. What the hell had she been up to, locking Reynaldo in his room and not wanting to let him see him? He had no answers anymore and he felt like screaming out. Rage filled him.

Something leapt up at Allen from the dark, knocking into him painfully. It made a wobbling noise in the dark at his feet, then thumped to a stop—a wheel from a car! Incredulous, he turned and saw the young punk, Raggedy Andy, up the slope of his yard with a tire iron in his hand.

"What the hell are you doing?" Allen shouted to him.

"I'm working on my truck. What's it to you?"

"Well your fucking wheel just banged into me…"

"What are you talking about?"

Allen pointed to the wheel at his feet. "I'm talking about this!"

"Oh. It must've rolled off when I was jacking the truck up. I didn't even know you were down there."

Allen looked up at the dark hulk of the truck on the barren lawn above. "What the fuck are you working on it at night for?"

"You should know, jerk! You wrote my landlord about the truck, didn't you?"

Allen frowned, vaguely remembering something about the truck. It didn't matter now. "I don't know what you're talking about."

The punk dropped the tire iron onto the ground and walked down the slope. Allen saw in him everything that had gone wrong in his life, everything that was squeezing him, destroying him. He swung wildly at him and missed as the younger man spun him around and threw him onto the dirt of the yard, pinning him. Allen realized he was using some kind of high school wrestling trick. Enraged, he managed to get to his feet. He and the punk closed again. Allen grabbed him by his jacket and the punk grabbed Allen's shirt front. Allen tried to throw him, but the punk was too strong and Allen heard the fabric of his shirt ripping. They circled, each trying to trip the other. Allen's breathing was ragged. "Why are you fucking with me, man?"

"Fuckin' with you? What are you talking about? You've caused me a lot of grief, motherfucker."

"Grief!" Allen laughed crazily. "You don't know the fucking meaning of the word."

Both men continued to circle each other warily, holding tight for fear the other would gain advantage. Allen tried to get a good look at the younger man's face but the corona of the streetlight behind him was blinding.

"What the hell happened to you?" said the punk. His voice was less aggressive now, less strident "You get in a cat fight or something?"

"None of your goddamned business," said Allen.

"Look," said the punk, "why don't you just chill out? I don't know what the fuck your problem is, but it ain't me."

The punk relaxed his grip on Allen's shirt and both men separated, putting some distance between themselves.

"You want to talk about this?" said the punk.

Allen was unsure of what he meant. "Talk about what?"

"Whatever your problem is, that's what."

Allen watched the punk warily. Could things get any crazier? What the hell was he supposed to do here, talk to some drug-using skater punk about how his family was coming apart and that he needed help?

"Fuck you," Allen spat. "I don't have anything to talk with you about!" He turned and went back down the hill to his house.

CHAPTER 31

FTER HER VISIT TO DOCTOR Neilson's office, Tawny drove to Rad's mother's house in South City. The test results were positive. After questioning Tawny briefly and probing her in a few places, Doctor Neilson pronounced her pregnant, about a month and a half now. Neilson had been fatherly as he assured her that, given her youth and health, he was ninety nine percent certain she'd have a healthy baby. Then he had called the nurse in to talk to her. Even as the nurse was handing Tawny the pamphlets on prenatal care, ultrasound scans, well baby care, etc., Tawny already knew what she was going to do.

Tawny parked on the Anderson's driveway next to Rad's mom's little Mazda van.

Florence, or Flo, as she always insisted Tawny call her, led her into the living room. Tawny's nostrils flared at the odor of something vile cooking in the kitchen.

They sat on the couch.

"I'm so glad you came by, Tawny," said Flo. "We haven't seen you in months."

Tawny nodded. "I know. I wanted to come by a couple times but... you know how it is."

Flo smiled. "Oh," she said, getting to her feet. "I wanted to show you something. Be right back."

Flo brought out a photo album and sat down. "Jack had tucked this away in the attic while he was redoing the bedroom. I had him get it down for me the other day." She opened the album, an array of about a dozen glossy, glassine-encased pictures on each page. They started with Rad's baby pictures.

As they cooed over some of the more fetching ones, Tawny forced herself to remember that she had come here to tell Flo she was pregnant and what she was going to do about it. The more she thought about it, the more she realized how crass and mean that was. Why the hell did she want to upset Flo? To punish her for what she and Rad had done? What was the point of that? It was better she didn't know anything about it.

Tawny continued to look at the pictures as Flo left and returned with a tray of shortbread cookies. Despite her embarrassment, Tawny found herself eating them one after the other, she was so hungry. They continued to make small talk as they turned the pages. They came to a picture of Rad sitting on a pony. It was so cute, so beautiful, that Tawny asked Flo to wait before turning the page. She wanted to study it.

"How old is he in that one?" she asked.

"Four," said Flo. "I remember the day like it was yesterday. Some Mexican guy came through the neighborhood with a little pony and a camera. He must have made an awful lot of money because every kid in the neighborhood wanted his picture taken on that pony." She laughed. "I remember being nervous about it..." Flo smiled in embarrassment and touched Tawny on the knee. "That's just the way I am. The pony was little and beautiful, with its blonde mane, but I could see it was skittish, its glassy eyes looking around everywhere. The guy just let the kids sit on it while he backed off a bit and took his pictures. I was a nervous wreck. I was sure that thing was going to take off with Rad on its back and go galloping down the street and onto the freeway or something."

They laughed.

"Rad wasn't scared though," said Flo, "he loved it."

Tawny nodded. "I can see that."

Flo pat Tawny on the hand. "Tawny, I'll never forget the one time at the Kmart. In the store, Rad had been bugging me to let him sit in the cart. I'd told him that he was too big for that but he wasn't dissuaded. Anyway, I let him climb in the front part of the cart with the packages. And then I pushed him out of the store and across the parking lot to my car. I was putting a package in the trunk when the cart must have started rolling. I didn't know it. When I turned around, the cart is rolling across the parking lot, picking up speed, heading right for one of the exits. And Rad is standing up in the front and just having a hell of a time, yelling, 'whoopee!' And there's this car coming! I screamed and ran after it but I couldn't catch it. Fortunately the car saw him and stopped. I felt like a damn fool, but at least he was all right. I was shaken up for the rest of the day."

"Oh dear," said Tawny. "Maybe that's where he got his love of skateboarding."

"Yeah," said Flo, "could be. When we got home, I put him in for his nap and had a stiff drink, I'll tell you that."

They laughed some more and Tawny knew that Flo must never know about it. Never. It would hurt her too much. Tawny would just have to deal with it herself.

"You know," Tawny said, "I better get going. I'm glad I was able to see you, Flo. I haven't seen you for a long while. And just because Rad and I are not together anymore doesn't mean we shouldn't maintain our relationship."

Flo held Tawny's hand as they stood. "I know, Tawny. Listen, you let yourself out, sweetie. I have to go check on my cooking." Before she walked out of the room her face grew sadly serious and she said, "I know you'll make the right decision."

Tawny nodded as she let herself out of the house. She felt confused. Did Flo mean 'make the right decision' in regard to her and Rad staying together or splitting up? That had to be what she meant. But Tawny couldn't get it out of her head that Flo knew more than she was letting on, and that *that* was the decision she was really talking about. That might explain her dragging out the baby photo album. Or was it all just one big coincidence?

The snake felt the call deep in the very molecules of its brain. It was as overwhelming as the call to mate, and as irresistible as the warmth of nearby moving prey.

The snake began moving slowly toward the light,

then paused where the channel of cooler air flowed swiftly into this place. It could not leave at this moment and must instead wait for the safety that darkness would provide. Periodically it lifted its head and swept it from side to side, tasting the air with its tongue. Never before had it experienced this confusion and urgency. It did not want to leave this place where food had been plentiful and regular, where heat had been adequate and constant, and its life quiet and solitary. But there was no resisting. The call continued and grew stronger and stronger.

The light faded to the point where the snake could safely slide out into the open. It poured itself along in the dark, passing several small prey and then a large one emitting much heat. But it did not, could not, stop.

The homeless man turned over onto his right side, assuming the fetal position in his sleeping bag. Obscured by some bushes and a low jumble of mesquite, he had been spending his nights here in the little no man's land between the backyards of the two rows of houses for almost a month. This night something brushed by his head in the blackness. Or did he dream it, he wondered as he lifted his head into the black coolness of the night and opened his eyes. Overcome by tiredness and the remaining alcohol in his blood, he closed his eyes again and forgot what had awakened him. He lay his head back down and quickly fell back to sleep.

Just before night began to dissipate the snake came to the place. It entered and immediately moved up the rough stony surface of the rise to the place where it was directed. It was promised that it would soon eat, and well. Confusion again threatened to overwhelm the snake, for although the entity that had called it here was powerful and close by, the snake could not detect its heat signature in the blackness.

As day slowly grew out of blackness, the snake waited patiently, tasting the air with its flicking tongue.

CHAPTER 32

FROM UP IN THE STANDS Rad watched the kids as they lined up to practice their foul shooting. Father Mike squatted down to coach the tiniest member of the team after he'd failed a second time to even reach the net. Rad thought again about his run in with Mister Peepers down the block. Initially he'd been really pissed off at the guy, wanting to slug him. But the guy's pathetic rage, his voice breaking, his rapid breathing and all the scratches on his face—all of it had affected Rad at some deep level and he had backed off. The guy seemed desperate, as if he was ready to die. Rad had never seen anyone in such a state before.

Father Mike stood up and caught Rad's eye. He started up into the stands

"So," said Father Mike, as he sat beside Rad, "did you think about what we talked about?"

Father Mike had seemed unconcerned about Rad's breakup with Tawny. The priest had instead spent most of their time together the week before talking about how important Rad's relationship with his parents was.

"Yeah," said Rad.

"And?" said Father Mike.

"My dad and I are supposed to get together for a burger and beer."

"Good."

The squeak and slap of sports shoes on the hardwood echoed off the gym walls. They watched as little Jay carefully lined up for his shot, then leapt as he launched the ball. It went in and the other kids shouted in approval. Several nearby boys high fived him.

"You know," said Father Mike, "when your sister first brought Jay here, he couldn't dribble two steps, let alone shoot. Now, look at him! He's got a lot of heart, don't he?"

Rad nodded. "You know I got in a kind of fight with the guy that lives down the block."

Father Mike answered as he watched the boys, "Did the police get involved?"

"No. It didn't go that far."

The priest seemed to feel it was not important as he continued to watch the practice. He turned to Rad. "You want to know the secret to life?"

Rad smiled. "Sure. I can use all the help I can get."

Father Mike leaned closer. "There ain't no secret, okay?" He laughed.

Rad smiled and nodded. "I'll remember that."

Father Mike slid off the bench and went down to the boys. He blew the whistle, signaling the end of the practice.

Rad climbed down from the stands and went over to Jay, who was pulling on his jacket. Before they could leave, Father Mike came over and gave Jay a high five. He slapped Rad on the back.

"Hang in there, Rad. Stay in touch and work on your relationship with your father, all right?"

Rad felt weary and beaten, but hopeful at the same time. He nodded and looked down at Jay. "You ready?"

Father Mike smiled at them and Rad felt the swell of hope inside. He and Jay headed out to the car.

Tawny had always been pro-choice and had no misgivings about going to Planned Parenthood. She knew where it was, having already been there four or five times for her pills. Strangely though, this time, the usual trio of protestors—a thirty-something bearded, wild-eyed man with a Southern accent, a young freckled fourteen-year-old girl, and an elderly nun—were not out in the parking lot waving at all who exited their cars. When Tawny went in the door she saw Jamie in the hall. Jamie, a young woman Tawny's own age, had been very friendly to her in the past.

"Tawny, how are you?"

Tawny realized it had only been a little over a month since she'd been here last. She wasn't out of pills and not due to show up here for another month or so. "Ah, I'm okay. But I have to see the doctor."

Jamie took her hand. She was very warm and physical, hugging and touching all who came within her orbit. "Are there complications?"

Tawny smiled. "Yeah. The big one, I think."

"Hmmm!" said Jamie, frowning. "Have you been taking your pills?"

Tawny tried to smile. "To the best of my recollection ... yes."

"Okay," said Jamie, "spoken like a lawyer. Well, sit down, Tawny. We'll get you right in."

Later, as Tawny lay on the examining table, the paper blanket pulled up to her chin, she wished the doctor wouldn't be so rough with his probe as he pushed it around on her belly. And the jelly they used for the ultrasound was cold and felt dirty to her. The doctor looked intently at the screen, never at her as he probed with the machine.

"Well," she said, "I suppose you concur with my doctor's assessment?"

The doctor grunted and continued to stare at the screen. Tawny craned her neck to see the monitor. "Can I see?" she said.

The doctor frowned and turned the machine off. "I'm sorry, we're just too busy. I've got thirteen patients waiting outside." He got to his feet and quickly washed his hands. Tawny sat up, holding the paper gown close about her.

"Get dressed," the doctor said, "and they'll schedule your procedure for you." He smiled a little forced smile and left the room.

Tawny dressed and went into a little conference room with Jamie. As they waited for the nurse, Tawny wondered what the procedure involved. She had never cared before.

The nurse came in with Tawny's chart under her arm. Jamie approached her. "Barbara, this is Tawny."

Barbara nodded without looking at Tawny.

"Tawny has a question," Jamie said.

Barbara raised her eyebrows as she looked at Tawny.

There was something in her eyes that put Tawny off; she was not sure what it was.

"What is your question?" Barbara asked.

"I was just, you know, wondering what will happen."

"Just some scraping," said Barbara, "elimination of the uterine contents."

Tawny felt uncomfortable in Barbara's gaze. "Well, what is it at this stage?"

Barbara shook her head. "It has more in common with a frog at this point." Barbara's smile chilled Tawny. "It's nothing, just a mass of cells."

Tawny again pondered what it was in Barbara's eyes that made her so uncomfortable. Superiority, that was it! Barbara was looking down on Tawny as if she were trash, as if this procedure were the only option for a woman of her class. She hadn't said that, of course, but the little smile on her face when she looked at Tawny, and the dismissive way she talked about it seemed to confirm it.

Barbara handed a form to Jamie. "Jamie will help you schedule your procedure," she said without looking at Tawny. "And she can help you with any further questions you have." Barbara walked out.

Jamie put the form in Tawny's chart and pat her hand. "Don't worry, Tawny. You'll be fine a day or two afterward. Let me go over some of that with you."

Tawny walked through the parking lot toward the car. Jamie had said that she'd have some period-like bleeding and cramps and there would probably be some feelings of depression afterward. But they had some medication for that. Tawny realized she was a little depressed about it already. She looked forward to going home and just chanting about it. And she definitely wanted to talk to Terri. Terri had said that she could get guidance about it. Guidance meant that you went to, and were counseled by, a senior member in the Buddhist organization about whatever problem you were having. Terri had said that no matter what they told you, in the end it was your decision. They would not tell you what to do. They would always counsel you to chant a lot about it. That was the biggest thing.

In the car, Tawny's thoughts went back to the nurse—what was her name—Barbara. She was like some kind of woman warrior automaton. "Just a mass of cells," she had said with that cold smile on her face, as if she'd like to do the procedure herself and just scrape it away. "It has more in common with a frog." Was that supposed to reassure her? Tawny had been so freaked out by Barbara that she couldn't wait to leave.

As she drove the freeway she passed a playground full of kids. Some of them were skateboarding, taking turns as they glided down an incline, watching each other. Rad's face suddenly flashed before her. This was 'their' problem, but he didn't know a damn thing about it. She thought of the four or five couples she had seen in Planned Parenthood, the men, boys, most of them, sitting close to their girlfriends, some of them holding their girl's hands. She imagined herself slapping Rad. Why the fuck weren't you there with me holding my hand? She hadn't told him, of course. And she wouldn't.

Her eyes teared up a little. She would never hit him, of course, not really; it would just be love blows. Ha! Despite her worries and fear she almost laughed aloud at the phrase. Love blows! Wasn't that what the president got? He'd had that chick coming in the White House and giving him regular blowjobs and he didn't even call it sex! If she and Rad had limited themselves to just that she wouldn't be in this predicament. But she could never let a guy just use her like that. She had wanted her arms around him. She had wanted more. And now she had it.

For a few moments Tawny allowed herself the distraction that the drama of the president's recent troubles provided, recalling her shock when she'd first heard about the whole thing. Before that she'd seen him a million times on TV, always coming out of some church somewhere with that big bible in his hand and that big smile on his handsome reddened face, a face that she and millions of other women daily imagined. Wow! Tawny gave a slight, almost-imperceptible shake of her head. But what the hell did all of that have to do with her problem, she thought angrily. Nothing. Not a damn thing!

As Tawny came in sight of San Bruno Mountain and South City she thought about Rad and how she used to admire his spirit. They talked a lot about spirit at the Buddhist meetings. Your spirit was your determination. It was the most important thing, they said. It was the spark. They even had a special name for it, Ichinin. Whatever you called it, Rad had it, even if he wasn't a Buddhist. First it was for his boarding.

He never gave up on that until it was obviously the end of the line. Then there was the Save the Mountain fight. He really got into that in a big way too. She thought of the last Buddhist meeting she had gone to. One of the women talked about how the real benefit of the Buddhist practice was seeing your life for what it was, not for what you wanted it to be. Only then could you begin to change it. This had come after a discussion of one of Nichiren's writings, *The Opening of the Eyes*. Tawny rubbed her belly slightly. Was she getting any benefit from this practice? Or was she only kidding herself?

She put some soft music on the radio. She smiled and rubbed her belly again, adjusting the seat belt so that it didn't chaff so much. In spite of everything, she felt a vague hope. If Rad hadn't gotten involved with that chick they could've gotten through this together. But she could still deal with it. She clenched her eyes as a single tear ran down her cheek. She shook her head sadly. Rad, why did you turn out to be such an irresponsible jerk?

The blue of the bay appeared on her right, the brighter blue of the lagoon on the left. Tears ran freely down her face. She thought again about getting guidance. She pulled some Kleenex from the box and wiped away her tears. The idea of getting guidance gave her more hope and made her feel a little better. She looked at her watch as she turned off the freeway. She wondered if Terri had cooked anything. The thing inside of her was hungry, the thing that bitch had said resembled a frog. The little frog was hungry and so was she. It was time to eat.

CHAPTER 33

CAPTAIN RICHARD TURNER, A DETECTIVE in the South San Francisco police department, sat stiffly, hunched forward in the lounge chair in the Collins' living room. The atmosphere in the house was strained. An abducted child was an awful thing to deal with, worse than a death. The couple sat on the couch staring down at the rug. The daughter, a cute little towhead, played with her doll as she sat in the mother's lap.

"Do you go to Green Park often?" Captain Turner asked the mother.

Tina Collins nodded. "The kids like the playground there. It's not as crowded as the one at the school."

"That's part of the problem," Turner said. "If there had been more people around we might have an ID on the kidnapper."

The mother said nothing in response.

"And you said it was really foggy?" he asked.

Tina Collins nodded. "I could see the bathroom building well enough when he went in there, but the fog came in thicker and then you couldn't see it. That's when I got Christine off the swing and we walked back down there."

Turner nodded. It had been foggy that day. In South City and Daly City sometimes patches of it rolled in so thick you couldn't see five feet in front of you. It caused a lot of fender benders and the auto body shops probably loved it.

He sighed. He'd gotten enough information to open the case. He wasn't happy to get one of these cases this close to his retirement. These things could go on for one, three, five years, like the Amy Kelly case. And he had only thirteen months to go before he got his pension and retired to his place in Redding.

Turner sighed and got to his feet. He looked at the family's photo on the mantle. He went over to it, turned to Mrs. Collins and pointed. "Do you mind?"

She blew her nose, then shook her head.

Turner picked up the framed photo. In it, Mr. and Mrs. Collins sat on a park bench with the boy and girl. The missus held the girl, Christine, in her arms. She looked to be two or three in the photo. And the mister held the missing boy, restrained the boy was probably more accurate. The kid looked like he wanted to chase after something. The mister had a smile on his face, but the boy was almost unaware of him, focusing instead on something in the distance.

Turner turned to the couple. "He's a good-looking kid. Nice color. Is he Mexican?"

The father shook his head. He looked drained of life, beaten. "His mother is from Guatemala, I think. She has a lot of Indian blood. We never did find out anything about the father."

"The mother was a prostitute," said Mrs. Collins as she rocked her little girl.

The detective looked at the father for corroboration.

Allen Collins shrugged. "We don't know for sure. It's possible I suppose."

"You say he's seven?" said the detective. "He looks awful small for seven."

Allen Collins nodded. "He was born premature and very small. The doctor said he would begin to catch up, maybe by the time he was eight or nine."

Captain Turner nodded as he put the picture back on the mantle. "Did he have any relatives in this country that would want him? Did anyone ever contact you about him?"

"No," said Mrs. Collins. "He had no one but us."

"He had nobody that we know of," added Allen Collins. "I suppose there could be somebody out there somewhere, but we... They didn't tell us anything about anybody other than the mother." Allen Collins looked back down at the rug.

"Well," said Captain Turner, looking at Tina Collins, "do you have the things I asked for?"

Allen Collins looked up at Detective Turner in confusion.

Mrs. Collins sat Christine on the couch and got to her feet. She turned to her husband. "I told the Captain I would give him some of Reynaldo's things."

Allen Collins nodded.

Tina Collins went into the bedroom and closed the door. She put some of Reynaldo's pictures and toys in a paper bag. As she reached for a Disney journal they had bought him, something told her to look inside. Most of the pages were empty, but a few were marked with

Reynaldo's scribbles, crudely drawn planes or ships, a few words, incomplete sentences. She turned to the last page and frowned. What appeared to be verse filled the page, five lines, block letters.

TODAY I WOKE UP WHEN THE
TREE SCRATCHED THE WINDOW

I WAS SCARED

I HEARD DADDY GET UP FOR WORK

I WATCHED HIM GO AND I WAS SAD

MOMMY WONT BE MEAN TO
ME WHEN DADDY IS HERE

Glancing at the door, Tina Collins tore the page from the book. She folded it and put it in her pocket. She put the Disney book in the bag with the other things and went back out into the living room.

Detective Turner took the bag from Mrs. Collins. He sighed as he looked at her and her husband. "I'll call you tomorrow to schedule another interview. We have to talk more about the day he disappeared, you know, go over the details a little more. Maybe there's something that slipped your mind and will pop back in by then. Things happen that way."

Back at his office, Detective Turner sat down heavily. He put the bag with the kid's things on his desk. On the computer screen he saw that he had some email.

There was a message from Fran Cleary, the Realtor up in Redding. She had the condo's escrow papers ready and wanted to know when he was coming up to sign them.

Turner took out the pedophile CD. It listed them all—where they lived, where they worked, their phone numbers. There were hundreds on the San Francisco Peninsula, all of them supposedly reformed, registered, and released by the system, and, more than likely, researching where they'd find their next victims—Boy Scout troop, little league, basketball team. He put the CD in the drive. While it was loading he pulled open the file drawer on his desk and took out a manila folder. He found Reynaldo's name. He looked for the phone number for the boy's birth mother's social worker. The birth mother was a head case, it sounded like. Never held a job, on welfare for years, a shut in but for counseling visits. But he didn't think she had anything to do with this. Still, he had to check into it. His mind went back to the Collins. The father had that faint scar on his cheek—got too close to the rose bushes while he was gardening, a fight with the wife, a girlfriend, or something else? He'd have to explore that a little. The mother Tina was obviously the one who wielded the buggy whip in the relationship. And something about her bothered him too. He would have to interview them separately, of course.

Turner turned back around to the computer and looked at the list of names. He picked up the kid's picture from the folder. Jesus Christ! Such a sweet-looking little kid. What kind of son of a bitch would hurt an innocent kid like that? He sighed. Thirteen more months of dealing with the dregs of humanity and sad stories like this and then he was retired, free. He would do nothing but go fishing, watch the sports channel, take trips to Reno, and the occasional shopping trips with Pamela. Thirteen months. Thirteen goddamned friggin months!

Turner picked up the phone. He'd better schedule the parents' interviews as soon as possible.

CHAPTER 34

TAWNY HAD BEEN SURPRISED WHEN Rad called and asked her out. She'd been hoping he would, and if he hadn't she would have called him. She had decided to talk to him about her situation, 'their' situation.

Terri drove Tawny to Tawny's old place. Tawny waved goodbye as she walked up the steps and knocked on the door.

"Wow!" said Rad when he opened it, "what did you do with your hair? It looks great."

"I got tired of the old color," she said. Actually, she had felt the need to dye it an auburn that closely resembled her original color. It was a statement that she felt good about.

"You want to come in before we go?" said Rad.

Tawny didn't want to take a chance on them ending up in bed again. "No. It's such a nice day, let's get going."

Rad locked the door and they walked down the steps.

"How's Ketsel?" Tawny asked.

"Eh, I don't know. I haven't checked on him lately. I called Gabriel last week and he said he would come and get him soon."

"Yeah," said Tawny, "that's always what he says. Where are we going?"

"You'll see," said Rad.

"A surprise. Okay, I'll play along."

Tawny smiled as she and Rad walked up the hill to the SamTrans stop. A bus came along not long afterward heading toward Daly City. Rad followed her up the steps, paying the driver and dropping down into a seat beside her. "What's happening at the job?" she asked him.

Rad shook his head. "Eh, nothing much. No big changes. Sometimes no news is good news."

Tawny nodded, then watched out the window as they passed one of the tree nurseries of South San Francisco. Then Rad took her hand.

"C'mon," he said, "this is our stop."

They got off the bus in front of the Eternal Green Cemetery on El Camino. The sun was full but not strong and Tawny caught the fresh smell of newly mown grass. Shaking her head, she looked at Rad as if he was crazy. "What is this? Some kind of joke? Why did you bring me here?"

Rad took her hand. "Tawn, c'mon... I told you it would be a surprise."

Tawny pulled her hand from his. "Yeah, it's a surprise all right... a date in a cemetery?"

"It's a tour, Tawn. C'mon, chill out. A Halloween tour of the cemeteries." He smiled and took her hand. "The tour bus will be here any minute."

Tawny frowned, but allowed him to lead her along. "A tour of the cemeteries?"

Rad smiled. "Yeah, it's a Halloween thing. You'll enjoy it."

A few moments later the tour step van arrived and they climbed aboard. Tawny relaxed further as she met the three other members of the Colma Cemeteries tour—a mid-forties divorced dad and his twelve year old daughter, and Doris, a plump, jolly woman in her fifties who had just moved to Colma from Philadelphia.

The fall weather was comfortable, the foliage beautiful, and despite Tawny's initial uneasiness, she enjoyed the rush of air into the van and the emerald green of the cemeteries and their ornate reproductions of classic architecture and sculpture. Soon they disembarked from the step van and met Katherine, the tour guide. They all stood on the curb as a white pickup truck filled with rakes, shovels, leaf blowers and lawn mowers rattled by on Hillside Boulevard.

Katherine turned to Tawny, Rad and the others. "This is one of the most popular stops on the tour," she said, "the Pet's Rest cemetery."

Doris turned to Tawny and her smile constricted slightly. "Oh, God. I had to have my little Tony put down two years ago."

The euthanasia of Doris's dog brought Tawny uncomfortably close to thinking of her own situation and the decision she had to make.

"What kind of dog was he?" she asked.

"A toy poodle."

Tawny nodded sympathetically. "You never replaced him?"

Doris laughed bravely. "I'm not going through that again."

Katherine and the single dad and his daughter started up the steps and onto the lawn of Pet's Rest cemetery. Doris, Tawny and Rad followed.

Some of Tawny's initial concerns returned and she was afraid the experience would be dark and depressing. But the cool fall weather, the open spaces, Katherine's interesting anecdotes on some of the better known residents of the cemeteries, and even jolly Doris's determinedly-upbeat banter, all began to lift Tawny's spirits.

Rad and Tawny fell behind the others to look at some raised beds of flowers. Then they approached the other three tourists who stood facing Katherine, who was standing before a flat black granite marker the size of a microwave that was set into the earth.

"This is where Tina Turner's little dog lies. The story goes that she had him laid in the box wrapped up in her favorite mink coat."

Tawny smiled at the thought as she looked down at the marker. She looked over at another a few feet away. A picture of two parakeets was carved into the stone— Pete and Repete, the epithet read, brothers, born together, died together. The epithet didn't say how. Tawny was amazed that people had gone to so much trouble and expense for two little birds. She imagined a lonely old woman had owned the birds. People needed love and companionship, no matter where it came from. They visited three more cemeteries and a half dozen graves of notables and then they were back on the van for the last stop on the tour—The Olive Grove Columbarium.

After the driver parked the van, Tawny, Rad and the others went into the marble courtyard. The day had waned and the high stone gates already blocked the sun, casting the stone courtyard in dark shadows. Tawny felt a chill and a great weariness came over her. "How many cemeteries did we visit?" she asked Rad.

Rad looked as tired as she felt as he turned to her. "Five, I think. There's more, but this is the last stop on the tour." Tawny nodded as she looked up at the dying light. She took Rad's arm and they went inside.

Katherine and the others had gathered around a nondescript black urn. Katherine was talking as Tawny and Rad approached. "This is the ashes of Ishi, the last wild California Indian." As Katherine recounted how Ishi had shown up naked, freezing and starving in a rancher's barn, Tawny stopped listening. She already knew the story, having read the book. She remembered how moved she'd been by it, and how saddened. They'd even removed the man's brains after he'd died for study, like he'd been just another species or something. She grabbed Rad's arm tightly and pulled him away. "Let's walk," she said.

The building consisted of corridors intersected by other corridors, and seemed to go on forever. Each corridor was roofed with tinted windows like a greenhouse. The sun had set and the light was muted and calming. They walked down an empty corridor and Tawny stopped and turned to Rad. "After this is over I want to go some place quiet." she said. "But not as quiet as this." She tried to laugh. "Some place where we can get something to eat and talk."

"Okay," said Rad. Some plaques a few feet away caught his interest. "Wow," he said, "most of these people died in the mid 1940s. Must be WWII vets."

Tawny nodded absently. Rad went over to examine one urn closely and Tawny walked off toward a beautiful arrangement of flowers well lit by a spotlights situated near the end of the corridor. She felt drawn to them like a bee. She needed flowers now, bright yellow, red, and blue flowers. She should have never agreed to this outing, she realized. It was too much; but it would soon be over.

She approached the floral display and saw with disappointment that they were imitation. She stared sadly at them and was about to go back to Rad when she heard a cry. It was a little boy. She listened closely. It was not the petulant crying of a spoiled child, or an angry child. She had never heard a child cry like this—plaintive and devoid of all hope. It came from around the corner. She frowned. He'd probably gotten separated from his mom on a trip to pay respects to a departed grandparent. That kind of experience can be pretty scary for a little kid. She looked back at Rad. He was still reading the inscriptions on the urn and apparently hadn't heard it.

Tawny went to the end of the corridor and turned left. Marble tiles stretched into the distance. There was no one there. She listened. The boy's cries were faint now, but still distinct. Was he in the next corridor? She walked to the end of the corridor and turned. The intersecting corridor was empty, but the boy's cries still echoed in the distance. Tawny felt faint and decided to go back. If a little boy had gotten lost back there, the security guard would have to go get him. This place was big and labyrinthine. She felt weary and sad. She started back toward Rad. He looked up when he saw her and came up to her.

"Take me back to the others, Rad. Please."

"Sure. Everything okay?"

Tawny said nothing as they walked quickly, their footsteps echoing sharply off the marble tiles. They turned a corner and saw the rest of the tour group. About thirty feet away from them a security guard spoke with a man in a black suit standing before a kiosk. She walked up to them, Rad beside her. The man in the suit looked at her and nodded.

"I heard a child crying back there," she said.

The man blinked his intelligent dark eyes and turned to the security guard. "Check it out and make sure nobody walked off."

The security guard nodded and left.

Tawny and Rad walked back to the tour group.

"What was that about?" said Rad.

Tawny spotted a ladies room off to the side. "I'll tell you in a minute." She went in.

When Tawny came out, the others had moved on and Rad was waiting for her. "They're around the corner," he said.

Tawny nodded. "Let's go. I've had enough of cemeteries to last me a lifetime."

"You don't want to wait for them?"

Tawny shook her head. "Let's go."

Rad smiled. "Okay. I'm sorry if it was too much for you. Let me tell them we're leaving."

They came out of the columbarium in the twilight under a gold and red sky. Small birds or bats, Tawny wasn't sure which, flitted in and out of the big eucalyptus trees nearby. "I'm sorry," she said. "I just couldn't stay in there anymore."

"Sure," said Rad, "don't worry about it. The bus stop is just two blocks down; we can walk it."

They started walking. "Are you sure you're okay?" he said.

Tawny nodded. "Yeah, I'm okay now. I heard a little boy crying in there while you were looking at that urn."

"And..." said Rad, with a wry smile.

"There was no one there, Rad."

Rad's face grew serious. "Katherine was telling ghost stories while you were in the bathroom," he said. "She said that that wing we were in is where all the preemies are buried, the ones from St. Claire's Catholic Hospital."

"I didn't hear babies, Rad. This was a boy, one particular little boy. He was lonely and scared, and crying like he had no one in the whole world to help him. I've never heard anything so sad in my life and it was tearing me up inside!" Tawny's eyes teared up

Rad gave her a worried look and took her hand. "C'mon. We only have a block to go."

They came to the bus stop and Rad pulled a bus schedule from his back pocket and studied it. "Should be one coming along in seven minutes."

Tawny nodded while she dried her eyes with a

Kleenex. Ten minutes later Rad stepped off the curb to look down El Camino. No big SamTrans buses were rolling towards them from either direction.

"Anything coming?" Tawny asked.

"No. I don't know what the problem is. They're usually on time." Rad looked over toward the little access road next to the cemeteries that paralleled El Camino. "There's a building over there," he said. "There's a sign; McCoy's. Must be a bar."

Tawny looked. "A bar? It's in the cemetery, Rad. It's probably a Funeral Home."

"No," said Rad, "it's not in the cemetery. It's on that little road next to it. What's it called? Anyway, we could get something to eat."

Tawny frowned. "After that tour and that... experience..." She shook her head. "I don't have much of an appetite, Rad."

Rad laughed. "Well, we could go and just have a few beers before the bus comes. You know, sit and talk."

"I can't, Rad," said Tawny. She looked nervously down El Camino.

"Why not? You give up beer for the Buddhists or something?"

"I'm pregnant, Rad."

Rad turned to her and swallowed hard. "Jesus! Really?"

She nodded.

"Mine?" he said.

Tawny looked at him, annoyance hardening her features. "Yes, Rad. There's never been any one else..." Her voice rose, "unlike you and her!"

"But... you were taking the pill! I don't get it."

"Yeah, well, I was, and I wasn't. You know the saying, shit happens." Tawny felt disgusted with herself for using such a crudity to describe what had happened to her. She wiped away a tear. "I don't know what happened. It didn't work, that's all."

"How old is it?"

"Almost two months."

Rad was silent for a while. "Jesus Christ!" He stepped out onto El Camino and looked toward South City. "A bus is coming."

Tawny said nothing.

"Well," said Rad, "what are you gonna do?"

"What am I going to do? Is that all you can say? Like you didn't have anything to do with this, like this is all my problem?" As she looked at him she saw hurt in his face. It tempered her anger, but only a little.

"Well," he said. "I mean, okay, what are we gonna do about it?"

"Nothing, Rad. I'm going to do nothing."

"Tawn," said Rad in exasperation, "you're not even two months yet. This is the time to get it taken care of."

Tawny turned to him. "You really don't care about me, do you Rad?"

Rad's face reddened. "Of course I do, Tawn. But be real. What the fuck are you and me and a baby gonna live on? My salary at the fucking skateboard shop? C'mon!"

Tawny's face was taut with anger and incredulity. "I thought maybe you had grown up some, Rad. That's why I agreed to see you today. I thought you would step up."

The bus pulled over to the curb with a squeal of tires and a hiss of the air brakes. Tawny shook her head and got on without waiting for him. He hurried after her.

CHAPTER 35

A LLEN COLLINS CAME HOME FROM work early. He passed Reynaldo's bedroom. Inside, Tina was putting Reynaldo's things in a cardboard box. The mattress had been stripped of bedding and was folded in half at the foot of the bed. The sight unnerved him.

"Couldn't you at least wait a while before you did that?" he demanded in a voice thick with anguish. "He's only been gone two days!"

"His room is a mess," said Tina, "and it stinks."

"Oh my God!" said Allen loudly. "After what's happened… and you're talking about his room? Oh, what's the goddamned use?" He walked out of Reynaldo's bedroom and back into the living room. He sat in the chair and put his head in his hands. Tina came into the room a few minutes later and sat on the couch. She said nothing to Allen and picked up the remote and turned on the TV. They sat in the room saying nothing while occasional waves of sitcom canned laughter washed over them. Finally Allen sighed loudly and got to his feet. He looked at her. She turned to him and said, "You don't do any of the cleaning around here. Why is that? You think I'm a servant?"

"What?" he said. His face contorted with rage. "After all that's happened you want to talk about house cleaning?" He put his jacket on and went out, closing the door softly.

Tina watched the TV for an hour after Allen had gone. She turned it off and got to her feet. She went over to the front window, parted the curtains and looked out. The van was gone from its space. She went back to the couch and sat, turning the TV back on. The sun moved slowly across the sky and after a while bold golden light was slanting in through an opening in the curtains. She got up and pulled the curtains closed, darkening the room. She sat down again and stared at the TV. She thought she heard something and turned off the TV. She went into Christine's room, but she was still well into her nap. She closed the door softly. She went into Reynaldo's bedroom. There was nothing there, of course. But his curtains were parted. She went over to close them and froze. A boy stood with his back to her in the yard by the fence. He was the same size and color as Reynaldo, but she could not see his face. She studied him as her heart began beating faster. She tapped on the glass, trying to get him to turn around. He did not move, continuing to stare out across the field. She went outside and around to the back yard. There was no one there. She went over to the fence and looked left and right, seeing nothing. The field below was empty. She walked around to the side of the house and her brows knit with suspicion. The crawlspace door had been unlatched and left slightly ajar. She looked around and satisfied herself that no one could see her. She knelt and pulled the crawlspace door up, looking inside. It took a moment for her eyes to adjust. She saw the reassuring sleeping bag shape of the bundle up where the crawlspace rose up slightly. She closed the crawlspace door and latched it and went back inside the house. Sitting down on the couch, she took the airline tickets from her purse and studied them. She and Christine would have to be at the airport bright and early for their flight to Costa Rica. She picked up the remote and turned the TV back on.

On Wednesday business was very slow at the board shop. Rad found himself thinking about Tawny and her situation. She hadn't told his mother anything about having an abortion and he wondered if she'd do it. Part of him found the idea distasteful; the fetus had some of him in it, his DNA. He knew there was more to it than that, but he didn't want to think about it. A big part of him just wanted it all to be over and done with. He felt sorry for Tawny but he couldn't help her or even make her feel better. She hadn't spoken to him at all the whole way back from the cemetery tour and he'd felt like crap. He still felt like crap most of the time. He wished he could take a trip for a couple months and come back and find it all over with, with maybe Tawny moved out of state, or maybe even married to someone else. That was really what she wanted, to be married. And he didn't have shit now, just enough money to pay the rent and that was about it.

Finally it was time to leave work. As Rad walked to Jen's dorm, thoughts of Tawny and her problem began to fade and thoughts of Jen grew, making him feel a little lighter. Jen made no demands on him. All she wanted was to be with him and to make it with him. He didn't think she loved him, not really, and he wasn't sure what he felt about her. He thought he loved her, kind of. He knew that he wanted to be with her a lot, and could hardly keep his hands off her.

When he got to Jen's door his erection was pushing painfully against his pants. He rang the bell and Jen let him in. He tried to kiss her but she backed away. He looked around. The little apartment smelled prettily of scented oil and there was no evidence of Cait. As he began taking off his jacket she said, "I tried to call you to tell you not to come, but you must have just left."

Rad smiled and pulled her close, running his hands down her back, kneading her buttocks. "Must have," he said.

"Rad," said Jenny, gently pushing him away, "look, I know this is our usual time, but today is not good for me."

Rad nodded and frowned pensively. "Got a test to study for?"

Jenny shook her head. "No." She looked over at the clock on the wall. "But I'm going somewhere at five."

Rad again put his arms around her and kissed her.

"That gives us about an hour and a half." He kissed her slowly and tenderly and she began to kiss back. Soon she was tugging at his belt, trying to unbuckle it. Cradling her head and shoulders, Rad put his arms through her legs, picked her up and carried her into the bedroom. After their lovemaking, they fell asleep in the afternoon quiet.

"Rad!"

Rad yawned and opened his eyes. Jenny was sitting up in bed. "Yeah, Baby," he said.

"Rad, you have to go. Come on." Jenny slid off the bed and stepped into her panties. She opened the closet and took a blouse off a hanger.

Rad sat on the edge of the bed and began putting on his underwear and socks. He looked at her closely. He'd never seen her like this, her mind evidently on other things, definitely not on him. "Got a date?" he said.

She frowned. "Nooo," she crooned. "It's a family thing, Rad. And somebody's picking me up in fifteen minutes. She sat in front of her mirror, smoothing something into her face."

"Jenny," he said, "I'm going down to the Dawg Friday night." He buttoned his shirt and tucked it into his pants. "Want to meet me there?"

Jenny's image looked at him from the mirror. "Rad... I'll call you, okay?"

It was the closest Rad had seen her get to anger and he frowned slightly. He put on his shoes and walked out into the living room. He looked back at the bedroom, tempted to say something else that would get her to 'fess up' to what was really going on, but he decided not to. He opened the door and almost bumped into a tall, handsome Chinese guy who was obviously about to knock. The guy smiled politely, trying to cover his discomfort and surprise.

"Hey... how you doin'?" Rad said.

"I'm doing just fine. And how about you?"

The guy's voice was refined, Rad realized, thoughtful, with no discernible accent and not peppered with 'hip-isms' like his own. It was a voice as finely crafted as his sweater, creased slacks and shined shoes, the highest quality, top shelf.

Rad nodded. "I'm good." He walked off.

CHAPTER 36

CHANNELED BY THE SAN BRUNO Mountains, the afternoon fog rolled above South San Francisco like a mighty river. Under it, Allen turned on his headlights as he drove down Second Avenue in a sort-of trance. Sometimes he thought of Reynaldo and Christine and Tina, and the family they'd once been, and then the pain became too much for him and he had to think of other things. He realized he was doing what President Clinton did—what did they call it, compartmentalizing—putting all the really bad stuff in the back of his head so he could concentrate on the important stuff that had to be done. Surely there were things that had to be done. He knew there were, but he couldn't think of any.

Every now and then an opening appeared briefly in the fog revealing bright afternoon sun. To the north and south, sunlit areas glowed like burnished bronze. Allen knew that in another couple of hours it would all be under fog.

He drove past the familiar façade of the big brick apartment building. As his eyes swept over it he thought he saw someone at the window of the sitting room that he had always imagined as belonging to a wise old couple. The window was, as always, lit with soft golden light. He decided to go see them.

It made no sense; he didn't know them, nor they him. Maybe they would tell him to get lost or call the police. But his desperate need to talk to someone, especially someone older and wiser than himself about his situation, overwhelmed his sense of decorum. He needed to hang his head and confess. He needed someone to listen to everything that had happened and tell him that it wasn't his fault, like he imagined Joel would have done. Maybe they would understand. If they didn't, did it matter? Did anything matter anymore?

Allen slowed. Spotting a parking space ahead, he pulled over and got out. He quickly walked back to the building and went in. A panel of brass mail boxes and buttons for the bells were set into the wall. Ignoring them, he looked around and spotted the door to the fire escape stairs. He went through it and up the stairs. He located the apartment relative to the stairwell. Four doors stretched down the tidy hallway in one direction, five in the other. It was very quiet and peaceful. He saw that the door was slightly ajar. He put his hand on the door knob and slowly pushed it open. He went in.

The white brocaded curtains were dirty; the two red upholstered chairs faced each other across the familiar fringed vase lamp which sat on a table with a marble top. The chair back facing Allen had a white tag sewn into it - GALLI PROPERTY MANAGEMENT. A white box with some wires coming in and going out of it—a timer for the lamp—sat below the table on a floor that was merely a slab of cheap pressboard with the manufacturer's name repeatedly printed in bands across it. Allen felt sick. He sat. The chairs wore a layer of dust like grey felt. On the opposite wall, a painting of an Italian wedding hung, with a couple posed before a table heaped with grapes, breads, cheeses and wine glasses under a bright sun. As Allen stared at it, the lamp's glow faded as sunlight flooded through the window, the fog having parted momentarily. The painting blazed in the light, revealing the brush strokes to be nothing more than uniform grooves and swirls that had been mechanically stamped into the mass-produced cardboard 'canvas.' Allen turned away and looked at the window sill. Unpainted, the wood showed indecipherable scribbling that had evidently been left behind by the workmen. Allen looked closer, seeing some measurements, a few scattered fraction-to-decimal conversions. Something longer, some phrase had been scribbled in pencil on the wall below the sill. He bent to read it—"What the fuck did you expect?"

"Oh God," he moaned. He got out of the chair, went out into the hall and hurried down the steps.

Allen drove for hours. He thought he had gone to Stowe Lake in the city and to Clement Street, but he wasn't sure which he'd gone to first. The radio was on the talk channel. A man was yelling about Vice President Gore's oil deal. Allen tried to remember what time it had been when he'd left Tina in the house and gone out. The news came on while he was on the 280 freeway flowing along with the commuter traffic. The talk was about some preacher having called

Clinton's behavior evil. Allen frowned. The word was archaic. Nobody believed in evil or hell or any of that shit anymore. The reporter went on about calls for the preacher to apologize. Some Republican senator came to the preacher's defense. Suddenly Allen saw McCoy's ahead. He slowed to pull into the lot.

Allen parked, turned off the car, and sat in the quiet. To the west, the fog was clearing up. The now-setting sun's slanting rays burned straight into his face. He got out of the van. As he approached the door he saw one of the biker guys that played pool in the back washing off a large Harley Davidson motorcycle with a hose. As Allen drew closer he saw that the bike was completely caked with dirt as if it had been ridden in the mud and left unwashed for days, or even buried.

Inside the bar it was cool and quiet, the light dim. Thoughts of Reynaldo and Christine assailed him as he sat down at his spot next to the taps, where Lou was sitting as usual, ready to serve him. He nodded a greeting to the hatchet faced old man. Lou pulled the ivory-topped chromed tap lever back, pouring a tall one for him. There was a soccer game on the TV. Allen had heard something about there being a tournament in town, somewhere down the Peninsula, maybe Stanford. He stared into the deep amber of the beer as if it might hold answers to the many questions that plagued him. Deep, male voices erupted in argument in the back room. A heavyset, muscled man, wearing a cut-off denim jacket, another Hells Angels biker type, came into the main room.

"Lucifer, did Harry ever show up?"

Allen's ears perked up. He'd always assumed that 'Lou' had been short for Louis, but Lucifer? The old man must have been in a biker gang in his younger days. That would explain a lot of things. Lucifer was the kind of name a biker type would pick. And it was likely that Lou had injured his leg on a motorcycle.

Lou nodded in the direction of the front parking lot. "He's out front trying to get all the dirt off his bike."

Allen's bladder ached and he got off the stool and went into the bathroom. He stared at the blurry image of himself in the mirror as he relieved himself. Leaving the bathroom, his curiosity got the better of him and he went into the back room where the loud-mouthed guys were playing pool. Just past the door two guys wearing leather jackets were pouring what looked like sugar into a plastic sandwich bag on the pool table. A high mahogany table off to the side had a dozen or so of bags neatly stacked. The men looked up at Allen briefly, exchanged glances, and then went on with their business. Allen thought drunkenly that it was probably dope, but it was none of his business and he pretended he hadn't seen anything. He nodded at the others standing around the pool table and returned to his seat at the bar

Allen's thoughts turned back to the soccer game and he quickly drained the tall glass of beer. A bone-numbing, familiar cold calm came over him. Reynaldo and Christine's faces, which had been breaking into his consciousness repeatedly, now faded into a nondescript blur. He turned to Lou. "Give me another, will you?"

As Allen drank, another one of the biker types

came in and spoke softly into Lou's ear. He went back into the back room and a cacophony of rough laughter erupted. Someone broke the cue set and Allen heard two balls drop into pockets. He turned his attention back to the TV and the soccer game. The announcer's voice rose with excitement as a player ran through a phalanx of opposing players straight for the goal. The goalie mightily hurled himself sideways but the ball sailed in just out of his reach. The crowd roared triumphantly.

"Damn, he almost stopped them," said Allen.

"Almost don't count," said Lou, an ugly frown on his face.

"Well, maybe. But the guy tried; he really did."

Lou looked at Allen with what Allen realized, was cold contempt.

"Trying ain't good enough either."

At that moment one of the bikers stuck his ugly head around the wall. Allen recognized him as the one called Harry that had been out front cleaning the mud off his bike. Harry called over to Lou, "Lucifer, you ready to get started?"

Lou looked at the broad windows at the front. Allen turned to follow his eyes. The sun had set and no more light came in through the edges. Lou got to his feet and Allen realized that this was the first time he'd ever actually seen him standing. He walked awkwardly and Allen looked down to see that he had a clubfoot.

"Yeah," said Lou, "get the guys out here. I'll lock the front."

Lou went over to the front door and began to bar it.

Allen got to his feet. "Wait a minute. I gotta get going."

Lou ignored him.

"What are you doing?" said Allen.

Allen heard the others coming into the room. He turned. There were about a half dozen of them, fallen angels every one of them. Harry carried a green canvas duffel bag and set it down with a rattle. It was full of baseball bats, both wooden and aluminum, like you'd see at a baseball game near the dugout. The others began pulling them from the bag, swinging them as they tested their heft and weight, as if warming up to go to bat.

Harry whipped the air with an aluminum bat. His eyes shone as he looked at Allen. Harry called over to Lou, "Never thought we'd end up doin' the Lord's work, did you, Lou?"

The others laughed heartily.

A small, Mexican-looking biker swung two bats simultaneously. He looked at Allen and smiled evilly. "Gonna hit a home run tonight!"

Allen felt the contents of his bowels liquefy. "Jesus Christ," he called over to Lou, "what the fuck's going on? I didn't do anything!"

Lou scowled. "That's right, wuss. You didn't do a goddamn thing. And now you're gonna pay for that."

Allen began sobbing. "I tried... but what could I do? I couldn't do anything."

Tina walked around to the back yard. The light was very bright, the setting sun burning into her eyes. The sounds of life were all around: children's laughter from the field on the other side of the fence, someone mowing a lawn a few houses down, a big 747 roaring up into the air over San Bruno as it headed out to the Pacific. She went around to the side of the house. She didn't think anyone would be able to see her over the tall fence. But it didn't matter as she had to look one last time just to be sure.

She knelt and lifted up the crawlspace door, propping it up with a stick. She cringed as she crawled inside. The light was very dim and it was quiet and peaceful as a tomb. The rat-proofing concrete was hard and rough and tore at her clothing. She crawled slowly toward the far side of the structure, finally spotting the bundle laying on the rise in the corner where it was supposed to be. Good. A tiny hole somewhere on the side of the house let the sunlight through, illuminating it like a spotlight on a stage. The plastic garbage bag was untouched and a fine sheen of dust had settled on it. The yellow cords securing it were intact. Good. She grimaced as she turned around and began crawling back. She thought she heard something behind her. Turning her head, she saw nothing. She blinked nervously as sweat burned her eyes. Ahead, the reassuring rectangle of light at the crawlspace door beckoned. She continued crawling, cursing the jagged concrete that bruised her hands and knees and snagged her clothing. She thought she saw something to her left. In the dim light, something dark seemed to be pouring by, like a thick column of ants? Or was it one big thing pouring along? Confused, she grimaced with determination and crawled determinedly toward the crawlspace door. A little boy laughed mischievously and the crawlspace door closed with a wooden clap. She crawled forward toward the door and something big threw itself over her with great violence, quickly wrapping her up.

Tina felt the thing tightening around her neck, constricting painfully like the automatic blood pressure cuff at the drug store. She lost consciousness. A moment later she came to and wondered if she'd left anything cooking on the stove. Her legs twitched convulsively as if she was trying to get to her feet and then she was still.

CHAPTER 37

RAD REVVED THE ENGINE AS he sat in his truck waiting for Tawny. The V-8 roared, then settled back to the torque-induced shuddering idle that he loved so much. He had started working for his dad in the business again and he had loaned him the money for a new set of tires and a tune-up. Rad thought about Jen. It was over, of course, but it had only been about sex. There had never been anything else there.

He turned on the radio, tuning to his favorite station. Tawny came out of the house and opened the truck door, pulling herself in. Rad smiled. She was such a cool babe. Visibly pregnant, but still sexy, and she insisted on doing stuff for herself. Rad knew his mother and father were right; Tawny was a solid choice for marriage.

Rad shifted into first and released the hand brake. He turned the wheel and was about to turn up the street when a black and white police cruiser rolled quickly past, pulling to a stop down the street in front of the yuppie's place, the one that they called Mister Peepers.

"Wonder what's going on down there," he said.

Tawny shook her head as she looked down the street. "C'mon. We're going to be late for mass."

Tawny was doing this for Rad. It had been his idea and she had wanted to encourage him. She had her Buddhism and she felt like she was getting something out of it finally. She felt happier and more confident then she had in a long time. And when Rad had told her he'd decided to go back to the Church, she'd been impressed and determined to support him too.

Rad drove to the top of the hill and turned onto Skyview Drive. The news came on the radio "... *A body was found in the bushes alongside Holy Cross Cemetery by an early morning jogger. The Colma man said that in the poor light of the fog it had appeared to be some discarded articles of clothing and other trash, but it was in the shape of a man and so he had stopped to take a closer look...*"

"Wow," said Rad. "We were there only a couple weeks ago."

Tawny shook her head, determined not to let this sort of thing darken her day. "Oh well, stuff happens, Rad."

They turned into the church parking lot as people were parking and leaving their cars and hurrying up to the steps of the church. As Rad pulled into a spot, the radio droned on, "*In another bizarre development, animal control officers and police reported a death involving a large snake...*"

Tawny reached over and turned the radio off.

"Did you hear that?" said Rad, as he set the parking brake.

"C'mon, Rad. I don't like to walk in late."

Rad and Tawny paused as they entered the church. The service was beginning and the priest, flanked by two altar boys, was poised to walk up the center aisle. After they started up, Rad and Tawny followed them, ducking into a row in the back behind a family with two small girls and a baby.

Rad looked around at the different faces—Euro/Castilian faces, American Indian-looking faces, Caucasians, a scattering of Asians, mostly Filipino, an elderly black couple. How many Sundays had he stood in these pews with his parents and looked around, wishing the mass would be over so they could go home and eat?

In front of Rad, the couple with the three kids seemed to have their hands full. Rad looked away from the wriggling kids and at the front of the church. For what he realized was the first time, he appreciated the architecture, almost as if he'd never seen it before. The altar. a polished granite slab longer than a surfboard, was situated under a magnificent nave with high, stained glass windows and clear glass that rained down bright white and colored light. Rad now saw this as the continuation of a line, a line going back thousands of years, Christianity, Western Civilization, his civilization. The name of his heretofore lapsed religion, The Roman Catholic Church, suddenly struck him with its full meaning. It harkened back to Roman times. Would he bring his son into this? Or would he be the broken link to it all? Maybe. Maybe not. And what impact would that have on the kid? He tried to wrap his mind around it but could not. Not now anyway, not yet...

Tawny watched a portly man approach the lectern for the reading from the liturgy. He opened up a large book. "For those who have died..." he intoned.

Tawny did not mouth the responses with the others, but listened carefully. She was here for Rad. He had wanted her to come with him.

"Lord, hear our prayer," answered the congregants.

Tawny looked around at the many young families in the church. She wanted her and Rad and the baby to be a family like that. As she looked at them she felt like a hungry person looking through the window of a restaurant at the diners enjoying their meal.

Four elderly churchmen wearing suits walked to the front of the church, genuflected, then started down the aisles. They reached into each pew with wicker collection baskets attached to long bamboo poles. Tawny removed a dollar bill from her purse.

As the priest readied communion, Tawny thought again about how much she wanted a family. And she wanted a home too, their own house, not a rental. The Buddhism seemed to be giving her hope. She put her hand on her belly as the baby kicked. She could already see their little one playing on the rug like she'd dreamed, maybe with a little brother or sister too. She looked at Rad. Would he get the hope and courage he needed from this?

"The Lord be with you," the congregants around her intoned in unison.

Was he mature enough, responsible enough, to be that husband? Maybe. After all, he did seem to have had some kind of realization and change of heart after talking to the priest. But would it last? She studied him, then turned her attention back to the priest. He said in a voice like singing, "In the name of the Father, The Son, and the Holy Spirit..."

The children in the pew in front of Tawny fidgeted and stared at her and Rad. There was something about the woman in front of Tawny that intrigued her, but she could only see her back and not her face.

"This is my body," intoned the priest. A bell tinkled.

Tawny stared at the girls. There was something familiar about them too, but she couldn't place them. One of the girls blushed and slowly turned her face away.

"This is my blood..."

Again the bell tinkled brightly.

People got to their feet and Tawny and Rad followed suit. The people raised their arms and outstretched them, holding hands.

"Our Father, who lives in Heaven..."

Tawny looked over at Rad and smiled as they held hands and looked around.

"...and grant us His peace..."

Tawny looked around, charmed and moved by the ceremony.

"Let us offer each other a sign of that peace..."

People began turning to each other, offering their

hands to shake. Tawny and Rad laughed as they faced each other and shook hands. The woman in front of Tawny turned and Tawny saw with shock that it was the Mexican woman who had passed her house every day for the last two years. They exchanged smiles and Tawny saw that she knew she was pregnant. And Tawny knew what that sparkle in the woman's eyes meant—she had pride in her kids and her man—her family. Hers!

"Peace," the woman said, extending her hand for Tawny to shake.

"Peace," said Tawny. The husband turned a wide handsome, mustachioed face. He shook Tawny's hand, then Rad's.

A few minutes later all the congregants had again turned their attention back to the front as the priests began serving communion. Tawny's mind was on fire with wonder. She had to find out more about this woman. She didn't even know her name. She resolved to follow her outside at the conclusion of the ceremony and speak to her.

Tawny and Rad moved with the crowd toward the church exits. Tawny kept her eyes on the woman and her husband and children who were just ahead of them as the crowd slowly moved out of the church. Once outside, the woman turned and spotted her. She came closer, smiled and extended her hand.

"My name is Yolanda, Yolanda Perez. And this is my husband, Ernesto."

Tawny smiled at the husband as Rad shook his hand. Both men stared off in different directions as people milled past them, slowly climbing down the steps and heading to the parking lot across the street.

Yolanda smiled again. "Every day when I'm going to work I see you. I should have said something."

Tawny nodded. "So should I have. You work late in the day, huh?"

Yolanda nodded. "I work for my mother who has a cleaning business. She watches my children." Yolanda looked wistfully across the street. She nodded toward her husband. "He's working two jobs. We're buying the pink house around the corner from you."

Tawny smiled and nodded. *Buying* the house! her mind repeated. All this time she had felt sorry for this woman, Yolanda, believing she was some poor minority living in a crowded apartment somewhere, scrubbing someone else's toilets, caring for someone else's children. Tawny wanted to go home and chant about all of it. It was a bit overwhelming. She wanted to talk to Terri and some of the Buddhist leaders about it too. She felt like she was learning a lot about her life and where she was, but it wasn't all encouraging. And yet, in a way, it was, because it was motivating.

"Well, we'll have to talk some time," said Tawny, "maybe when I see you on the street."

Yolanda nodded and smiled. "Okay. Well, bye."

Rad took Tawny's hand as they started down the steps to the sidewalk.

"Who is that?" he said.

"Her name's Yolanda. They live right around the corner from you, I mean, from us."

"Wow," said Rad, "that's awesome! I've never seen them around before."

Tawny nodded. "She's younger than me and she already has three little children."

Rad looked at her. "You'll have one to hold soon."

She smiled. "Yes."

Tawny recalled Yolanda and Ernesto and their children. They seemed really natural about their lives and their family. They would probably have a long life together, long after their kids had grown up. And what about her and Rad?

Despite her happiness over their reunion and their plans to marry, a tiny part of Tawny still wondered if she and Rad would be together forever. Didn't half of all American marriages end up in divorce? Despite that, for the sake of the baby it was best if he had a mother and a father; she was certain of that. It was natural, the way God or the life force, or nature, whatever, intended it, like growing old, like gravity. She was stronger and happier now. Maybe it was the baby. Maybe it was Rad and his awakening. No. It was in her. Maybe it was the Buddhist chanting. She was taller, rooted more deeply, like one of those trees on the mountain they'd cut down. And this little boy inside her was loved so much already. She would never, ever, let anyone hurt him and she would do everything she could to see that he had a good life, no matter what happened between her and Rad.

Tawny frowned as sharp pain rippled across her abdomen. Rad put his arm around her shoulder. "You okay, Babe?"

Tawny looked at him. There was a hint of a tear in the corner of one of his eyes, as if he too was pondering their future and worrying about whether or not they'd be able to pull it off. "I'm okay," she said and smiled. "He keeps doing kick flips in there. He takes after you."

Rad threw back his head and laughed loudly and uproariously, "Oh that's so cool! C'mon. Let's go home."

THE END

ABOUT THE AUTHOR

Paul Clayton is the author of a three-book historical series on the Spanish conquest of the Floridas— *Calling Crow*, *Flight of the Crow*, and *Calling Crow Nation* (Putnam/Berkley), and a novel, *Carl Melcher Goes to Vietnam* (St. Martin's Press), based on his own experiences in that war.

Carl Melcher Goes to Vietnam was a finalist at the 2001 Frankfurt eBook Awards, along with works by Joyce Carol Oates (*Faithless*) and David McCullough (*John Adams*).

Clayton's last book—*White Seed: The Untold Story of the Lost Colony of Roanoke*—is a work of historical fiction.

Paul currently lives and writes in California

CPSIA information can be obtained at www.ICGtesting.com
Printed in the USA
LVOW05s1656160514

386133LV00001BA/51/P